AIN'T SUPERSTITIOUS

D1520155

Third Flatiron Anthologies
Volume 4, Fall/Winter 2015

Edited by Juliana Rew
Cover Art by Keely Rew

Ain't Superstitious
Third Flatiron Anthologies
Volume 4, Fall/Winter 2015

Published by Third Flatiron Publishing
Juliana Rew, Editor

Discover other titles by Third Flatiron:

License Notes

www.thirdflatiron.com

Contents

Editor's Note

by Juliana Rew

We've always loved bluesman Willie Dixon's tune, "I Ain't Superstitious," and think it makes a great theme for a short story anthology, especially as fall rolls around and thoughts turn to Halloween, All Saints', and Día de los Muertos. Our writing prompt called for stories involving luck, prophecy, and magic. We found that these topics brought forth a new pool of writers from the horror and dark fiction genres, and we're glad to get them. Welcome to our lucky thirteenth edition. We are doing a full-size double issue this time.

We open with the strange world of Amy Aderman's "Salt and Bone," in which the savage sea contains demons that can only be soothed by playing magical instruments carved from bone.

Witchcraft is of course an old standby in the world of superstition, and some witches are indeed evil, as in Gerri Leen's "Spellcasting." But we do like our witches resourceful as well as powerful, as in Maureen Bowden's "Confrontation on the Big One Three" and Judith Field's "Ambrose's Eight-plus-Oneth," The magical realism of E. E. King's "Pandora's Piñata" is a fine antidote to the heartbreak of love stolen by a curse.

And since cats, especially black ones, hold a special place of honor in the superstition pantheon, we invite you to join Ken Altabef's cat, "Jester," on a late-night outing for "A Little Mischief." But we can't leave out the horses of the Apocalypse, so take Bruce Golden's "Upon a Pale Horse" for a ride.

In a way, destructive feelings, such as guilt and phobias, are a form of superstition, with a fine pedigree dating back to greats like Edgar Allan Poe. John

Hegenberger's "The Necromancer" and Will Morton's "The Candlestick" present instructive tales about men who didn't do the right thing. In Andrew Kozma's offbeat "The Apple Falls Upward," we are pulled into a dysfunctional friendship between two men, one apparently mental.

Since the Age of Enlightenment, it's become the norm to reject belief in miracles, revelation, magic, or the supernatural. But it's only human to feel that delicious frisson of fear when things get a little strange. Thus we feature a healthy dollop of straight horror in this collection. Spencer Carvalho's ambrosial "Coffee Lake" is just a little too good to be true, and Lyn Godfrey's "Pantomimus" convinces us of the folly of whistling in a circus tent. Dennis Mombauer's "The Plague Well" might answer that question you've been wanting to ask. And don't forget to attend the "The Annual Scarecrow Festival" with John Paul Davies. Oh, wait. You can't, it's cancelled.

We need the occasional break from the horror of it all, and our "Grins and Gurgles" flash humor offerings this time are Sarina Dorie's "Nine Ways to Communicate with the Living" and Benjamin Jacobson's "Schrödinger's Schrödinger."

Other humorous contributions for this round include Kevin Lauderdale's "James and the Prince of Darkness," a rollicking P. G. Wodehouse spoof; K. T. Katzmann's "Sam, Sam, and the Demoness," superstition done Jewish-style; and Adele Gardner's "Wolf Call," a unique celebration of Elvis's birthday.

We point you to a trio of wonderful stories that reflect their region or origin. Jacob M. Lambert's "Across the Styx of Norway" stars a dying Native American who seeks to cross the Northern Lights off his bucket list, and Sean O'Dea's "Wind Chimes," a particularly Colorado story, features neighbor-on-neighbor feng shui in suburbia. Argentinian author Gustavo Bondoni's "Gualicho Days" proves once again it's not nice to try to fool Mother Nature.

Editor's Note

Sometimes it's just plain satisfying to see right conquer might, even if it's pure fantasy ("It could happen, right?..."). James Aquilone proffers "A Day to End All Days," a satisfying beat-the-devil tale. A. P. Sessler's "What Is Sacred to Dogs" gives us a sweet little hellhound who helps a preacher clean up (and clean out) his congregation full of sinners.

We were greatly moved by Christina Bates's poignant "Dead Men's Drinks," in which a mother hopes for one last conversation with her daughter, and we truly hope she gets it.

Finally, we close with "O Shades, My Woe," as one of King Arthur's knights gets his come-uppance for serving his master far too devotedly. It's a classic ghost story that will stay with you a long time.

So, as dogs begin to bark all over your neighborhood, lock all the doors, put on a recording of Frank Zappa's "Zombie Woof," and settle in for a good, old-fashioned scary read. Third Flatiron's "Ain't Superstitious" anthology proudly showcases an international group of new and established speculative fiction authors, who let their imaginations run wild.

*****~~~~~*****

Salt and Bone

by Amy Aderman

You can't ever *destroy* evil spirits—they have as much right to exist as we do, so we can only chase them away for a little while.

That's what Kate said. But Mrs. Carlson, my math teacher, said of course anything could be ended if some people would just work hard enough. I figured Kate knew better, though, seeing as how she was the one who'd been playing her bone flutes up on that cliff for years now.

She made the flutes out of deer bones. There were more deer than you could shake a bow at just a little ways inland, and my uncle liked to hunt. The venison went in the freezer, the fur got turned into rugs, and Kate got the bones. Something for everybody.

(When I was little, Ryan next door tried to make me cry by saying Kate locked up children in her house on the cliff and carved her flutes out of their bones. I broke his nose.)

Nobody was supposed to bother Kate when she was working. She might lose her concentration, and a spirit might capsize a boat, and then somebody might drown, and you wouldn't want to be responsible for making somebody *die*, would you?

I asked her about that once, after all of the boats returned to the harbor and all of the fishermen had stepped back on land on their own two feet.

Kate let out a weak puff of laughter. She was still sitting limply in her chair outside, and her short hair was damp with sweat. "The spirits take up all of my attention. I'm not saying you should throw a party and light firecrackers around me, but one person hasn't got much chance of breaking my focus."

And that was that.

By the time I reached high school, I visited more often. I didn't like to drive all the way to her house. It seemed like the spirits only paid attention to the ocean and the boats, but I worried they might do something to the brakes or the engine.

The best time to visit her was on a stormy day, when the fishermen couldn't go out. The spirits were still there, but there weren't any people on the water for them to attack. They always seemed to forget that Kate existed when she wasn't playing her flute. I don't know why, and I'm not sure she did, either.

I remember one day I stopped by her place in spring. It wasn't raining yet, but the sky had been cloudy all morning, and it was too choppy for the boats to go out. I'd been bored and skipped school with my friends after lunch. Sarah's parents weren't home, so she and Sam went to her place and there wasn't anybody else to hang out with. Kate had been doing what she did for so long that I think sometimes she forgot things like school existed and that she should have been telling me not to skip. Or maybe it was because she had so much responsibility already that she couldn't be bothered to care.

Anyway, the wind was so strong that my hair got blown into knots by the time I got to her place. It was a little house that'd been built after she came here and agreed to protect our boats; it didn't have many rooms, but the back of it was covered with windows, so that she could always see the ocean. The house was painted yellow. One time I asked if the color protected it from the spirits.

She laughed. "No, I just wanted some brightness in my life."

I sat with Kate by all those windows and watched her carve yet another flute. She probably could've done it in her sleep by now.

"How many of those have you made?" I asked.

"I don't know anymore. I used to keep count back when I got started, but that was ages ago." Kate tapped her knife on the table as she thought. Bone shavings were scattered across the wood in front of her. "If you were asking how many of the flutes have broken, I'd say at least a thousand, but I've made a lot more than that."

I glanced at the basket that held her unused flutes. There were about a dozen in it. I'd seen pictures of carved flutes other people made that had beautiful designs etched all over them, but Kate's were always plain. It didn't feel like there was any point in trying to make hers look special when she always had to keep making new flutes because the spirits broke them.

"Did you always make them?"

"Not at all. I used to buy them when I was just getting started—I wasn't much older than you, then. But it didn't take long for me to figure out that they work best for the person who makes them. They last longer, too."

"What's the longest you've ever had one last?"

"A week. But that was a very slow week. You have a lot of questions today—thinking of joining us?"

"No way. Besides, guitars are more fun, and you can't make one of *those* out of bone."

Kate grinned and settled more comfortably into her chair. "You'd be surprised what somebody can make when they have enough imagination."

...

I shouldn't have gone there. Even though Kate had told me I wouldn't be a distraction, I knew better than to hang around when it was going to be a busy day for her. I really did. It was a beautiful summer day: not a cloud in the sky, and the water was glass-smooth. All of the fishing boats would be out today and even a few people who would dare to sail or paddle around the harbor, just for fun. But it was the first day that my father was going fishing again since he broke his arm, and I couldn't stand just waiting at home with Mom.

I parked in my usual spot and ran to Kate's house. She sat in her wooden chair on the cliff. The ocean stretched out before us, and I saw the fishing boats scattered below. Her eyes were closed. She was already playing and the music hovered on the air around us.

I looked out onto the water. The boats had sailed far enough that now they were lowering their nets for today's catch. It would be a good day for bringing in plenty of fish, if the spirits didn't take control. The spirits never ran out of ways to meddle: they might capsize the boats, or send waves crashing over the fishermen when the water was calm not twenty feet away, or tangle the nets, or fill them with stones lifted up from the cold ocean bottom, deeper than any of us could swim.

Kate's music rippled like water. Her bone flutes had few holes, but she made them sound better than anything we played in music class. I didn't understand how something so beautiful could stop those evil spirits. I wondered how she had figured out which kinds of music worked best.

Dad and the others wouldn't be safe at home for a while yet. If you worked on one of the fishing boats, you had to learn that fine line between getting the largest catch possible for the day, and losing all of it because you stayed out one minute too long and couldn't fight the spirits any longer. I sat down but couldn't keep myself from pulling up handfuls of the thick grass.

The fishermen continued their work. The ocean began to grow restless around them. When I looked at Kate, I saw that she had opened her eyes but stared straight ahead. The rest of us could never see the spirits, only what they did, but I thought she could see them.

She'd told me that on days when the spirits weren't so strong, she might get only a few small cracks in that day's flute and she'd be able to keep using it for a while longer. But today she couldn't have been playing for more than an hour, and already I could see hair-thin cracks stretching all around the bone.

I knelt at the edge of the cliff and looked down. The waves tossed the boats around more and more, but they splashed highest against the part of the cliffs directly below us. They reached closer and closer to me as I watched, until a few drops of the salt spray landed on my lips. The water never really grew that warm, even in summer, and it tasted cold.

But I stayed put and watched. The boats must have been well anchored, because they didn't drift far.

There was a sharp *snap*. I jumped up.

Kate's flute had just cracked into at least a dozen pieces. She reached down and grabbed a new one from the basket wedged between her feet.

The minutes stretched on, feeling ten times longer than when I was waiting for school to end. The sun must have been crossing the sky, but it felt like that warm day was going to last forever. One of the boats was almost done pulling a full net aboard when it plummeted back into the water. The scales on all those fish gleamed in the sun right until they sank beneath the waves. The net of the next closest ship swung out into the air but was hauled back aboard.

Another crack. Kate swept the pieces of bone from her knees and played on.

A few of the boats started to return, the ones that always played it safe. They were the poorest but almost never lost a fisherman. Even with them back in the harbor, there were still plenty of people on the water for the spirits to torment.

Each flute broke faster than the one before. Soon there was only one left in the basket. Kate still hadn't looked at me, but I ran into the house. Six more flutes were completed. I laid all of them at her feet.

It wasn't at all windy up on the cliff, but a few of the boats started to be swept back and forth. One spun around in circles. I could see its fishermen holding on to the railings. Kate forced the spirits to make it stop, but by that time its catch was lost. That boat turned homeward.

I couldn't decide which was worse—watching what was happening on the water or seeing Kate grow more tired as her flutes kept shattering.

The rest of the boats returned to the harbor, one by one. The boat Dad was on was the last to turn back, as usual. Mom was always trying to get him to sign on to another boat, but the captain was his best friend.

They were moving so slowly! Even though there was only the one boat left, it didn't look like the spirits were going to stop anytime soon. Another gust of wind swept past us, pushing the boat back out into the ocean as it tried to sail home. The waves tugged it farther onto the deep water as Kate paused to pick up her next flute. It was the last one. She met my eyes for the first time as she brought the flute to her lips.

The music had been fast-paced since I got there. Now it slowed down until it sounded something like a lullaby. It was softer, too. I didn't know how the spirits could hear it all the way out there.

The wind began to die down, and the boat was able to creep inland. Then the waves pushed it back again. It reminded me of when the little kids played tug-of-war next door. I could have laughed, if it wasn't Dad and his friends trying to get home.

Kate didn't stop playing. The music was pretty, like when the water was calm and I walked out on the pier, and I could see deep down because the sun was shining. Even though all of us knew better than to tempt the spirits, at times like that I wanted to jump in and feel the water on my skin, and see how far out I could swim. There had to be good things in the ocean, too.

Her playing slowed down, and now she held the same low note for a long time. The waves flattened out like a hand was pressing down on them.

My father's boat lurched into the harbor.

Kate fell silent. I looked at her. Chips of the bone flutes were spread across her lap and the ground in front of us. She squeezed her fingers the tiniest bit, and the flute she held fell apart.

"Well," she said. "I haven't had a day like this in a long time." Her voice cracked, and her lips looked dry. I brought a glass of water and refilled it twice before she was done drinking. I had to hold the glass for her because her fingers were so stiff.

She didn't say anything for a while after that. We just sat there and looked at the ocean. Well, I looked. Her eyes were shut, and I couldn't tell if she'd fallen asleep. I'd have to tell Dad that they shouldn't go out tomorrow, since she had to carve more flutes.

Everything looked so calm now. The boats finished unloading today's catches. We'd see some of the fish in the store soon but the rest would be shipped away to places where the people didn't have to worry about their families being attacked by spirits when everyone was just trying to make a living. I wondered where the spirits went when they weren't bothering us.

After a while, Kate stirred. She took the basket that had held the spare flutes and brushed the shards from her lap into it. When she stiffly started to pick up the pieces of bone from the ground, I went over and helped.

"I need all of them," she reminded me.

"I know."

Finding the bones wasn't as hard as it could have been. The pieces of the flutes mostly dropped straight down when they broke, and none of them were smaller than my thumbnail. I still had to crawl on my hands and knees to make sure I'd found everything, but at least the pale bones stood out against the bright green grass.

When we were done, she asked, "Would you take care of it today?"

"Sure."

Kate smiled and handed the basket to me. "Thank you. Things would have turned out much worse if you weren't here." She went into her house before I could say anything. I wondered which she would do first: carve more flutes or pass out.

The pieces of bone softly clicked against one another as I drove to the beach. Later on, the place would be full of children splashing in the shallows (but only in the shallows) and my classmates sunbathing, but nobody came near the ocean so soon after the boats had been out. Strangers never imagined that something might be wrong with it.

I only stopped walking when the water was just about to touch the tips of my shoes. After I had a good grip on the basket, I tossed the bones as far out as I could. For a few moments they bobbed on top of the water. I waited.

A large wave rolled up, sucked all of the bones into it, and rolled out again. Not one flute piece was left behind.

Even Kate wasn't certain what happened to them, only that the offering seemed to keep the spirits happy for a little while. Every now and then, a couple of pieces would be washed back ashore. The bone would be polished and its sharp edges smoothed out like sea glass. I had one that I'd made into a necklace. For luck.

I sat down in front of the quiet ocean and waited for my friends. We would keep watch together.

###

About the Author

Amy Aderman is a Librarian in western New York. One of her favorite things about writing is doing research for her stories. Her short fiction has previously been published in *Daily Science Fiction.* Her first fantasy novel, *The Way to Winter,* is a retelling of H.C. Andersen's fairy tale, "The Snow Queen."

*****~~~~~*****

Coffee Lake

by Spencer Carvalho

Jack walked through the graveyard late at night. He shined his flashlight over the headstones as he searched for a particular grave. He was looking for the one with a coffee tree planted over it.

The Oromo people of Africa had a tradition of planting a coffee tree on the graves of powerful sorcerers. It was their belief that the first coffee bush sprang up from the tears that the god in heaven shed over the corpse of a dead sorcerer.

Jack wasn't in Africa. In fact, he had never been to Africa. He was in Brazil. Some Oromo people had immigrated to Brazil and brought their traditions along with them. Jack decided to seek out the coffee tree, because coffee was his obsession. He worked for an American company that exported coffee from Brazil and had made many trips there. On all his trips he always asked the locals about where to find the best coffee. This time, he'd found something online about a cemetery coffee tree that intrigued him. It stated that perhaps the coffee tree absorbed the decomposing elements of the supposed sorcerer it was buried over, and that enriched the coffee flavor.

Jack found the coffee tree over a grave. He stood and stared at it. Though it was rumored that the tree yielded the best coffee in the world, rumor also had it that anyone who disturbed the grave or coffee tree would be cursed. Jack wasn't Oromo, and he wasn't superstitious, so he didn't pay attention to that part of the legend and picked the just-ripening coffee berries. He sealed them in an airtight bag and brought it back to his hotel room, where he used his personal coffee kit to process the seeds, which he then roasted, ground, and brewed into a cup of coffee. He tasted it and was disappointed. It tasted like regular coffee. There was nothing special about it. He still had not found the world's best coffee.

The next day he met up with Tyler. Tyler worked for a rival coffee company that also exported from Brazil. Jack and Tyler were friendly, as friendly as rivals could be. With limited foreign language skills, they were often bored on their trips, so they would hang out together to kill the time. They met at a restaurant for lunch. Jack told Tyler about the cemetery coffee.

"You too," said Tyler. "Yeah, I tried that myself. Disappointing, huh? If you would have told me what you were planning, I could have saved you the trouble."

"There has to be something better," said Jack. "There must be something special out there. I refuse to believe that I've already had the best coffee I'll ever taste."

A local Brazilian walked over to where they were sitting.

"Excuse me," said the man. "My English isn't so good, but I speak a little, and I heard your story. Many people have been fooled by the coffee in the graveyard, but the best coffee in the world can only be found at Coffee Lake. Have you not heard of this?"

Jack and Tyler had no idea what he was talking about. They shook their heads.

"They say that in the Amazon there is a whole lake made of coffee. There are vast fields of coffee plants growing wild and warm springs, and in a special part of the jungle the two meet up and make a lake of coffee."

"Have you actually seen this lake?" asked Tyler.

"No," said the man. "I have only heard tales. I don't go into the Amazon. It is a strange place. Bad things happen there."

Jack and Tyler eventually left and made their way back to their hotel rooms. They stayed at the same hotel. Many of the hotel staff spoke English, so the hotel was considered to be American friendly. On the elevator ride up to their rooms, Jack turned to Tyler.

"Coffee Lake," said Jack.

"Yes, it's quite ridiculous," said Tyler.

"It's weird that he didn't ask for money. I thought at some point he would try to get money from us to scam us."

"He probably just wanted the attention. He's just some crazy guy telling stories. Forget about him."

The next day Jack woke up and went through the normal morning ritual of checking his phone and his email. After that he went to Tyler's room to see if he wanted to do something. Jack knocked on Tyler's door, but there was no answer. He left and came back an hour later and knocked again. Still no answer. Jack went down to the front desk.

"Excuse me," said Jack. "Have you seen my American friend? His name is Tyler Jergensen. You may have seen him with me."

"He checked out earlier today," said the employee.

Jack instantly realized what was happening. Tyler had left for the Amazon to search for Coffee Lake. He knew that if the lake actually existed and if Tyler found it first then he would be able to purchase it from the locals for his company.

Jack called Tyler's cell phone. Tyler didn't pick up, and the call went to voice mail. Jack booked a flight to the Amazon. Tyler had a head start but not much of one.

Jack found guides who had heard of the coffee lake, but none of them knew where the lake was or if it was even real. One guide said that there was a tribe with dark teeth and lots of energy and that they knew where Coffee Lake was.

The guide led Jack into the Amazon. It wasn't very far before Jack's cellphone stopped working.

They ventured further in by boat and after a few days left the boat to travel on foot. The guide showed Jack a field of wild coffee plants. On the other side of the field was a tribe. The tribe fit the story Jack and Tyler had been told. He rejoiced that he'd beaten Tyler there. Even the older members of the tribe moved with the speed of much younger men. Their village was surrounded by coffee plants. Coffee seemed to be more than a drink to these people. It was a major part of their lives. Jack had learned that long ago in East Africa and Yemen coffee was used in native religious ceremonies. It seemed that this tribe had some of the same beliefs. Jack wondered if it was a coincidence or if this tribe knew some secret about coffee that was only also known by a people who died centuries ago.

An elder member of the tribe approached Jack and his guide. The elder had noticed the way Jack looked at the coffee plants with admiration. Jack talked to the elder through his guide, and they reached a deal. Jack gave the elder a portable coffee maker, and the elder drew a map in the dirt that showed them the location of Coffee Lake. Jack compared the dirt map with his topographical map and marked where it was supposed to be.

Jack and the guide went deeper into the jungle. They stopped when something flew out of the trees and nearly hit them in the head. It was a black blur that flew by them. The guide crouched down. At first Jack thought it was a bird. Then when one flew right by his face he could see that they were bats.

"What is it?" asked Jack.

"Day bats," said the guide. "The coffee, it makes the animals overstimulated."

"If we run really fast we should be able to get past them."

"No. This is where I stop. I won't go any further."

"Fine. I'll meet you back at the village."

Jack ran past the bats. When he was clear of the bats, he began walking again. It was now just him alone in nature, albeit an unusual part of nature. The plants around him looked like coffee shrubs but were larger. The coffee trees seemed taller than normal. Then the smell hit him. It was the smell of fresh-brewed coffee. He followed the scent. He saw a break in the trees and ran to it. When he reached the treeline, he saw it. Jack had found Coffee Lake.

It was a small lake with brown water. It wasn't brown from mud. Jack had seen muddy waters many times before, and this was a different shade. This was a familiar shade. It wasn't as dark as a normal cup of coffee. The coffee-to-water ratio was off. There was a little too much water, but still the smell was amazing. Even diluted, it was the strongest smelling coffee he had ever experienced. He pulled a cup out of his pack and got as close as he could to the lake. It was tough, because there was thick jungle up to the edge of the water that was much higher than the water level. He had to hold onto one of the tree roots and reach down to fill his cup. When his hand entered the water he could feel the temperature. It was warm but not too hot. It reminded him of a hot tub. The idea of a hot tub filled with the world's best coffee excited him. This place, Coffee Lake, was his holy grail. He almost fell in but managed to pull himself back up.

Jack raised his clear cup to check the coffee. There were no bugs crawling in it. He ran it through his portable purifier just in case. As soon as it was purified, he tasted the coffee. It was magnificent. He leaned against a tree and enjoyed the best cup of coffee he had ever had.

Jack looked around, expecting to see Tyler show up. He wanted to see the look on Tyler's face, the look of defeat when Tyler realized he was just a little bit too late. But there was no one around. He was alone in the jungle.

The idea of a hot tub filled with the world's best coffee persisted in his mind. It was a strange idea, but this was a once-in-a-lifetime chance. He took off his pack and his clothes. He moved to the edge of the treeline. He was a few feet above the water level, but he would be able to use the tree roots to pull himself back out.

Jack smiled and jumped into the water. It was warm, and the smell was even stronger in the lake. Jack started to wade around and then noticed something horrifying. It was Tyler, trapped in the tree roots at the edge of the lake. Tyler's tongue was hanging out of his mouth, and his eyes were lifeless. Tyler's arms were tangled in the roots, as if he was trying to climb out of the lake when he died. Jack's mind raced with possibilities. Maybe the tribe attacked him and dumped his body in Coffee Lake. Maybe he was injured by one of the jungle animals but made it to Coffee Lake before he died from the injuries. Maybe the coffee was too strong and it gave him a heart attack. Even if he didn't drink any of it he still absorbed it through his skin. Then Jack realized that he was also absorbing coffee through his skin. All these thoughts faded away, however, when Tyler's corpse bobbed up. The lower torso was missing.

Jack felt a sharp pain in his side. It felt as if he had been nicked by a chainsaw. Then he felt it again and again. His last thought was the realization that Coffee Lake was filled with piranha, piranha with dark teeth and lots of energy.

About the Author

Spencer Carvalho has written short stories for various literary magazines and anthologies. His stories have appeared in the anthologies *Undead of Winter, Horror in Bloom, Moon Shadows, Sanity Clause is Coming,* and *State of Horror: North Carolina.* To find more of his stories check, out his Goodreads.com page.

*****~~~~*****

Confrontation on the Big One Three

by Maureen Bowden

My name is Jacquetta Moon, and I'm a witch. Forget hooked-nosed crone, think young and fit: pre-Raphaelite hair, sooty eye makeup, and purple nails. That's me. I do, however, have a bad-tempered black cat, a mole in my armpit, and a long memory, but I prefer to live in the present.

It was five thirty on Friday afternoon, and I was about to shut up shop, namely 'Vesica Pisces' on Glastonbury High Street: retail outlet for occult artefacts. Rosie Routledge stumbled through the door, colliding with the carousel of feathered dream catchers. She's a sweet child, but all knees and elbows and with a tendency to be clumsy.

"Sorry, Rosie," I said. "I'm closing."

"It's okay, Jacqui. I don't want to buy anything. I've come to see Bill the Bad Cat."

Bill lay sprawled across my glass case of rabbit's foot earrings. He was in need of some serious grooming. Matted black fur, speckled with grey, sprouted in tufts and spikes between bald patches, like a worn-out yard-brush that possibly supported its own eco-system. He opened one yellow eye, surveyed us, hissed, and closed it again. "He's asleep, and he hates to be disturbed," I said. "You know what he's like when he's angry."

She grinned. "Yeah, Mama says she doesn't want to spend another four hours with me in the Accident and Emergency waiting room, so I've come prepared this time." She delved into her Marks & Spencer recyclable Bag for Life, and produced a bottle of Dettol and a packet of Band-aid. "And my tetanus jabs are up to date."

The pricking of my thumbs alerted me to the imminent arrival of another visitor. He, she, or it was closing in on my kitchen. "I have to leave the shop for a while, Rosie," I said. "Don't annoy Bill, and try not to break anything."

"Don't worry," she said. "I'll be careful."

I wasn't reassured, but I hurried through the door into what Rosie calls 'backstage.' The air shimmered like a heat haze, and Hekate, goddess of witchcraft, manifested at my kitchen table. "Hello, Katie," I said. "What's up?"

"Bad news, Jacqui. Matthew Hopkins is back. He reincarnated eighty years ago, and he's finally tracked you down."

I laughed. "Well, there's not much call for a Witchfinder General these days, at least not in Somerset. He can't burn me at the stake, can he? It's illegal."

"So what? The man's barking mad, off his trolley, and away with the west wind. The forces of law and order won't stop him. He's been after your blood since you evaded him in the seventeenth century."

"Huh, some evasion. I had to kill myself to get away from him. I'm not going through that again."

"Don't be melodramatic, girl. You were well on the slippery side of seventy, so you didn't need much killing. Drop of hemlock, wasn't it?"

"Yes, but that was then, this is now," I said. "I like the twenty-first century. I have a thriving business, television is marginally better than the travelling mummers, well, some of it, anyway, and Jed, the mechanic from the local service station is a hummer in the hay."

"Spare me the details, please."

"Fine. The point is, I'm staying put. Can't you get rid of Matthew? You're supposed to be the almighty goddess."

She shook her head. "Like every deity that humankind creates, I can only assert myself through mortal hands. You have to do the dirty work." She cupped my face, turned my head towards her and forced me to look into her eyes. They were beautiful, but they held such sorrow that they seared me with pain. I closed my own eyes to shut it out. "This is more important than one young witch's social life," she said. "Make us both a coffee, and I'll explain."

I listened as I put the kettle on. "The Witchfinder General feeds on women's suffering, because he has a superstitious fear of them, and it's solidified into hatred. He was drawn to this century, because his own ideology is mirrored in events taking place throughout the world. Women are being oppressed, enslaved, tortured, mutilated, and murdered because they are women. Matthew Hopkins' spirit nurtures these obscenities and sustains them."

I handed her a mug of coffee. "Are you saying that if we get rid if Matthew it will solve all this?

"No, Jacqui. It will take many years to put it all right, but it will be a start: a chance for a glimmer of truth to penetrate a great lie."

I sighed. "Tell me what to do."

She sipped her coffee and scowled. "For a start you can put some sugar in this stuff. I doubt if your hemlock tasted as bad." I added three spoonfuls to her star sign mug. She took another sip. "That's better. Now, the first thing is to protect yourself. Is your familiar up to the job?"

I nodded. "He's old, but vicious. He'd have your arm off on a good day."

"Excellent. You should also wear an amulet. It's mostly psychological, but every little helps."

"What about a weapon?"

"I was coming to that. Matthew is fuelled by self-righteous rage. The most effective way to neutralise it is to confront him with innocence."

"I think I'm a good person, Katie. Won't that do?"

"I don't doubt your goodness, but innocent you are not. I remember your dalliance with Kit Marlowe in the

1590s, and I'd rather not know about Jed from the service station. Can you enlist the assistance of a child's unblemished soul?"

We were interrupted by a clatter, a feline yowl, and a human yell, from the vicinity of the shop. I suspected that Rosie was in need of the Dettol and the Band-aid.

"Yes," I said. I believe I can.

"Good. I'll leave you now. Prepare yourself."

"Hang on. When will he be here?"

"Do keep up, Jacqui. What's the date a week today?" I glanced at my Johnny Depp calendar. Of course. The Big One Three. I'd be facing my adversary on Friday the 13th.

Hekate's image had already faded, so I returned to the shop. Bill lay on his back, snoring, with his legs in the air. An upturned display stand lay beside him, and assorted talismans, plastic pixies, and skull-shaped joss stick holders were scattered across the floor. Rosie was sitting in the midst of the debris, dabbing a claw-inflicted gash on her forearm with a Dettol-soaked handkerchief. I dressed the wound with a band-aid. "Would one of your magic potions make it better?" she said.

"Yes, but Dettol works just as well."

"Do you have any spells to stop me getting scratched or bitten again?"

"Yes. Stay away from the cat."

She giggled. "I know you don't mean it. Bill likes me most of the time, and I really like him."

"How old are you, Rosie?"

"Ten."

Old enough. I'd been younger when I first encountered evil. "Do you like me too?" I said.

"Yes, I think you're pretty, and I want to be a witch when I grow up."

"Right. I'll give you a bit of practice. Can you come here next Friday? I need your help with something."

30

She grinned. "Something witchy?"

"Yes."

"Great. I'll come after school."

I spent the next six days preparing. I rummaged through my shed-work reproduction of Pandora's Box, in which I kept assorted junk, and pulled out the rusty horseshoe that had fallen off the shop door in last autumn's hurricane. I polished it up and nailed it back in place, with the opening at the top to catch good luck. I located my amulet fashioned from Morgan le Faye's toenail cuttings, and hung it around my neck. Finally, I began practising an incantation that would place a mystic firewall around Rosie and Matthew, preventing him from drawing strength from the prejudices and beliefs of like-minds. He would have to face the onslaught of Rosie's innocence alone. It would be an equal fight, one to one.

On the morning of Friday the 13th, I tackled Bill the Bad Cat. "Listen, fleabag, I may need you to protect me until Rosie gets here. Do you think you can stay awake long enough?" If a cat could smirk, I swear he did. I added a spoonful of coffee to his saucer of milk, hoping the caffeine would energise the old stinker, and then I crossed my fingers and touched wood.

At 3:30 pm the door burst open, and an octogenarian voice whined, "Jacquetta Moon, bride of Satan, prepare to meet your doom." I turned to face the Witchfinder General. In his previous incarnation he'd worn a cloak and a big hat, and he died young. In this one he was wrinkled, bald, bent, and wearing a belted raincoat I believe I'd seen in Oxfam's shop window. It was at least two sizes too big for him. He would have cut a comical figure, were it not for the zealot's passion that shone in his eyes.

"Ill met by sunlight, Matthew," I said. "What kept you?"

"You hid yourself by your black arts, witch, but I found you by the sign of the Evil One above your door." He cackled and held up my horseshoe.

I laughed, and it wasn't a cackle. "That's a good luck charm, you idiot."

"I am not fooled. You nailed it upwards, to resemble the horns of The Beast. Look. I shall reverse it." He turned the horseshoe upside down, as I'd hoped he would.

"Well done. You've spilled the good luck and the consequences will be on your head."

For a moment I saw doubt in his eyes, then his arrogance reasserted itself. "I have no need of luck. I shall avenge the evil you have inflicted on mankind through your female wiles."

"Nothing changes," I said. "You always blamed every problem on women, including Cromwell's warts, but beware. I have protection." Bill swaggered out from behind the counter and hissed. "Hell spawn," Matthew shrieked. He delved into one of his raincoat's pockets and pulled out a hipflask. "This vial of holy water will reduce you to dust."

"Holy water, my. . . artefacts," I said. "It's out of a tap, and it won't bother anyone, unless they're allergic to fluoride or they've got rabies."

He unscrewed the top of the flask and hurled its contents over Bill. I don't know if it was the caffeine or if the holy water sent his arthritis into remission, but the faithful old Hell spawn leaped through the air and sunk his fangs into Matthew's neck. During the writhing and screeching that followed, Rosie crept in unnoticed. Matthew wrenched Bill away from his neck; Bill slithered down the raincoat and began gnawing at Matthew's ankle. Rosie manoeuvred my shed-ware Pandora's Box from its spot by the wall, to stand close behind Matthew, then she clambered on top of it, raising herself above his height. Matthew fumbled in another pocket and produced a gun.

This was a disturbing turn of events. Not even Morgan's toenails could protect me from a bullet. Rosie was delving into her Bag for Life. To distract Matthew, I said "Hey, have you got a licence for that thing?"

"Of course I have," he said. "I joined a gun club." While I was pondering on why gun club membership didn't require a certificate of sanity, Rosie found her bottle of Dettol, held it above her head, and brought it down on Matthew's skull. Whack! He dropped the gun and keeled over. Bill fled back behind the counter.

Rosie jumped off the box. She dipped her handkerchief into the spilled Dettol and began dabbing at the blood oozing from the gash on Matthew's head and the teeth marks on his throat. I chanted my spell, ring-fencing them from all outside influences. She was unaware of it, but she was about to do battle with my enemy simply by being herself.

Matthew opened his eyes and groaned. Rosie said, "I'm very sorry that I hit you, but I had to stop you from hurting Bill. We should be kind to animals. They depend on us to take care of them."

He glared at her. "That animal is a demon."

"No, he's not," she said. "He's just old and grumpy, like you."

"Who are you, child?"

"My name's Rosie Routledge. What's yours?"

"Matthew Hopkins, Witchfinder General of all England, and I must destroy that witch." He pointed a bony finger at me.

Rosie stuck a band-aid on his neck, "I can tell you're very angry. My Grandpa says anger makes people sad. Would you like to stop being sad, Mr. Hopkins?"

He looked at her as if he was seeing another person for the first time. Maybe he was. "I don't know how," he said.

She smiled. "Grandpa says the best way is to grow things. He grows carrots."

"Why?"

"He says bringing things to life makes him happy, and people will always need carrots. Maybe you could grow something."

The furrows on Matthew's brow deepened. He had never been receptive to innovation, but Rosie had awakened his latent sense of adventure. "Could I grow garlic?" His eyes flashed with a new obsession. "It wards off vampires, you know."

She glanced at me. "Does it, Jacqui?"

I shrugged. "Dunno. I never met a vampire."

She said to Matthew, "Grandpa could probably tell you how to grow it. Let's go and ask him." She helped him to his feet, and turned back to me. "Is it okay if I come back tomorrow to help you with that witchy stuff?" I nodded, and hand in hand, the child led the born-again vampire slayer towards a new destiny. I made a mental note to warn the local Goth community about a mad old man in a raincoat who might increase their street cred by clobbering them with cloves of garlic.

I picked up Matthew's discarded gun, carried it into the back alley, and dropped it down a manhole. When I returned to the shop, Bill was dozing in a pool of Dettol, surrounded by broken glass. "Thanks for your help, old friend," I said.

He opened his eyes in his own good time, balanced his bulk on arthritic legs, raised his tail, and with the nonchalance of advanced age, emitted a blast of flatulence. He then yawned, lay on his back, legs in the air, and with a rasping snore, sank once again into oblivion. I wafted my hands about in an attempt to disperse the methane, lit a joss stick, and placed it in a skull-shaped holder located in close proximity to his rear end.

###

About the Author

Maureen Bowden is a Liverpudlian, living with her musician husband in North Wales. She has had fifty-four poems and short stories accepted for publication by paying markets. Silver Pen publishers nominated one of her stories for the 2015 international Pushcart Prize. She also writes song lyrics, mostly comic political satire, set to traditional melodies. Her husband has performed these in Folk clubs throughout England and Wales. She loves her family and friends, Rock 'n' Roll, Shakespeare, and cats.

*****~~~~~*****

The Plague Well

by Dennis Mombauer

Deep down in the forest, everything was black. Harubai and Tsubada's flashlights turned the roots and branches into a twisted tunnel of shadows, following a path that had long been overgrown into obscurity.

"Did we really need to come here at night?" Tsubada was following his slightly older friend and nearly stumbled over some hidden rocks, which reared up from the gloomy forest floor like a reef.

"Yes, I've told you a dozen times. The legend clearly states that we need moonlight." Harubai had a queasy feeling in his stomach, but it was an exhilarating, adrenaline-producing kind of queasiness. "Only then will the Well answer our questions—and if any night will work, it's this."

High above them, scraps of night sky shone through the treetops, cinereal from the full moon, but this brightness was diluted before it reached the undergrowth. There was rustling up there, followed by a flapping sound, maybe from some small nocturnal bird.

"So the Well is in this town, and the town is abandoned? Nobody lives there anymore?"

"Again, yes. There was a plague a few hundred years ago, and it depopulated the village. It's a ghost town, if you will, with a magical well."

"Do you really believe that somewhere around here, there is a well that can answer questions?"

"Not somewhere. Here." The trees cleared before them to reveal the ruins of a village, pale and spectral in the moon's shimmer. There were cottages and hovels reduced to almost nothing, with trees growing from their floors, roots worming their way between old stones, moss and lichen covering the remaining walls. The village square had been overgrown by grass, and the paths leading in and out were barely visible, swallowed by the surrounding forest.

"Maybe it's true, maybe it isn't, but it's an adventure either way, just to be here, especially at night."

Both boys felt a chill crawl up their bones and cover their skin in goosebumps, while they stared at the ruins, then at each other.

"I guess." Tsubada turned off his flashlight and slowly walked out in the open.

"There is the Well." Harubai overtook his companion, his own lamp flitting over stone foundations and rotting planks. An old gate with faded varnish stood at the bottom of a hill, which was circled by a grass-veiled path and crowned by a blackened spot of earth, marking the site of some building that had vanished a long time ago.

Things scurried away from the lamplight and the boys' approach, mice or insects hidden in the tall weeds. There was no wind, but the trees around them swayed and whispered, while the moonlit ruins remained as still as an old photograph.

"It doesn't look that special to me." Tsubada's voice was quiet and faltered among the noises of the forest, betraying his words.

The well seemed ancient, a round brick-built shaft leading down into the earth, with opaque water that was free of plants, except for a few algaic fingers creeping up at its edges.

"I think it looks very special." The flashlight wandered along the uneven rim of the well and glided over motionless water, before Harubai finally turned it off. "I bet if we measure the whole village from one edge to the other, we would find the Well to be exactly in its middle. And it doesn't smell or anything. . . the water's still fresh." Harubai laughed nervously. "And maybe, it'll answer our questions."

"Yeah."

They both stood at the well's rim and gazed down, their own reflections drifting pallidly on the water, as if sculpted from drowned flesh.

"Do we speak the questions out aloud or just think them? How would this even work?" Tsubada shivered as coldness rose out of the well, like fog steaming over the surface of a mirror.

"O great Well, please answer my question: How can I win Ayafu's heart?"

A drop from above splashed into their reflected images, fragmenting them in a series of concentric circles. Another drop fell, and suddenly rain pelted down, breaking the water of the well into a confusion of cracks and fractures.

"Let's get out of here, under the trees!" Tsubada started to run but came to a halt again after two steps, ignoring the heavy rain.

There were lights around them, lanterns swaying under the porches of buildings and from behind shuttered windows. Where there had been overgrown ruins and rubble before, the boys could now see undamaged houses, sheltered gardens, and polished wooden floors.

"How—" Thunder rolled across the stormy sky and swallowed Tsubada's words. The rain was soaking them to the skin.

At the base of the hill, the free-standing gate gleamed in bright vermilion, visible even through the heavy downpour. A path circled up from it to a wooden shrine, muddy but completely cleared of vegetation. There was someone standing at the entrance of the shrine, but as if the boys had stirred him up, he vanished inside.

"Hey, you there, by the Well!" The shout came from the porch of one of the biggest buildings, from a bald-headed man in a plain robe. "Come on, come on. Do you want to be drowned?"

Ain't Superstitious

Harubai's and Tsubada's feet splashed across the village square, needing no further invitation.

"There you are, come on. This is no weather to be outside." The lantern revealed the man's eyes as white orbs, unable to see, and Harubai wondered how he had heard them over the rain. He had a slim case—a flute?—slung over his back and turned his head in a strangely animalistic fashion, as if he was trying to localize something with his ears.

"What's happening here? Where did all this come from?"

"The people, you mean? The village is being overrun by refugees. No one can continue south, because the road's been flooded. Haven't you seen the encampments at the entrance? What a horrible night they must have, out there in the storm."

"Refugees?" A very unsettling realization dawned on Harubai, a realization that wasn't possible and couldn't be true.

"From the plague. Where did you come from, overseas? Everyone is fleeing the plague, to the fortress city in the south. It's the greatest tragedy of our time—all those lives lost, all those souls carried away. Robbed me of my voice, it has."

"What do you mean? How can this be?"

"We should go inside, talk there." A sign next to the curtain-covered entrance showed an ink-washed tree with hundreds of bats hanging from its branches, and a lettering that read, "The Howling Tree."

"Yes, thank you. Give us a moment, please? Really, thanks for all your help—go in, we'll follow you in a bit."

The blind flutist nodded and made his exit through the curtain, leaving the two boys alone on the porch, surrounded by the rain-shrouded village.

The Plague Well

"What are you doing?" Tsubada's eyes were wide and unsteady, his hands nervously combing his dripping hair. "We have to get out of here!"

"Easier said than done." Harubai strayed around the porch, touching the wooden support beams, testing their physical reality. "Do you know where we are? *When* we are? How do we get out of here, Tsubada? We can't just walk into the forest and hope for the best!"

"The Well!" Tsubada sprinted into the storm again, disappeared, and returned a minute later, splashing water all around him. "The Well brought us here, it has to take us back!"

"Why?" Harubai stopped, his face radiant in the lamplight. "Why did it bring us here, Tsubada? What did you ask it?" He shook his head. "Maybe we are being shown something. Maybe the Well only works in moonlight, and the storm is blocking it. Maybe there is no way back."

"But we are where I think we are, right? Back when the village was still alive, when the plague swept through it?"

"Looks like it." Eyes seemed to be staring at them from behind every window, ears listening behind wooden walls and drawn curtains. Both boys shivered, suddenly not on a harmless nightly adventure anymore but in another world entirely, a world with real death waiting.

"What if we catch this plague? Is there a cure by now? Do you know what it is?"

Harubai shook his head again, his mouth too dry to speak.

"Harubai? Are you all right?"

"Yes. . . yes, yes, everything's fine. Let's get inside, talk to the people, see what's happening here." He brusquely turned to the entrance and slipped through, with Tsubada following him quickly.

. . .

People sat on mats around low tables, standing in groups throughout the room or leaning on the bar counter, a barely worked tree trunk with multiple snags jutting out. Most of the tenants were occupied in their own conversations and business, but some watched Harubai and Tsubada as they made their way to the wooden bar. A man sat at a back table alone, even though the inn was crowded, his hand resting on a monstrous sword. A merchant displayed an array of goods at another table.

The innkeeper, a sturdy woman in her forties, gave them an appraising look.

"You are young."

Harubai thought fast. "Our parents died in the plague. We're going south, to our uncle." What were they doing here, surrounded by people with knives and swords, and probably some carriers of a deadly contagion? Tsubada was right, they needed to get out!

"Have a drink on the house, boys. Let's pray the rain will stop and the roads become traversable again. I don't like all these people backing up here, what with the plague and all."

She put down two mugs of water before them, then tended to another guest.

"What do we do now?" Tsubada stared at Harubai as if he expected him to have all the answers. What could they do? The well had transported them here, but would it bring them back? What if it didn't?

The merchant with his wares on the table gestured them to come over, and they hesitantly approached. Tiny carved sculptures of ivory were arranged before him, albino bats of differing sizes, with their wings folded and their eyes painted bright red.

"Amulets, to protect against the plague." The merchant noticed their looks and smiled encouragingly. "You want one?"

"We don't have money."

"This little animal here is yours." He offered Harubai an ivory bat the size of two fingers, with a cord strung through a hole. "It may be bad business, but in times such as these, we all gotta stick together and share our talents, right? We should do what we can to help others, to make this easier for everyone." He winked at them, then turned around: "Hey, flute-man, play a song for us."

Expectant silence set in as all eyes turned toward the blind flutist.

"I'm sorry, I can't."

"Why not? You are a flute-man, aren't you?"

"Yes, but I only know happy songs, and in times such as these, it doesn't feel right to play them."

"Play them! Especially now, we need something uplifting."

The flutist shrugged and hung his head, until the room returned to its former background murmur and private conversations—only to be startled when a group of people burst in the door.

"The refugee camp is being flooded! We need help! A mudslide has carried away half the road!"

Several villagers jumped to their feet, but stood in place, obviously uneasy. The flutist raised his head again, speaking softly: "We should all stay here, until after the storm. As long as we are inside, nothing will happen—the gods protect us, don't they? It's not as if a little rain would bring down the shrine."

"He is right." The villagers settled down again, glad for an excuse not to run out into the weather. "We are sorry, but we can't help you. It doesn't make sense that more people get lost in the storm."

"But we need help! There are women and children out there, and—"

A flash of white brightness surged through the window from outside, followed by apocalyptic thunder, as if the sky was being ripped open above them.

"What was that?"

Everyone streamed out of the inn, and Harubai and Tsubada were pushed by the rest, onto the porch and further. The whole village was lighted in red reverberations, licking across every house wall like hungry tongues, staining the lantern light to that of burning torches.

A fire consumed the shrine up on the hill, its flames sizzling and smoking in the rain but not being extinguished.

Lightning! The lightning has struck the shrine!" The cry reproduced itself among the crowd, but no one seemed willing—or able—to do something. "Where is the priest?"

Harubai remembered the figure at the shrine's entrance, turning away as they had looked up from the well, and he shuddered. Even though his clothes had somewhat dried by now, he still felt cold, and this was not the only thing that made him shiver.

"There is a demon among us." Someone whispered the words to himself, maybe the ivory merchant, and others joined in. "There is a demon among us."

Harubai slinked to the side and pulled Tsubada with him. The burning shrine made all faces appear flustered and angry, towering above them with restless eyes.

"A demon has brought doom to the village! Someone here is the demon!"

Now everyone stepped away from each other, even if it meant getting further out into the rain. The innkeeper crossed her arms above her breasts, the swordsman suddenly had a hand resting on the hilt of his blade, and numerous people grabbed their bat amulets. Another bolt of lightning came down somewhere over the forest and bathed the whole scene in stark white for a second, before being dispersed by the thunder.

"Help!" In the milling crowd, a man broke down. He was covered in glistening sweat, red-colored by the fire. Harubai realized it wasn't sweat at all, and suddenly tasted acid in his mouth.

"There is no help." The swordsman drew his weapon with a grim expression, and drove it right into the dying man's chest. Harubai dry-heaved, and saw Tsubada do the same at his side. "He is infected. We are all infected, everyone who was in the inn. The demon has tricked us. No one will leave this town alive. The gods have forsaken us."

Harubai gripped Tsubada's shoulder, digging his fingers into his friend's flesh. Tsubada's lips were moving without sound, and he trembled as if he would collapse at any moment.

"The demon is among us! We must find it and kill it!" Regardless of whoever said it first, it soon echoed across the gathered villagers and refugees in a murderous chant.

"We must find it and kill it!" It was hard to tell who shivered from the wet cold and who from aggression, but the entire crowd was in motion, watching each other, the forest, the burning shrine on the hill.

"A priest once told me that demons don't have a sense for art, that they are incapable of creating something beautiful."

"A flute-man who doesn't play. . ."

Swiftly, a free space formed around the flutist in his plain robe, like the sea receding after a high wave. "He told us to stay inside! He prophesized that the shrine would burn down! He didn't want us to help the refugees! He is a stranger!"

"Are we infected?" Tsubada's voice was a whisper under the roaring of the storm and the crowd, which encircled the flutist with increasing hostility.

"I don't know. How would I know? We can only hope that we aren't, and that we can somehow get back again. There has to be a way, something has transported us here, and it can transport us again. The Well–"

Harubai stopped as he saw the crowd closing in on the flutist, led by the swordsman and a couple of muscular young workers.

"He is the demon! The demon has to die!" Several men grabbed the flutist's arms and legs, repeating the phrase over and over. "The demon has to die!"

As Harubai and Tsubada watched in helpless horror, the mob carried the flutist through the rain and toward the well.

"Let me go! I'm not a demon, I'm just a wandering blind man! Help me, please!"

"The demon has to die!" The villagers gathered momentum, then heaved the struggling flutist over the well's rim, plunging him inside with a splash.

The rain stopped, the clouds cleared, and moonlight flooded over the village.

...

"Hey, you there!"

Harubai and Tsubada flinched as the voice resounded across the village, hitting them like a whip.

"You look like you have seen a ghost." A man stood between two of the ruined houses, dressed in walking boots and a camouflaged outfit with several pockets. He bore a vague resemblance to the ivory merchant from the inn, with a hunting rifle slung over his shoulder. "What are you doing out here in the middle of the night?"

"We wanted to see the Well, to get our questions answered!" Tsubada blabbered out the words before Harubai could think of a better story. They shouldn't be here at all, especially not at night, and the huntsman seemed to sense that.

"Ah, following the old legend, yes? What question did you ask that the answer disturbed you so? As far as I understand it, it's supposed to answer only one question anyway, isn't it?"

"One question?"

"What happened here. It is said that the spirit of a travelling flute-man still resides in the village, and that everyone looking into the Well's water will see his last night on earth. He carried the plague with him, the story goes, and the townspeople drowned him for that, but it was already too late. The flute-man died, and the plague swallowed the town, with all the souls in it."

"Is it certain that this flute player brought the plague into the town?"

"This plague. . . " Tsubada interrupted before the huntsman could answer. "What were its symptoms?"

"According to historical records, exhaustion, shivering, feelings of coldness, and delusions. The infected began to see and hear things, blinding lights and bright wings in the darkness, a sensation of being hunted. And then, suddenly, their whole bodies would bleed, and they would die."

Harubai and Tsubada looked at each other, then back at the huntsman, remembering all that had happened.

"You should go home now, back to your parents. Where do you live?" He smiled at them, showing rows of white teeth that shimmered in the pale moonlight. "I can bring you home, if you want."

"No, no." They slowly backed away, the resemblance of the huntsman to the ivory merchant now stronger, almost unmistakable. "We'll find our own way home, no problem. Thank you very much."

They turned and ran blindly through the overgrown village remains and toward the forest, where their path was barely visible. Something flew up from the undergrowth before them, something with albino wings and tiny red eyes. The boys shivered again, more violently this time, and stopped at the edge of the woods.

"What is happening? I don't want to die!" Tsubada had tears streaming over his cheeks, and Harubai fought to prevent himself from crying. "We should have never come here!"

"Don't. . . don't be afraid. Nothing has happened, we will go home now. Here, dry those tears." As his friend wiped his face, Harubai looked back. The huntsman was gone, no trace of him visible anymore, but all the trees between the ruins had white bats hanging from their branches, an abundance of animated, breathing, wing-flapping fruit.

"Everything is all right now. . . " Harubai's voice trailed off as he saw Tsubada's face. His tears had turned red, like iron entirely consumed by rust, dripping down his chin and into the hungry moonlight.

###

About the Author

Dennis Mombauer, born 1984, grew up along the Rhine and today lives and works in Cologne. He writes short stories and novels in German and English and is co-publisher and editor of a German magazine for experimental fiction, *Die Novelle – Zeitschrift für Experimentelles* (http://dienovelle.blogspot.de/). He has current or upcoming short story publications in magazines and anthologies, including *Heroic Fantasy Quarterly, Plasma Frequency,* and *Psychonymous II: Verzogen.*

*****~~~~~*****

Across the Styx of Norway

by Jacob M. Lambert

He let his gaze shift upward—to the sky, where the phosphorescent, neon green hues of the Aurora Borealis seemed to flow in ghastly silence. The night was cold, and as the wind beat against his copper skin, numbing both his lips and cheeks, static filled his ears. And in that static, the gnarled voice of his grandfather: *Only whistle if you're ready.*

Sighing, Michael lowered his gaze back to the vehicle.

It was haunted.

It had taken him three days to reach this point: a day on the boat, then another on the plane, and finally, by taxi—the road. The latter started as an endless, meandering rectangle the color of scorched earth, but eventually forked, then straightened—then forked again, until becoming a dirt road. Like the cancer metastasizing in his abdomen, the roads slowly crept along, invading small towns, then branching outward, infecting others.

The taxi didn't reach the car rental place until four in the afternoon, Svalbard, Norway, time, and it was four-thirty before an old woman with a desiccated, liver-spotted face approached the jaundiced service desk, asking him if he needed help.

"Yes, I need a car," Michael said. The women nodded, offered a smile, and disappeared through a beaded walkway, leaving him puzzled half-leaning over the counter.

Breathing in an eye-watering mixture of turpentine and stale coffee, Michael gazed from from the counter, over to a small room on the left: a waiting room—equipped with white plastic chairs and a black-and-white television set. Unsatisfied, he turned and faced the large

49

glass window behind him. He could see the adjacent town of Longyearbyen three hundred yards away from the rental store. The store sat on top of a slope, and Michael could only make out the arched roofs of the town's houses below and the massive snow bowl that enclosed them. He tried bending at the knees so he could see Mt. Hiorthfjellet in the background, but two things obstructed his vision: the large pink letters written across the glass—and second, a man with long, stringy gray hair peering back at him.

"You need a car?" the man said, his English accented but nonetheless clear.

After placing his long black hair into a ponytail—and raising the hood of his wool jacket—Michael nodded. "If it's not too much trouble. Only need it for a couple hours."

"Where you heading?"

He'd hoped he wouldn't have to answer this question, but here it was, floating like a black cloud between them. *I'm here to cross out the last item on my bucket list, sir—to see the northern lights. Then blow my brains out on the mountain. But don't worry: I won't get blood in the upholstery. That I promise.*

"Just to see the lights. I've always wanted to see them. Ever since I was little."

"You picked the perfect time, too," the man replied, then motioned for Michael to follow him around the corner. "November's the best time. February's good, too—but nothing like now. You headed to the mountain for a better view, I imagine?"

"Yes, sir."

"Well, I hope you aren't expecting nothing fancy, cause all I have is this," the man said, pointing in the direction of a red car covered in rust, dents, and scratches. The back two tires were almost flat, and the headlamps resembled calcified windowpanes—with large cracks running through both.

Sudden warmth spread over Michael's scalp, and he could feel his heart thumping inside his ears, a pulsating sensation that made his head heavy. "I asked for a Honda Civic. The travel agent said you had a Honda?"

"Who? No Honda here—only this."

"I don't remember his name, but he said—"

"There's only my wife and I. And we have only two cars: this one, which we bought at an auction—and our personal vehicle. But if you *are* going to take *this* one, I must show you something. Please, follow me."

Exasperated—and freezing—Michael rounded the building, walked to where the man stood on the right side of the car, and hovered over him.

"See this stain here," he said, pointing to a massive red splotch on the back seat's upholstery. "I thought I should tell you there's blood on the seats and floor back here. Nothing bad happened, but I just thought I'd tell you. If you don't mind, don't try to clean it out, okay? I'd rather you left it alone."

Nothing bad happened. . .

The words played and replayed in his mind—with each reiteration somehow sounding more and more ridiculous.

Don't try to clean it out, okay?

Was this really happening, Michael thought? Or was this another fever dream—like back on the boat, where he'd thought he heard someone screaming in the water? The freezing wind and pain in his stomach told him that he wasn't dreaming, but the eerie, drone-like quality of the man's voice suggested nightmare. And the content of that voice only verified the possibility of the latter. If it wasn't a dream—though he wished that it was (even a terrifying one)—then this was the moment the man would brandish a knife, turn around, and. . .

"So—this alright?"

51

Coughing into his palm, Michael shook his head. "It will have to do. How long before the sun goes down here?"

"An hour, hour-and-a-half at most."

"Alright, how much?" Michael reached into his pocket and removed his wallet.

The man frowned, making him look like a sun-bleached raisin, and shrugged. "Ten dollars—American."

"*Really?*"

He shrugged again.

"Okay, and American's all I have," he replied, placing the money in the man's upturned, steady hand.

"Remember what I said: please leave the stain alone. You don't need to fill up the gas, either. I'll have my wife do that later."

"No problem," Michael said, taking the keys and starting the car—cranking it on the first turn: something that surprised him enough to make him smile. He then climbed in and shut the door, but before he could pull away, the man knocked on the window.

"One more thing: my name's Kent, like Clark Kent. If you break down—which I'm sure you won't—just give me a call. You have a phone?"

"Bought a disposable one when I came into town."

Kent placed his hands on his narrow hips and arched his back, stretching. "Good. My number's on the registration. Call me if you need help. You shouldn't, but that car's never gone up to the mountains. It will make it, but just keep me in mind if you need help."

For the third time that evening, Michael nodded.

"And *don't* mess with that stain. It adds character."

…

Halfway up the mountain, the Geo-look-a-like started overheating.

Cursing the vehicle and slamming on the steering wheel offered nothing more than a headache and throbbing palm. But Michael continued pressing the gas

52

anyway, though he could feel the frame of the car vibrating under his feet—making his heart flutter.

Once he'd reached flat ground, however, stress on the vehicle abated enough for the temperature gauge to rest slightly *under* the large H.

It wasn't smoking, but he could hear sizzling, like sausage casing right before it snapped. He turned on the radio, hoping to drown out the sound. But the only thing that came through the buzzing side speakers was static, static, and garbled laughter mixed with static. Next, he rolled down the windows, but the mountain air instantly numbed his face, forcing him to—

With a final shudder, the Geo-look-a-like started smoking.

Thank God I slowed down, he thought veering to the right, to the side of the road.

Michael parked the car, opened the door, and stepped out into the icy mountain air. As he walked to the hood—though he didn't know what for (he was tribal police, out of Michigan: not a mechanic)—he caught a glimpse of the sky beyond, just over the next hill. A brilliant luminescence painted the landscape an ethereal green—as if the above aurora were greedy, intertwined souls reflecting in a massive mirror, hoping to duplicate itself.

"It's more beautiful than I thought," Michael said, vaguely aware of the radio's static gaining volume behind him.

He took a step forward, then another, then glanced over at the car one more time before deciding he'd walk. As he ventured further away, however, there was a loud pop, like several balloons exploding at once, and a voice—deep and incredulous—shouting at his back, cutting though the previous static.

"All you have to do is give it a minute, son. Give it a chance to cool down."

He didn't see anything, and the static—that was now deafening—had come back. Heart beating rapidly everywhere but his chest, Michael approached the vehicle on knees held together with gelatin, and squinted, half drawn to the aurora, half to the car. *Another fever dream, here? In the middle of nowhere? At least there's no pain.*

"There isn't yet—but it won't last. Trust me," the voice said again, in between bursts of static from the radio, as if tuning itself.

Now I'm hearing voices in the radio? Great—one more thing.

"Will you just get in the damn car and get us closer to the lights? We've been waiting years for this, and you ain't taking *that* away."

"*We?*"

"Yes, *we*—and you ain't crazy: I'm speaking through the radio, like that movie where the son talks to his dad in the past. Yeah—like the movie. But I *ain't* your daddy, and you *ain't* my son. And this most definitely *ain't* the past. Now c'mon. Let's get moving."

Michael felt his jaw drop. And in that same moment, he thought of the laughter he'd heard in the static only a few minutes ago.

It wasn't the radio—but it was. Just not a station or anything.

"If it helps, just think of me as the car's frequency. Can you dig that? If not—try something else. Think of it as memory foam, and I, like everyone else here, happened to leave my *impression* on it. That help you some?"

Michael shook his head.

"Alright, alright. We'll figure it out when we get there, deal?" the voice said, and then faded, leaving behind the same ear-splitting static.

Instead of question it—though he couldn't formulate a logical sentence if he tried—Michael returned to the Geo-look-a-like and, after placing it in drive, floored the gas pedal. The car lurched forward, stalled, and caught traction, the tires producing massive plumes of smoke as they tore into the pavement, sending sediment—and energetic squeals—into the darkness.

"Where do I go?" Michael said, gripping the steering wheel and squinting through the dirty windshield.

Nothing—only static.

"Hello?"

Again—nothing, then, as the aurora's full breadth filled his vision, the static cleared. "Up the hill. A little closer, then stop at the top, underneath it, and open all the doors, so we can finally get out of this damn car."

Once he reached the summit, Michael did exactly that. And when he'd finished, he stepped away from the vehicle, far enough that he could see both the aurora and the car.

He let his gaze shift upward—to the sky, where the phosphorescent, neon green hues of the Aurora Borealis seemed to flow in ghastly silence. The night was cold, and as the wind beat against his copper skin, numbing both his lips and cheeks, static filled his ears. And in that static, the gnarled voice of his grandfather: *Only whistle if you're ready.*

Sighing, Michael lowered his gaze back to the vehicle.

It was haunted.

All four doors of the car remained open, light from the interior spilling out into the darkened, isolated road—music now blaring from the radio, a dissonant classical tune. Michael could now see the people through the dirty windshield, their shapes flickering in and out of focus like the batteries of a dying hologram. Then they were out: exiting the not-a-Geo, dozens of them, into the street—where they circled the car, their eyes fixed on Michael.

Every one of them wide-eyed and exuding an expectant smile.

"Only when *you're* ready, son," the voice said. He wore tattered blue jeans, a white shirt, and had a long, uneven beard. A huge serpentine laceration snaked along his right thigh, removing any equivocality that he had last *sat* in the vehicle.

Again, his grandfather's words: *the light will take you, Michael. But only ask it when you know the time's right. Our people always know. Only whistle when you're ready.*

Warm tears streaming down his numb cheeks, Michael returned the smile of those gathering around the Geo-look-a-like. And a few moments after that, he— averting his attention to the aurora—took a deep breath, pressed his lips together, and blew between them.

Even into the early hours of the next morning, one could still hear the resounding high-pitched whistle coming from somewhere near Mt. Hiorthfjellet, but most passed it off as ringing in their ears—while others, the more *superstitious*, knew it involved the northern lights.

Kent—like Clark Kent—heard it, too.

And he couldn't help but smile.

About the Author

First place recipient of the Scott and Zelda Fitzgerald award for short story, Jacob M. Lambert has published with Dark Hall Press, *Midnight Echo: The Magazine of the Australian Horror Writers Association,* and more. He lives in Montgomery, Alabama, where he teaches music and is an editorial assistant for The Scriblerian and the Kit-Cats, an academic journal pertaining to English literature of the late seventeenth-and early eighteenth-century. When not writing, he enjoys time with his wife, Stephanie, and daughter, Annabelle.

*****~~~~~*****

The Necromancer

by John Hegenberger

November 29

Watched the original "Invasion of the Body Snatchers" last night. Had seen it before, of course, years ago—when I was still alive.

It's the one where some alien vegetable form takes over citizens of Santa Mira, California. Silly movie. Old, too. Reminded me of a lot of those other vampire legends. People have a whole mythos about outside intelligences taking over their bodies, using things like voodoo, and stealing their freedoms. Glad I don't have to worry about those superstitions any more.

Got enough to sweat with selling life insurance. Ever since the perfection of Necrotech, folks know that their bodies will be sold and used again after they're dead. It's not a curse; it's a business. The money from the sale goes to the survivors, so who cares about life insurance any more? Still, that's my job: finding clients, meeting in their living rooms, and explaining actuary tables. Good thing they don't know I'm a Deadman, or they'd never sign. Tough duty, but that's my programming. It's quiet, safe, and leaves me plenty of time to be with the family and watch old movies.

December 21

Went to church again. Don't know why they bother with that foolishness. When you're dead, you're dead. Strange concept: the Holy Spirit. It's invited into a person's soul. "Fill us with the Holy Spirit," they sang. Why do these things continue to bother me?

January 1

Remembered something. During downtime at night, thought of other experiences than my own. How is that possible?

Seemed as if I worked at a clinic, or biolab. Lots of controlled samples. Beakers, flasks, enhanced lymphocytes. How could I know that? Deaders aren't supposed to dream.

February 4

Vid reports. According to the news programs, the human brain slows down after ten minutes of intense observation of the vid screen. Gale and Tommy took me to the theater. Crowds of people paying to sit in a large darkened room and have their minds affected by wide, colorful images of stimulating events and rich, loud sounds. Gale said I was too analytical. Tommy thought that was a good sign.

"Don't you feel anything?" she asked.

Shrugged.

Her eyes began to fill with tears.

Tommy took our hands and walked between us. "It'll be all right," he said. Can't remember the name of the movie, but the title ended with a number.

February 10

Drugs. Don't mind eating, but this alcohol has a blindingly painful effect on my system. Neighbor across the hall smokes tobacco. Tried it once; hurt my awareness and perception.

March 6

Don't understand Gale's art. Told her, and she thought I meant paintings or sculptures. Don't understand any art. Music, dance, poetry, architecture.

Seems like mass hypnosis. Generation-fostered hoax. What purpose does it serve these people?

March 11

Didn't have all these problems when I first became a Deader. Everything was peaceful then. No worry. No guilt. Gale was upset, but she handled it well, considering. Tommy was a real trouper. He'd have made a wonderful lab tech.

Wonder why I think that? They keep telling me I worked in a lab. Even took me there one time. Seemed a little familiar, at first. Then decided it was something I'd seen on the news, a movie. Left me cold.

March 15

Caught Gale crying again last night. She'd been out with Norman, but had come home alone, tipsy. She called me into the bedroom and made me put my arms around her. Her eyes searched for something in my face. Held her as she instructed. Did everything she said, but felt nothing. She held my face in the palms of her hands. "This has to stop," she told me.

"What?"

"I need you, Andy. You've got to come back to me."

"I'm here."

"No, you're not!" she cried and pushed me away.

Sat in a chair until she fell asleep.

April 2

Getting closer to the answer. Read a book about zen by Alan Watts. What is reality? Tricky business. Simple converging lines in two dimensions "suggest" a third dimension, depth. Esthetics. If we don't know what life is, then what is death? Anti-life? Anti-atoms in my blood?

May 23

Sex. Somehow my body seems to move by itself. Watched it, but couldn't get it to follow my instructions. Almost automatic. Who's in charge?

May 25

Sleep. Another "bodily function." Includes dreams. Dreams bother me. Their power is a lot like the movies or vids, only much more secret and personal.

June 7

Gale is fed up.

"The government has paid to keep you in a home," she said, "and I can't fight it any longer. I have my own life to live. Don't you see? It's not your fault. It would have happened anyway. Besides, it's not so bad. They use Deadmen for lots of menial tasks. Bus driving, baby sitting, even forgodsakes caddying! You've got to get over it, Andy. Maybe the therapy will do some good."

June 8

Deadmen. Some people trade and collect them. Kids get them for Christmas now. Deadmen on Mercury. Deadmen in college, taking exams. Deadmen used as memory banks. Deadmen used to beat up bullies. Deadmen in the police force. In the hospitals, monitoring patients. In the movies. Deadmen as a protein substitute. Deadmen as a "living" art form. Deadmen in college, giving exams.

June 20

Undergoing therapy.

Psychology unifies and combines most of the other mysterious elements. The lies, the sex, the dreams, the drugs, the various aspects of Reality and Truth. Having experienced quite bit of this now, I find that there are thousands of variations and opinions regarding Reality.

Must choose a Reality and then act accordingly. If I do, I'll appear to be "cured," and they will leave me alone. But, I'm not insane; I'm dead! Don't they understand? I didn't cause all these Deaders to be walking around; I'm innocent.

Not so sure I want to leave this place. Didn't like selling insurance anyway. Besides, I can learn a lot about psychology, this way. The only problem is the shock therapy and the drugs. They keep giving my body things that make it uncooperative. And call me Doctor Westfield.

July 12

Dying. But how can this be? Am already dead, aren't I? Aren't I? How can I die, if I'm already dead?

"You're not dead," they tell me. "It's all in your mind. You've suffered a withdrawal. Your guilt for having perfected the Deader made you empathize with all the bodies that had been reanimated."

"Yes," I say. "It's my fault."

"No, there is no fault, Dr. Westfield. What you've done has helped mankind. You've freed us all from mindless labor. You've shown the way to eternal prosperity. Admittedly, there have been problems, but that's exactly why we need your help."

"My help?"

"Yes, we couldn't create one without you, Dr. Westfield. Your achievement set the standard. The economy is booming. "

"But it's all so complex. The dreams, the media, the art, the sex. . . "

"We'll help you. Your wife and son will help you, too. You'll be all right. You'll see."

November 8

I know what they meant. It's difficult to deal with life and all its confusions. I refused for a long time to accept my responsibilities. It seemed as if the Deaders had

61

it easier, but when you're dead, you're dead. I know that now.

We flew to Stockholm for the award ceremony. Gale and Tommy loved it. I felt foolish in a rented tuxedo accepting the prize. But I got a chance to meet and compare notes with several important colleagues, who heralded me as a man of genius. But I know better; I'm just a man who saw a job that needed to be done. A man who advanced the technology one step farther along its endless progression. Nothing to feel guilty or proud about.

November 23
We watched another movie tonight. An ancient superstitious nonsense called "Frankenstein." But it made me wonder if it's possible for Deadmen to achieve free will. I plan to begin analysis on this question in the lab tomorrow morning.

About the Author

John Hegenberger has published before in *Galaxy* and *Amazing*. He will soon have a new SF novel published by Rough Edges Press, *Mutiny on Outstation Zori*. Check out also his trilogy of novels coming from Black Opal Press about TripleEye, the first private eye agency on Mars. His newest novel, TRIPL3 CROSS, launched in August.

*****~~~~~*****

Pandora's Piñata

by E. E. King

It happened in a Mexican village, the kind known as Pueblos Mágicos, magic towns.

Like hand-painted Easter eggs, each magic town was similar, yet unique.

Some nested on the shores near oceans bluer than the turquoise necklaces the old women hawked to tourists on white sand beaches.

Others were high in desert mountains, where deep canyons seared the dry ground. Once a year, when the rains came regular as sunrise, the arroyos rushed with water, turning the barren hills green. On rocky crags, barbed cactus exploded in delicate, fragrant blossoms that lasted but a single night.

A few dotted the midlands, cobbled streets circled rocky hills like spiraling orange peels. Weathered crucifixes shaded rutted lanes.

All were small, ancient places unchanged by the passing of centuries. In these towns anything might happen. Lightning might strike twice in exactly the same place. Children would dream of flight and awaken to torn shirts, their floor littered with flamingo-pink feathers.

In other towns nothing happened. And in this town of which I speak, it was nothing that made it magic. A nothing so perfect bluebirds roosted on the ground. Fledglings could hop out of their nests and stroll into the forest to search for worms, without even bothering to spread their wings. It was a nothing so undisturbed even the roosters didn't crow at night, which as anyone who's ever been to Mexico can tell you is very nothing indeed.

It was a nothing so peaceful that bulls never fought. No one spurred the naked feet of birds and made them fight. No one could conceive of an idea so cruel and

63

unnatural. Stray dogs were well fed. Not one had mange or fleas. There were no stray cats; all had homes and were so fat and sleepy they did not bother to catch birds. This was a good thing, because as I've mentioned, the birds preferred to walk.

The only beings not wholly content in this place where nothing was magic were the worms and the old witch woman, Yadira Arevalo, who lived beneath a worn stone bridge that arched over a barren arroyo.

Each magic town has its individual customs. In this one, in the *Zocalo*, the central square, hundreds of piñatas dangled above narrow streets. Over clay skeletons and skins of cardboard, bright loops of tissue paper clothed burros and lions. Brilliantly colored Micky Mouses and grinning demons swayed perilously in the gentlest of breezes. Every year on the first night of Día de los Muertos, the piñatas were smashed.

On that night the children, faces painted like grinning skulls, were blindfolded. They spun round and round. Shrieking with joy they twirled, swinging hard wood bats, hoping to smash ceramic bones and release candied guts into the streets. The tiniest girls were always the most vicious.

Día de los Muertos lasted three days. These were spent gardening and picnicking on ancestral graves. Children offered up pinwheels and candy. Women cooked for weeks and baked for months in preparation. Men brought their finest cigars and tequila to share with the beloved dead.

But one year, in this pueblo where nothing happened, something extraordinary took place. The first night of Día de los Muertos came twice.

Afterward no one remembered the second coming, no one except for Yadira Arevalo.

After all, she had summoned it. For years she had saved the bones of fragile creatures and distilled the juices of rare orchids. For decades she had hoarded the tears of young girls and kept the cries of women who died in childbirth safe in airtight Mayan baskets.

Late, late at night, after the piñatas had been pulverized, the sweets collected, and most eaten. When children slumbered fat and happy in their beds. When parents dozed exhausted by the reveries. Yadira gathered together all the pieces of the shattered piñatas and carried them off to her home beneath the bridge.

Under the white full moon, she sliced off the tip of the little finger on her left hand and, mixing it with tears, pain, and bones, made offerings to the ancient gods of death and carnage. In the stillness of the village, the gods listened. In the calm of the nothingness they came. Swiftly as desire they turned the clocks back.

Yadira stuffed the broken piñatas with dreams as colorful as the tiny woven dolls peddled by indigenous women in the *Zocalo*. She wove them back together with tendons of memory, readying them for the second first night of Día de los Muertos. She wiped the town's memories clean as newly sewn communion frocks.

Beneath a second full moon, the blindfolded children swung wooded bats, harder than reality, shattering the inner clay. Dreams poured out, dispersing like sparks, before reaching the ground, clouding the air with the acrid scent of desire.

The magic gushed through the streets, dangerous as sudden rains in the deep, dry arroyos that surrounded the town.

A boy wishing for a pony might arrive home to discover his house a stable. A man craving wealth would find his wife turned to gold. A girl wishing for a husband could find herself betrothed to an *anciano* older than her grandfather.

Amelia, a visiting American, was swept away by the unexpected deluge of dreams made manifest. She had been strolling the winding streets, wishing for an exotic romance, even though Matt, her childhood sweetheart, waited back home.

Matt was as faithful as an albatross—birds so true they will circle the world to return to their mates. But Amelia was not thinking of Matt. She was not anticipating her homecoming. Instead she was imagining muscled brown arms and glossy black hair.

Stumbling into the *Zocalo* she fell, deep and hard as the wooden piñata shattering bats, for the first man she saw. He had soft night hair, eyes dark as secrets, and was strumming a silver guitar.

Amelia couldn't understand the lyrics, but it was clear he was playing a love song. She didn't know that *desamor* meant not love but heartbreak. She didn't realize that desire provides a sandy foundation for anything lasting. Although Amelia was majoring in music, she didn't notice that he was out of tune.

She didn't stop to investigate, or she might have discovered that the musician already had a wife, a mistress, and twelve children scattered round the country, messy as sugared *pan dulce*.

Instead, she marched right up to him and laid her fingers on his strings. The man smiled up at her, and who would not? She was twenty-three and blond as sunlight.

The silver in his molars added gleam to his grin. Amelia was dazzled.

Things are going to go badly, you can already tell. But what is a story, or indeed a life, without difficulty? Misadventure is more interesting than happiness. It is why angels are boring and God is a bore. It is why heroes are unmarried and seductresses smell sweeter than ingénues. The devil has better stories, and everyone knows he's a better musician. God hands out harps to anyone who'll take them, but the devil choses his instruments with care.

Ricardo's smooth hands stroked chords in Amelia's chest she didn't even know existed. She tasted red wine and inhaled the heady scent of night cactus.

She forgot Matt, even though they had been born only four days apart and had been friends from before the time of memory.

Ricardo glistened, inviting as a warm ocean. She didn't realize that he was too flashy for everyday wear. He was a piece of cheaply gilded jewelry that would slip through your fingers, leaving them glittering but empty.

Amelia moved in with Ricardo, although he did not move in with her. He found her a job teaching English at a private school in town. He'd visit once a week, then depart with a kiss sweet as lemonade.

"I must leave you now, my darling," he'd say. "My heart breaks every time I do, but I must travel to the city to play."

"I could come with you," she said. "I hardly make any money at that school. I'm sure I could make more doing translations online."

"If only you could, my love, my life would be complete—but alas, the children need you, and you would never desert them. You are selfless, darling."

Amelia hated the children. They were as rich and as rotten as week-old menudo. She was poisoned by guilt.

Meanwhile Matt wrote. He sent daily email, texts, and skypes. Amelia blocked her ears with wax and disconnected her internet.

He sent carrier pigeons, who winged their way from the Midwest to the middle of Mexico, collapsing exhausted on Amelia's porch, hearts beating faster than a hummingbird's. Amelia ignored them.

At dusk Yadira crept out from under the bridge and carried them home. She wrung their necks and drained their blood into old salsa jars for use in love potions. Plucking off their tattered feathers, she roasted their naked bodies over Matt's unread epistles. The burnt words drifted into the night, making young girls dizzy with the smell of heartbreak and longing.

Ain't Superstitious

Matt waited, but his birds did not return. He had read of pigeons navigating wars and across oceans to return to their mates, but his, it seemed, were as faithless as Amelia.

Matt had always played the guitar. Now, with nothing to distract him, he began to write and record songs. Plucking his battered guitar, he whispered into the mic as if it were a lover.

When I call your name only wind replies
The words scald my tongue and that's no lie
Your memory tastes like sorrow and regret
No matter how I try I can't forget.
I call your name only wind replies
I call your name and hear only sighs.
I know I will never find another you
But you, you will never find another me
You'll regret it girl
Don't forget me girl
I'm alone in the night I don't know why
I love you babe that's no lie

Matt's music went viral. Asian girls swooned over his blond hair and round blue eyes, so different from their own. Latin girls appreciated his lack of machismo, so different from their fathers'. African girls admired the way his fingers drummed, faster than cicadas, round the smooth heart of his instrument.

Yadira collected the sorrow in these songs and the yearning they inspired. She wove them into colorful ribbons, which she gave to unmarried girls. They were charms, she said, which would be sure to draw husbands. And they did. She did not mention that trinkets made from regret and bad decisions almost never attract true love. She did not tell them that a wedding is not an end but a beginning.

The married girls did not talk either. They were too busy at home, cooking, cleaning, and caring for children. They were too embarrassed to show their bruised faces, split lips, and battered limbs.

Because this is a story and not life, you might expect Amelia to hear Matt's music. She would return and battle for her man, driving away his pretty, adoring, but essentially vapid, groupies.

But, because sometime fiction is almost as hard as life, especially when a witch is involved, this did not happen. Instead Amelia got pregnant, and Ricardo abandoned her.

Matt's fame grew. He collected girls like charms for a bracelet, but never opened his heart.

In the village where all had been content save Yadira and the worms, now only Yadira was satisfied.

She had become strong from the music of misery. She was a muse to the melancholy, a genius to the grieving. Under her inspiration romances turned to tragedies, and comedies blackened. Even the lightest work developed a Russian flavor. On the pages of books, lovers quarreled, children sickened, and the dog always died.

Thus, the town that had been magic for nothing, because a center for art and heartache.

Matt, whose songs had become increasingly depressing, went out of fashion. He developed a virulent case of writer's block. His mind was not just miserable, but empty. His agent suggested a vacation.

"Why don't you go to Sunny Mexico," Matt's agent said. "Why not go now, and celebrate the Day of the Dead?" Matt agreed. It sounded like his kind of holiday.

As usual the town square was bedecked in piñatas. It would take much more than misfortune, misery, death, or even magic, to alter the traditions of an ancient pueblo.

Yadira had grown complacent. She no longer bothered to gather the death cries of pregnant woman, or the sobs of shattered children. She let the rare orchids, whose juice was so useful in the making of concoctions, live. It was too much work to climb the steep, dry hills and scale the rough, tall trees where they thrived. Besides, why bother? Nothing had changed, nothing would change. An emotion in motion will stay in motion, and an emotion in depression will stay in depression. This was Yadira's law.

But laws, like piñatas, are meant to be broken.

Amelia had taken her daughter, Maria, to the square for the inaugural night of Día de los Muertos. Maria was five. It was the first time she would be big enough to heft one of the piñata smashing bats.

Ricardo was there, as always, playing his silver guitar and crooning. He was off key, and Amelia knew it. Her Spanish had improved. She understood the meaning of heartache, of regret. The full moon rose. For an instant the brilliantly colored tissue skins of the hanging animals and demons glowed like dreams. A cloud drifted across the moon, or perhaps the moon hid. Either way, the result was the same. In near-darkness, the children went wild. Like blind armies, they battered the hundreds of piñatas to bits.

Matt watched from the balcony of a nightclub. A straying breeze caught the ash from his cigarette, creating small black eddies in the sky. He felt like he had seen it all, even though he'd never been to Mexico.

Just then Maria shattered one of the hundred piñatas. Candy fell about her like hail. She laughed with so much joy, Amelia couldn't help smiling too.

A fragment of piñata flew through the air and grazed Matt's hand. It cut him so deeply a drop of blood dripped from the wound into the screaming crowd.

Just then, so unexpectedly it might have been magic, the moon peeked out from the cloud. Amelia's hair had turned white, but in the moonlight it looked like sunshine. Her face was worn and weathered, but in the dim light, lines smoothed by laughter, she looked like a girl.

Matt, gazing down to watch his falling blood, saw their joyous upturned faces. He heard a new song in his mind. This one had a happy ending.

About the Author

E.E. King is a performer, writer, biologist and painter. Ray Bradbury calls her stories "marvelously inventive, wildly funny and deeply thought provoking. I cannot recommend them highly enough." She has won numerous awards and been published widely. She's been the recipient of many biological research and art grants.

She's painted murals in Los Angeles, California, and Spain, worked with children in Bosnia, Korea, Los Angeles and San Francisco, crocodiles in Mexico, frogs in Puerto Rico, egrets in Bali, mushrooms in Montana, archaeologists in Spain, and butterflies in South Central Los Angeles. In her spare time, she gardens and raises egrets, kittens, or whatever small creature comes her way.

For more information, visit her website at www.elizabetheveking.com

*****~~~~~*****

A Day to End All Days

by James Aquilone

When I kicked the homeless guy in the gut, I didn't even scuff my alligator-skin boots. The guy drunkenly got to his feet, swayed like a blade of grass in a hurricane, looked up at me with whisky eyes.

I glared at him.

He got the message and dashed back up the alley. I thought about hunting him down, and breaking an arm or a leg, but I didn't feel like running. Not in that heat. Staten Island in July has to be worse than the sixth circle of Hell.

I was still holding the scratch-off ticket. I pressed it against the brick wall, scraped off the last square with my thumbnail, and a wet-eyed kitten appeared. Looking just as dumb and pathetic as the homeless guy. Un-*fucking*-believable. That was the third kitty I had uncovered. All told, I had won fifteen thousand dollars!

I shoved the winning scratch-offs into my pocket, and thought about the audacity of a stranger asking me for a handout—ninety-three cents, actually; he was very specific about it.

Not today, buddy. I was sick of playing Mr. Nicey Nice. This was going to be a day of reckoning—despite a few early bad omens.

I took the ferry to work.

Work was at the Donnelly Library in Midtown Manhattan. It was a slim building, squeezed between a Starbucks and an arty gift shop. With the Moderne Museum across the street, the café and gift shop received hordes of tourists and hipsters. The library, though, was mostly patronized by pale-skinned office workers. They disgusted me. I worked in the basement, in the media room. No one went down there, which suited me fine. But there was this one girl.

Her name was Jessie. She came into the library most days around lunchtime, read film books, occasionally photography books or Doctor Who novels. She worked at the Starbucks next door. She had no idea poor Peter Palumbo existed.

When I entered the media room, she was sitting at one of the tables beside the CD collection. She was reading. Today her hair was purple. She wore a nose ring, an emerald stud that shone like a tiny dragon's eye, and thick-framed glasses. She looked like some kind of circus pixie. I just wanted to eat her up.

I came stomping down the aisle toward her, clearing my throat conspicuously. But she stayed focused on her book. As I got closer, I noticed she was wearing headphones. Most likely listening to something upbeat and about death. I was about to kick the back of her chair, when Linda said, "Neil wants to see you." Neil was the manager of the media department. Linda worked the checkout desk.

She was behind the counter, removing books from a large canvas bin and placing them in a book cart. I stood beside her.

Linda looked up. "Neil said it was important."

I glared at her.

"What are you doing?" she said. Her hair reminded me of a den of snakes. That was the only thing I liked about her.

I said, "Gazing into your soul."

"What's gotten into you, Peter? You weren't always a jerk."

"All things change, Linda. Even your old reliable Peter."

"Yeah, well, I liked the old you better. I think those horror stories you write have gotten into your head. Or have you been reading those self-help books upstairs? *The Seven Habits of Highly Effective Douchebags?*" Her laugh was piercing, like a shriek from the abyss.

"Linda, do you want to know how you're going to die?"

Panic washed over her wrinkled face. "Weirdo," she said, and returned to sorting books. I went into Neil's office.

Neil Likpudlian was a great big fat guy, with eyes like black jujubes. He was in a constant state of trying to catch his breath, as if he had just climbed to the top of the Empire State Building.

"Peter, Peter pumpkin eater," he said. "Sit down."

He sat at his desk, hunched over a plate of chicken wings stained with a gooey, bloody red liquid.

I sat.

"It's eleven-thirty in the a.m., Petey. Kinda late, isn't it?" He raised his eyebrows, leaned forward in anticipation of an answer. I said nothing. He waved it off, gasped his fat-man gasp, held up a hand as if to say, "Wait, a minute," caught his breath, picked up a wing, and gnawed it like a beaver, the blood-red sauce slithering down his adipose hand. "I'm sure you have your reasons for being three hours late. Maybe you can't see your watch now that you've stopped wearing glasses. Contacts?" He giggled. A man should not giggle. "Anyhoo," he said, "I want to talk to you about your career."

Could he be firing me? God, I hoped so.

"You've been here a long time, Petey. Some might say too long." A laugh bubbled up from his blubbering throat. "And, well, I've been sorely aware that in all that time you've never once had a promotion. Shame. Real shame, Petey. The phrase 'dead-end career' comes to mind." Again, the terrible fat-man laugh. I smiled. I liked the sound of that phrase, "dead-end career." Something lyrical and ominous about it.

"Couldn't be helped," he said. "Damn budget cuts and the like. Well—and this doesn't leave the room— we're up for another round of cuts. Ten percent of the staff this time. But there's a silver lining. Always a silver lining, right? Your very own Neil has been promoted to manager of Donnelly *and* the Midtown Library—after they fire both managers, of course. Seems they're making too much. So, what this all means is we need a new media manager." He paused.

I said nothing. Bile was rising in my throat.

"You're getting that promotion finally! Opportunity is knocking, old Petes." He grabbed another chicken wing, inhaled it, and then he rapped hard on his desk. His bobble-head Gandalf the Grey bobbled its head. He gagged, chicken-wing juice leaking out of the corners of his mouth. "Are you ready to get up and open the door? I know you can be quite bashful, Petes."

I got up and punched him in his fat throat. Then I took an early lunch break.

Jessie had left by the time I exited Neil's office. So I decided to pay her a visit.

...

I sat in a big, cushiony chair in the corner of the Starbucks. It was overrun with creatures in Brooks Brothers suits, dull soulless things gazing blankly into smartphones. The place smelled like burnt asphalt. I watched them, imagining how each would die. A tall, bespectacled executive type sat next to me. He droned into his phone like a chittering locust. His death, in three months time, will come swiftly, like an eagle swooping from the sky to pluck its supper from the river. He will be intoxicated on Jack Daniel's and Oxycontin, he will be on a lake, his children watching, his mistress watching, he will be skimming along the water in a jet-ski, he will collide with a motorboat full of teenagers, the propeller vivisecting him from crotch to chin. I snickered at the thought.

"What's so funny?" a voice asked. I looked up. It was Jessie. She seemed out of place in her green apron.

"Inside joke," I said.

"I know you, right?"

"No. You don't know me at all." I winked.

"The library, right? You work there."

Probably not anymore, but I said, "Smart girl."

"Oh, hey. It's funny that I've never seen you in here before."

"I've never been here before."

"Really? I'm in the library almost every day. You must have seen me there."

Ol' Peter Peter Pumpkin had seen her in his nightly fantasies. He had his eye on this siren with a nose ring for some time. But the old reliable Peter never uttered a word to her. Peter Peter wrote stories about her, too. Right now, three novels—unique manuscripts—were floating around the various publishing houses of New York, fantasies about a purple-haired emo girl who battles demons and incubi and ifrits and all manner of supernatural nasties. They were written in blood. I sent them special delivery first thing in the morning.

She said, "It's strange. I never really noticed you before. Why is that?"

"I walk in the ways of darkness."

She smiled. I touched her then. Perhaps too soon. But I couldn't help myself. I reached out, innocently, a light touch on her forearm. She didn't pull away. I let it linger for only a moment.

I said, "Want to know how you'll die?"

She smiled awkwardly but didn't back away. She was supposed to back away at that point. "Not particularly," she said, and smiled again. But this time it wasn't awkward but sweet. That smile was an abomination. I had nasty plans for that smile.

"It's not very interesting, actually," I said, and flashed my most charming smile. "It's not as if a lunatic hunts you down like a wild animal, captures you, devours your flesh, and leaves your bones for the wolves to gnaw on."

She threw her head back and laughed.

I glared at her.

I defiled the temptress in the employee bathroom, three times. She insisted. Afterwards, I told her how she'd die. I had lied to her before. She *would* die in a most spectacular and cruel way. Just not at the hands of a maniac. It would be a brain tumor exploding through her skull while she flew to Hawaii on her honeymoon.

When I returned to the library to clean out my desk, I heard a croaking from Neil's office. I walked past the door, and the blob came stumbling out. I was about to strike, when he extended his hand. But before I could grab it, twist it, and snap his ulna, he said, "I have to thank you. The medic said I would have been a goner if you hadn't dislodged that chicken bone from my throat. I owe you my life. You're like my guardian angel. How did you even know I was choking?"

The bile reached the back of my tongue. I said, "Your life, Neil Likpudlian, is worth less than a flea turd. Your time on this earth is quickly fading. You will die overwhelmed with panic and terror, blood dripping red and dark from your orifices. You will lie, gasping, on the cold floor, a vile stench rising to your flared nostrils as your bowels evacuate and your life runs out through your ass. Your funeral will be a sad, pitiful affair."

Neil looked confused, as if he were trying to figure out a tough mathematical problem. Finally, he said, "Oh, Petes, you're probably right. I really do need to lay off the fast food. Anyhoo, I'm giving you my bobble-head collection, which you've always admired. Think of it as your promotion gift."

I went home, cursing my luck.

Home was a cramped basement apartment in the Bulls Head section of Staten Island. Most of the place was taken up by paperbacks and magazines. Some of which weren't pornographic. The life of Peter Paul Palumbo was pathetic.

The phone rang.

I hoped it was Jessie, Jessie shouting and raging about how she hated every miserable bone in my body.

"Is this Peter Paul Palumbo?"

"In the flesh."

"This is Margaret Hutcherson from Hexen Publishing. I want to talk to you about the MS you sent us."

Please, say you want to press charges, black list me from the publishing world. Time was running out.

"We've read your novel *Jessie and the Jorōgumo Queen,*" she said, "and we—*love*—it! Where have you been hiding? We're ready to offer you a three-book deal. We adored that the manuscript was written in fake blood and the paper you used—what amazing texture—felt like animal skin. This is exactly what we've been looking for. It has weight, a living quality to it that you can't get with an e-book. We're actually losing a bundle with e-books, you know."

Black bile rushed up my throat and geysered out of my mouth. I hurled the phone across the room and stomped on the ground like a madman. Everything was wrong.

Then they went wronger.

I received a text message from Jessie: "Had a great time! You're an animal!!! Call me ;)" A great time? Did I not perform the Iron Maiden *and* the Angry Dragon? Divulged the terrible details of her death?

I looked at my watch. Goddammit! The day was over.

I had failed.

...

As per our agreement, I vacated Peter Palumbo's body.

The plump geek stood before me. He beamed. It sickened me.

"I thought you'd try to pull a fast one and destroy my life or something," he said. "But this is great. I got so

79

much more than I bargained for. Usually you hear that deals with demons go the other way, but you really came through."

I lowered my boney, black head, retracted my wings.

"Confession time," I said. "This whole 'renting a soul' business is a scam. Supposed to be a scam, anyway."

"But you said you guys no longer bought souls. You only rent them for a day now, and then you'd grant me a wish: get me published. You did exactly that."

"Don't be so fucking naïve, Peter. Once I took possession of your soul, I was *supposed* to destroy your life within the allotted twenty-four hours, which subsequently would have plunged you into an all-consuming madness, and, in the end, we'd get your soul forever. It's pretty simple. When it works, of course. Which it didn't."

"Why didn't it work?"

"It's me. I am a guardian angel. *Was* a guardian angel. I became a demon after some crap with those vindictive cherubs; it's not important. This was my first job. But the guardian angel mojo in me is too strong, apparently. Every time I tried to hurt you, I ended up helping you. You wouldn't want to make another bargain, would you? Double or nothing? They're going to crucify me when I get back. And I'm not talking figuratively."

"Don't think so."

I began pacing. My wings fluttered like a spastic housefly. "Do you have any cigarettes? Booze?"

"I don't."

"I know that. I know everything that was in your sad head. I was just hoping I was wrong. Everything else had gone wrong today."

"Look, you seem to be a great guardian angel. Why don't you just go back to that?"

"You know the forgiveness crap in the Bible?"

"Yeah."

"It's just that. Crap. Once you're out of Heaven, you're done. I can't be a guardian angel again, and I suck as a demon. I'm screwed."

Peter's face scrunched up like a puckered anus. The blob was thinking. "You want my soul for eternity, right?" he said.

"Yes, yes! Are you offering it?" A glimmer of hope.

"No. But you made all my dreams come true, and I don't want to see you get punished. Now that I have a book deal I'm not going to need my old job. Hell, I don't need my apartment either. You can have it all. Take my old life. It's all yours."

Live as a frustrated writer in a basement apartment in Staten Island? I thought about it for all of a second. "I'd rather take my chances in Hell," I said, and descended to the Underworld. If I was lucky, they'd only tear out my entrails for ten thousand years.

About the Author

James Aquilone is an editor and writer, for fun and for profit. His fiction has appeared in *Nature's Futures*, *The Best of Galaxy's Edge 2013-2014,* and *Flash Fiction Online,* among other publications. He would sell his soul if anyone was willing to buy it. James lives in Staten Island, New York, with his wife. Visit his website at jamesaquilone.com

*****~~~~~*****

Upon a Pale Horse

by Bruce Golden

France, 1087

Smoke billowed above the town of Mantes in the fullness of the sunset. But the sunlight and all its sundry colors were blotted out by the unbridled burning of the hamlet. The battle had raged all day, and yet there were still pockets of resistance, where vehement defenders refused to lay down their arms. Their fight was futile. The outcome of the incursion had never been in doubt. The forces of William, King of England, formerly Duke of Normandy, formerly William the Bastard, were too many. . . too strong. They were seasoned, ferocious warriors clashing with uninspired French troops and untrained townspeople.

The brutal sacking of Mantes had begun.

Under normal circumstances, William wouldn't have allowed the pillaging of a town in the region where he was born. But he'd ordered it to make a point to Philip, King of France, as well as to his own son Robert, who'd once more turned against him. Transgressions against his sovereignty would not be tolerated.

No longer the great burly warrior, William approached the smoldering town a rotund old man whose eyesight was failing him. Once unequaled as a horseman, he now kept his pale war horse reined in to an ambling gait instead of a triumphant gallop. He hadn't even worn his hauberk, because he'd grown too fat and it made him uncomfortable. He wasn't worried. He would need no chainmail on this day.

Next to him rode his young son, Henry. He'd brought him along with the intention of teaching him the art of warfare, but his heart wasn't in it.

Henry noticed the look of grim dissatisfaction on his father's face.

"What is it, Father? What troubles thee?"

William spit the dust and ash that had gathered in his mouth and replied in the guttural voice he was known for, "I tire of war, Henry. I've been fighting my whole life. It seems so long ago that I took England for my own. Now I'm back in Normandy, the land of my birth, fighting again to retain what's mine. It seems war never ends. Remember that when I'm gone."

"Yes, Father."

One of his captains rode in from the front and stopped next to William.

"We've taken the town, sire."

"That of it which does not burn," replied William.

"Those *were* your orders, were they not, sire?"

"Yes, those were my orders. See to it, Captain."

The officer rode off to ensure the king's orders were carried out.

As they moved into the town, the raging flames grew higher, burned hotter. The scarlet glare of the conflagration turned the pallid gray tint of William's horse to a hellish hue. The carnage was all around them. William watched Henry's eyes, his expression. He was heartened to see his son's distaste for the slaughter and destruction.

A structure near the king abruptly collapsed amidst a blaze of sparks and flaming planks. A shower of hot embers splayed out in front of the king. His steed reared violently, kicking its hooves into the air in protest, its amber eyes shimmering with fear.

Instead of being thrown back off his mount, the stirrups that held William, the same stirrups he'd improved his legendary cavalry with long ago, thrust his upper body forward. His gut slammed into the broad pommel of his saddle. So great was the force, even his girth did not protect him.

The pain shot through him like a dozen arrows. He fell. The pale horse did not hesitate. It raced off across a bloody, trampled field with stony indifference.

…

Five weeks passed, and the king's injuries had not healed, even with the ministrations of the priors of Saint Gervase. In fact, William's condition had worsened, and he knew he lay on his deathbed.

Lying there he recalled his wife, Matilda, who'd died years earlier, and his son Richard, who'd been killed in a riding accident when he was not much older than Henry was now. Soon he'd be joining them both.

He called forth his ministers and issued his final proclamations. He would leave Normandy to his oldest son Robert, despite his treachery. But the crown of England would go to his second son, William Rufus. Little did he know this division of his kingdom would create the stage for enmity and conflict for centuries to come. A legacy of violence and strife would haunt him even in his grave.

He ordered large sums to be given to his son Henry and his daughters. Other monies were to be given to the church and to the poor. He also ordered that all of his prisoners be released, including his half-brother Odo, who, in a vain attempt to become pope, had defied William's orders and attempted to corrupt his vassals.

In the king's last moments, his son knelt by his bedside. There were tears in the boy's eyes.

William joked to Henry, "Well, the bastard will soon be dead." He started to laugh, but the pain was too great. "Be not like me," he told his young son. "For war and death have been my standards. Let them not be yours.

"May God forgive me, for I have taken that which is not mine. I am stained with the rivers of blood I have shed."

With that repentant statement still fresh on his lips, William the Conqueror died.

85

Maryland, 1682

William Calvert was in a hurry. He wanted to reach his home in time for his son George's 14th birthday celebration. His business in Charles County had taken longer than he expected, so he was pushing his horse harder than usual, slapping its flanks with the reins whenever it threatened to slow its pace.

To his left a wall of morning fog had begun to dissipate. Despite the cool air and the patchy clouds, sweat ran down his back and chest. It was warmer than usual for May, and he could feel it would be downright hot before the day ended.

His wife, Elizabeth, had expected him home days earlier, and was likely worried. As the daughter of Governor Stone, she was raised to be punctual, and expected it of everyone else. However, Calvert's position as Secretary of Maryland and member of the House of Burgesses often required him to travel, especially in these times of Catholic and Protestant conflict.

He didn't understand why the zealots of each sect couldn't just live and let live. Religious freedom in this new world had been a dream of his father's, and his grandfather's. It was what drove his grandfather, the original Lord Baltimore, to petition the king for the right to colonize the region he named Maryland. But it seemed some people couldn't be happy if their neighbors prayed differently from themselves.

It had been a long, quiet ride, intruded upon only by the staccato beat of his horse's hooves. Soon he'd reach the Wicomico River. Once he crossed it he'd be back in St. Mary's County, just an hour's ride from home and the loving embrace of Elizabeth—that is, if she wasn't too upset with his tardiness. She called him Colonel Calvert whenever she was angry with him, though he hadn't used his militia title in years.

He spotted the river ahead of him. He'd find out soon if she were glad or mad. He really couldn't guess which it would be.

The Wicomico appeared to be swollen from the recent rains, but he'd forged it before. He slowed his steed as he reached the river's edge, and despite the animal's brief trepidation, guided it slowly into the water.

By the time he reached mid-stream, the river was lapping at his waist. His horse struggled to keep its head above water, snorting its displeasure. The current was as strong as any he'd felt, and when his mount lost its footing and began to swim, he was jerked from the saddle.

He struggled to reclaim hold of the animal, but it kicked away, trying desperately to regain its own foothold. He was close enough to see the fright in the beast's tawny gold-flecked eyes, but not close enough to grasp it.

He tried to swim, but his clothing held him down. The current pushed him further and further away. Just before he went under, he saw the pale gray horse reach the river's bank and dash up the slope onto dry land.

Massachusetts, 1808

Solomon pulled the cinch tight to secure his saddle, then led the horse by its bridle out of the barn. The cold morning air blew from the beast's nostrils like smoke. It stamped its hooves restlessly, its gray head high and alert, its bronze eyes rich with anticipation.

It had been a while since he'd been riding. Various health concerns had kept him out of the saddle, but today he was looking forward to it.

His old friend Joseph Varnum was going to be in Worcester, and he hadn't spoken with him since he'd last been in Boston.

Joseph's status had long ago risen from his quiet days as a farmer with little formal education. He'd served with valor in the American War of Independence from

England, eventually rising to the rank of major general in the state militia. Now, 14 years after first being elected to represent Massachusetts in Congress, he'd become the Speaker of the House of Representatives.

Joseph wasn't just an old friend. He'd become a man Solomon greatly admired. As long as they'd known each other, they'd both been vehemently opposed to slavery. And ever since Joseph had entered Congress, he'd been an outspoken opponent of negro servitude. He'd even submitted to Congress a proposition to amend the Constitution—a proposition that would abolish the slave trade. It took him two years, but finally the proposition was passed by both houses of Congress. Now it was up to the states to ratify the amendment. It would take three-fourths of the state legislatures to approve the new law, but Solomon was hopeful it could be done.

He wanted to speak with his old friend about the chances the amendment would be added to the Constitution, and to congratulate him.

"Solomon Willard, where do you think you're going?"

It was Lydia. He was hoping to ride off before his wife spotted him.

"I'm riding into Worcester to see an old friend," he replied, pulling himself up onto his mount.

"You're too old to be riding into town like that," said Lydia. "Let me get Micah to hitch up the wagon for you."

"I'm 52, not 82, Wife. I can still ride a horse."

She stood there frowning at him.

"I'll be back before dark."

His youngest sons, Isaac and Archibald, playing with their dogs out in the south field, spotted their father and came running.

"I want to ride! I want to ride!" they both squealed as the dogs barked at the boys' enthusiasm.

Solomon's old pale horse, which surely had heard dogs barking and children shouting before, nonetheless became agitated by all the noise and the frenetic activity around it. It nickered and reared up unexpectedly. Solomon was thrown backwards, landing head first. His neck broke on impact.

Missouri, 1888

It was a long way from Kansas City back to Atchison County. Two riders making the journey had stopped to rest, when the sky began to darken and the wind rose up to whistle through the trees. Their horses stood grazing in the nearby meadow.

"You think the Cowboys will ever field a good team?"

"I don't know, Charlie. They sure didn't look too good today. They've been in last place all year."

"The Browns sure beat up on them," said Charlie.

"That's why they're in first place, and are probably going to win the American Association pennant again this year."

"I don't know why St. Louis always has to have such a good baseball team," said Charlie. "It ain't right."

"Right's got nothing to do with it. If the Cowboys had Tip O'Neill and Jocko Milligan hitting, and Ice Box Chamberlain hurling the horsehide for them, they'd be in first place instead of the Browns."

"Look at that," said Charlie, pointing at the heavens. "We'd better get going, Richard." As he said it, the first few drops descended upon on them. "Then again, maybe we should hunker down until it passes."

"There ain't much shelter around here," replied Richard. "And it don't look like it's gonna pass anytime soon. It's coming in from the south. If we get going, we might beat it home. Anyway, I'd rather ride in the rain than sit in it."

Ain't Superstitious

They mounted their horses—Charlie on his sorrel, Richard on his pale gray—and galloped off.

They heard thunder in the distance as the rain gained in intensity. The wind was at their backs, and so was the storm, pushing them, prodding them to ride even faster.

When a bolt of lightning flashed up ahead of them and the thunder cracked loud enough to hurt their ears, Charlie shouted, "Shit! That was close."

Richard didn't respond. He just kept riding.

They'd gone less than a mile, when it became obvious they weren't going to outrun the storm. But there was nothing for it, save to keep going. By the time they passed into Atchison they were soaked through and through, chilled to the bone.

Richard looked over at his brother-in-law and smiled. Charlie smiled back. They were thinking the same thing.

Richard's wife, Carrie, had warned them about the storm. She had a sixth sense about such things. He and Charlie knew they'd hear it from her to no end when they got home.

The last thing Charlie saw before the lightning flash blinded him, and the force of the electrostatic discharge knocked him from his horse, was Richard smiling.

It had been so close, the thunderous explosion so loud, Charlie's ears were ringing with it. He picked himself up and checked himself for injuries. Finding no broken bones, he looked for his horse. What he saw instead was Richard. Both he and his pale gray were on the ground, smoke rising from their bodies. His brother-in-law was as still as stone, and there was no spark of life in the horse's amber eyes. The streak of lightning that had just missed Charlie had struck Richard and his horse.

###

About the Author

Novelist, journalist, satirist, Bruce Golden's short stories have been published more than 120 times across 15 countries and a score of anthologies. *Asimov's Science Fiction* described his second novel, "If Mickey Spillane had collaborated with both Frederik Pohl and Philip K. Dick, he might have produced Bruce Golden's *Better Than Chocolate*—and about his novel *Evergreen*, "If you can imagine Ursula Le Guin channeling H. Rider Haggard, you'll have the barest conception of this stirring book, which centers around a mysterious artifact and the people in its thrall." You can read more of Golden's stories in his upcoming collection, *Tales of My Ancestors.* http://goldentales.tripod.com

Bruce notes: History has recorded that Richard Greenville Golden, Solomon Willard, William Calvert, and William the Conqueror, also known as the first Norman King of England, Duke of Normandy, and William the Bastard, all suffered equestrian-related deaths just as described herein. That it might have been the same horse they were riding is pure speculation.

All four men are also direct ancestors of the author of this abbreviated tale. Said author has only been on horseback a couple of times in his life, but he continues to use the same mode of transportation he has for the last 30 years—a 1965 Ford Mustang.

*****~~~~~*****

Wind Chimes

by Sean O'Dea

It doesn't look much like mashed potatoes, but with the care and attention with which it was slung, I am sure it will taste better than it looks. The overly gracious volunteers who serve it have a tendency to smile too much. Probably because they don't want us all to figure out just how unsanitary the food here really is. You might assume a lot of things by looking at me here with my warm meal and charitably donated clothing, but if I told you my actual story, you probably wouldn't believe me.

Picture a two-story house at the top of a cul-de-sac in a charming, suburban neighborhood. Inside, you will find my lovely wife Lisa, and our two wonderful children, James and Samantha. No dogs. I'm allergic to dogs. The attached garage houses an obnoxiously large SUV, and a small, but efficient hybrid. My lawn? It's impeccable. By far the greenest on the block. What was my secret? Saving the fresh-cut green mulch from the mower bag and sprinkling it on top of the browning spots.

How did I afford all this? Corporate auditing for a prestigious software firm. Admittedly, I am the guy with the loosened tie hanging off the coffee-stained shirt that my wife forgot to iron. I am the guy in the office who women never flirt with, and the guy who always manages to burn his popcorn in the break room's microwave. I work my ass off. Why? To earn the bonus that takes my family on vacation every year.

One Saturday in August, a fight with my wife over the broken garbage disposal snowballed into a fight over my utter incompetence as a human being. Eventually, she shooed me out the door. And locked it.

"Hey, Rob," my neighbor said, as he closed the trunk of his glistening red BMW.

"Heya. . . Rich. What's up?"

"Well, work has me pretty busy these days." His perfectly groomed hair refused to move as he nodded to his license plate that read, "NEW VP."

"Oh, right, that big promotion. I forgot." *Dick.*

"Yeah, that's right. Hey, I should probably tell you, we'll most likely be moving next spring." He pointed subtly to the gated neighborhood on the hill. I nodded. Their proximity kept my property values higher.

"Wow, that's really great." *Dick.*

Rich's wife interrupted us. She managed to kiss him passionately, despite her oversized, designer sunglasses.

"Oh, hey, Rob!" Rich's wife finally acknowledged me.

"Hi, Margaret," I replied, noticing her low-cut running top. I'm quite certain she *never* ran.

"Rob, how long have we known each other? Call me Meg!"

"Sorry, yeah."

"Well sweetheart," Rich continued, "Why don't you head down to the country club, I will catch up with you later." She flinched as he squeezed her backside.

"OK," I interjected, "I'm heading down to the hardware store. . . so, I'll see you later." *Dick.*

With every step down the aisles of the hardware megastore, my temper subsided. I always viewed such places as a sort of sanctuary, a place where even a corporate auditor could seem macho. After perusing countless aisles, I inadvertently ended up in the garden department. There, I noticed a sale on wind chimes. After testing countless models, I decided on the midsize *Lakeshore Melody* in the key of D.

The chimes dinged as I pulled them out of the trunk of my car.

Wind Chimes

"Hey, man," Jim said, walking across the street. He wore his crisp white socks and Birkenstock sandals. "Nice wind chimes." He arrived in my driveway and adjusted his gray pony tail.

"Hey, Jimbo, how are you?"

"Where you gonna put that thing, Rob? Cause you know. . . " Jim pointed all around. "It's all about the *feng shui*."

"Are you really interested in how I arrange my furniture?"

Jim laughed. "No, man, *feng shui* isn't just about your furniture, it's about man's interaction with the universe. How the elements of heaven and earth flow through our everyday lives."

"You want a beer, Jim?"

"Yeah, man."

I handed Jim the wind chimes and disappeared into the garage. I returned to the driveway with our usual folding chairs and two cans of cold beer. We sat in our familiar driveway setup—beers perspiring in our seats' built-in cup holders.

"Where'd you put the wind chimes?"

Jim pointed to the lone ornamental tree—the focal point of my prize-winning lawn. The wind chimes hung silently from a lower branch, the wooden pendulum dancing subtly within its musical prison. "Not sure that's what I had in mind, Jim."

Jim took another swig from his beer and belched quietly into his hand. "No, no, that's what you want. You see, it redirects the flow of the negative *chi* that's flooding in your front door." Jim's hands snaked through the air, mimicking the path of the *chi*. "Haven't you been noticing more negativity in your house lately? Don't lie, either! I've been noticing you and Lisa fighting more."

"The trials and tribulations of marriage, Jim. I'm sure you remember what that was like."

"No, it's more than that. Ever since they built the community pool up the street, it seems like the flow of negative *chi* was redirected." Jim leaned over and hit my arm. "Think about it man! They built that pool in June, which rerouted all the negative and positive *chi* that flowed into this very cul-de-sac. And look what happened! Richie Rich here gets a big new promotion. What's-her-face, the neglectful mother, wins a big alimony suit over her ex-husband, and you and Lisa start having marital problems. I'm telling you man, it's all *feng shui*." He paused again to gulp his beer and adjust his cargo shorts. "Wind chimes are an essential element in directing *chi*. If you hang them there, it should reroute the flow of all negative energy, thus promoting more positive energy to enter your house. You should notice improvements."

"Where does the negative *chi* go?"

Jim did some impromptu calculations. "I guess it funnels it around to Rich's place, man."

"So Rich is going to have all the negative *chi* now?" I couldn't help but laugh at the assumption.

"Robert." Lisa appeared. She wore her old college sweatshirt with her dark brown hair in a tight ponytail. A telltale sign she had spent the afternoon deep-cleaning the house. "I'm sorry I got so angry at you earlier. I'm just stressed out about getting this house ready for James' birthday party."

"Yeah, I'm sorry too."

"Hey, Lisa," Jim interjected.

"Hi, Jim. Well, I will let you boys finish whatever it is you were doing. Did you want me to grab you more beers?"

"Yeah, sure honey, two more beers would be great." Lisa grabbed two beers from the garage fridge and shuttled them to us before going back inside.

"You see," Jim said as he cracked open another beer. "The positive *chi* is working already, man."

...

I leaned over the kitchen counter basking in the morning sunlight and watched the coffee slowly drip into the pot. I could hear the kids watching TV. Familiar arms caressed me from behind.

"Last night was wonderful," Lisa whispered.

I smiled in remembrance.

Lisa kissed me. "Hey. How about breakfast? Scrambled eggs, toast, and crispy bacon just the way you like it."

"Great. I'll grab the paper and see what the kids want." I made my way through the living room, where my children lay sprawled out in pajamas, hypnotized by a cartoon.

"Dad," James said, his eyes never leaving the television. "Something's wrong with the neighbors."

"Yeah, OK," I replied as I grabbed the front door knob. "Listen, your mother is cooking us all breakfast this morning, do you kids want anything special?"

"I want pancakes." Samantha raised her hand.

"Pancakes. Check." I opened the front door.

I heard the familiar sounds of birds chirping, dogs barking, and sprinklers running. I bent over to pick up the paper, and noticed Rich's lawn littered with everything that should have been in his closet. The surrounding hedge seemed to be flowering with expensive shirts and ties, while custom golf clubs littered the lawn. *Whoa.*

A few houses down, Jim came walking out of his garage in his trademark white shirt tucked into beltless khaki cargo shorts, ready to trim his own hedges.

"Jim!" I whispered loudly while scurrying down the cul-de-sac in my bathrobe. "Jim, look what happened."

"Morning, Rob. What's going on?" Jim said, focused on his bushes.

"Look at Rich's house, man!"

Jim tipped his sunglasses down. "Looks like Richie Rich got evicted."

97

"Jim!" I pointed. "Did we do that?"

"What do you mean, with the whole redirecting negative *chi* thing?"

"That's exactly what I mean, Jim!"

"Well, it's hard to say. I mean—maybe?"

"Maybe!?"

"Yeah. I mean, if the energy flow were changed, we could've catalyzed things, maybe made his actions more apparent to. . ." Jim looked at the lawn again. "Meg."

"That's great, Jim. We decide to mess with the natural order of things, and we ended up ruining Rich's life? Are you kidding me!?"

"Well, Rob, the guy is kind of an asshole," Jim said. "Besides, that bad energy *could* still be flowing into your house."

"No! You know what? This is coincidental. I'm not buying any of this flowing energy stuff. I'm sorry." I started walking back to my house.

Jim yelled when I was half way home. "Hey, you wanna drink some beer later?"

"I'll be out after breakfast," I yelled back.

…

Jim was already sitting in my driveway. My chair was set up with an unopened beer in the cup holder. "How was breakfast?" Jim asked.

"Really good, actually." I got a view of Rich's trashed lawn as I sat down.

"So listen, Rob, I thought about our conversation earlier, and I think I found the perfect remedy."

"Really? Does it entail removing the wind chimes from my tree? Because they look ridiculous there."

"No." Jim pointed to Rich's front porch. A small decorative mirror framed with wood hung to the side of the front door.

"A mirror?"

98

"Mirrors are vital to *feng shui*. They can deflect negative *chi*. So earlier, I grabbed an old mirror I had laying around in my garage and hung it on their porch."

"You're kidding, right?"

"Nope. Problem solved. Good *chi* for everyone."

"You smoke entirely too much weed."

Rich tiptoed out to his lawn and began cleaning up all his belongings. "Oh, hey there, guys. Sorry about the mess this morning," he finally said.

"Oh, no problem, Rich," I replied.

Jim lifted his beer can. "No worries, man."

"Yeah well, you know Meg," Rich laughed. "So you know. . . sorry about the mess here. I'll get it all cleaned up."

Jim and I swung our head in unison as Meg came strutting through the front door.

"Hi, honey," she said. Rich stopped his cleaning to kiss his wife. Passionately. *Dick.* She finally pulled away. "Oh hey, Jim, thanks again for the mirror. I think it looks really great in that space."

"Yeah, that's no problem Meg," Jim yelled.

"Are you kidding me?" I whispered to Jim. "Am I supposed to believe now that because they have some little mirror on their porch, their lives got better?"

"Pretty much. That's *feng shui*, dude."

By the time we finished our second round of beers, the cul-de-sac came alive with lawn mowers, the operators marching up and down their lawns like a suburban drill team.

"So Jim, I'm confused," I said watching all the mowers being exchanged for weed whackers. "Where is all the negative *chi* being deflected now?"

"Yeah, kind of in that direction." He pointed. "I think? No worries, though."

. . .

I sped down the neighborhood parkway after a long day at work. I white-knuckled the steering wheel and neglected my constantly vibrating cell phone in the passenger seat. The nine missed calls were no doubt Lisa reminding me that I was missing James's eleventh birthday.

As the sun set, I finally pulled into my cul-de-sac. Unfortunately, a black Mercedes blocked my driveway. As a matter of fact, a multitude of fancy cars forced me to park in the only empty spot down the street. I grabbed my briefcase, and walked over to Rich's open garage, filled with cigar smoke.

"Hey Rich," I yelled, "Do you mind having someone move the Mercedes blocking my driveway?"

Rich excused himself from the well-dressed crowd. "Rob, how are you, buddy?" Rich intercepted me in his driveway and put his arm around me. "Listen, I got some serious clients and fellow executives here tonight for a poker game. Do you mind just leaving your car in the street tonight? Thanks, man, I appreciate it."

I realized he had subtly walked me back to the sidewalk. "No, Rich, I want to park in my own garage, OK?"

"Hey, you like cigars? I got a box of *Arturo's* in the house. How about it?"

"No. I don't even smoke! Now move the car!"

"Great! I will send over the cigars tomorrow." Rich patted my back and began walking towards the garage. "Thanks again, Rob!"

Dick!

"Robert! Where have you been? I've been trying to call you. You are missing your son's birthday, and I can't handle all these boys by myself."

"Sorry, honey," I replied.

...

I waited for Lisa to fall asleep before I snuck out of bed and made my way downstairs. I carefully stepped around eight boy-filled sleeping bags in the living room, then heard a familiar voice. "Dad? What are you doing?"

Wind Chimes

"Moving my car into the garage. Go back to sleep, James," I whispered.

I walked over to Rich's front window. I peered into Rich's house like it was a fishbowl, gazing upon a school of pompous executives gathered around a table, sipping fine scotch. *Dicks.*

I took down the mirror from the side of Rich's front door.

Seven o'clock in the morning. A house full of hungry boys. Lisa began mass producing waffles, and I escaped the chaos by taking refuge in the garage. Eventually, I decided to peek out at Rich's lawn. It was clear.

I walked down the driveway to retrieve the paper. I pretended to inspect it. Really, I looked for any sign of bad luck. All I found was Rich opening the door in a monogramed robe. He walked out and waved. "Morning Rob!"

I nodded.

Rich paraded towards his *Wall Street Journal.* He sighed deeply. "You know what I love about good scotch?" he said, "It doesn't give you a hangover."

Another figure appeared at Rich's front door. An older Asian woman stepped onto the porch and began shaking out a small rug.

Rich noticed my attention. "Oh, that's Sue Wyn. Our new maid."

I smiled and waved, but the hawk-eyed housecleaner simply fixed her gaze on me. The wind chimes rang calmly and interrupted. Her gaze snapped to them.

I spent most of the week researching *feng shui* at work. I decided it was bullshit. Superstition. Except for when I pulled up to my house that afternoon, an exterminator's van was in the cul-de-sac. Rich was outside talking to the green-uniformed pest controller.

"What do you mean you can't do anything?!" screamed Rich.

"I'm sorry sir, but the black-tailed prairie dog is an endangered species, it would be illegal to trap or poison them. You gotta call the Division of Wildlife."

"Hey, Rich. Everything OK?"

"Goddamn prairie dog colony underneath my house. I swear these things just appeared overnight!" Just as Rich finished his sentence, a chirping prairie dog ran across his lawn.

I closed my front door just in time to hear the exterminator's van drive off. Lisa and the kids were peering out the living room window.

"Can you believe this?" Lisa exclaimed, "Prairie dogs? I mean, what awful luck!"

"Yeah." I snickered.

"Rob?"

"Hmm?"

Lisa looked at me sternly. "Robert, did you do something to Rich and Meg's house?"

"No, no, I swear. I didn't do anything."

My son piped up. "Then, why did you steal his mirror, Dad?"

"You *stole* his mirror?" Lisa asked.

"Yeah, I mean, no. . . not really.

"It's under the sink, Mom," James announced.

"Okay, look. I can explain."

"Kids, go up upstairs," Lisa commanded.

The ensuing fight led to me spending the night on the sofa with strict orders to return Rich's mirror in the morning.

The sunlight flooded the living room and woke me up early. I snuck over to Rich's porch. Quietly, I re-hung the mirror. Trying to straighten the damn thing, someone pulled back the curtains and startled me. The wizened Chinese face disappeared and promptly reappeared at the front door.

"You steal his mirror," the woman said.

"No, no. I was just returning it. Geez, you startled me there."

"He no need mirror now. I hang up crystal instead."

I turned to see the hanging string of crystal prisms in the window.

"He better off now. Better than with mirror. Gophers go away now. Now you go too."

I walked down to Jim's house and knocked on the door. He answered out of breath, wearing only black yoga pants.

"Hey, man, what's up?"

"Right. . . hey, what do crystal prism things do in *feng shui*?"

"Crystals? They're kind of weird; they can actually disperse and sometimes amplify the *chi* directed at them in multiple different directions. Why?"

"Rich's maid, man. She must know this stuff too. She hung up a string of crystals on Rich's porch.

Jim peeked out his front door. "Huh, there's no telling where that negative *chi* is going now, man. Serious *chi* warfare."

"So is my house ok? What do I do now?"

"Listen, man. Stop by later this afternoon, I'll figure something out."

I went back to my house, where Lisa toiled in the kitchen. She remained emotionless. "Honey, I'm sorry about last night, I returned the mirror this morning. Can you forgive me now?"

"Your work called, Robert, you're supposed to call them back."

"On a Saturday? That's weird."

…

The storm clouds engulfing the sunset mimicked my mood as I drove home from my last day of work. The company merged, and I got laid off. *Allegedly* receiving a severance. All my shit sat in company-provided boxes in the back seat. I pulled into my cul-de-sac and noticed Jim out in his yard installing a fountain. I stopped and got out of my car.

"Jim, what are you doing?"

"Look man, I was doing some calculations, and I think those crystals are spreading that negative *chi* all over the cul-de-sac. This is my defense."

"A fountain?"

"Water. It's another way to redirect *chi*." Water from the fountain blew into Jim's face as his ponytail flapped like a windsock. "You should be okay, though," he yelled, "Your wind chimes should deflect most of it, too."

"Okay," I yelled back. Lightning flashed. Thunder cracked. I could feel raindrops as I ran back to my car, where my cell phone was ringing.

"Yeah, hello?" I yelled.

"Rob. It's Lisa."

"Hey, you know there's a storm moving in."

"Rob, I'm at my mother's house with the kids. I don't think our problems are getting any better right now. . ."

I looked up at my yard, phone to my ear. My wind chimes were missing. *Fuck.*

I dropped the phone and rushed out. I barely made it to the garage when a bolt of lightning struck my roof.

. . .

"You gonna eat those mashed potatoes, friend?" asked the fellow homeless man next to me.

I ran my spoon through them before making my decision. "Yeah, man, you can have 'em." After taking the milk off, I slid my tray over.

"Thank you, friend. Good karma will surely come your way."

"Karma, huh?"

Wind Chimes

He took a bite of my mashed potatoes. "You know, karma. The eternal cycle of cause and effect, the idea that good deeds will come back to you and bad ones, well, you know."

"Yeah, I know," I said. "Why don't you take my milk, too?"

About the Author

Sean O'Dea teaches philosophy and world history at an all-girls high school in Denver, Colorado. His first novel, *Peacemakers*, a historical scifi thriller set in 1914, was published in March of 2015, with the sequel, *Warmongers*, slated for a January 2016 release. You can follow him on Twitter @Sean_M_ODea.

*****~~~~~*****

James and the Prince of Darkness

by Kevin Lauderdale

"James?"

"Sir?"

"I am in a bit of pickle, James."

"Indeed, sir?"

"I seem to have sold my soul to the Devil."

"*Indeed*, sir."

Careful readers will not have missed my valet's emphasis of that particular "indeed." James rarely emphasizes, and when he does, it indicates an enterprise of great pith and moment.

Diabolism is not the usual topic of conversation to be found at my breakfast table. Ordinarily, as I peruse my copy of the *Times* and examine the morning post, James stands by ready to assist, and he and I engage in a spirited discussion of the news of the day.

Anyone sharing my toast and marmalade can expect yours truly, Reggie Brubaker, to be up to snuff not only on the weather, but also which horses at Kempton Park are worthy of a solid turf investment.

And as you sip your Lapsang souchong, while looking out of my breakfast nook's window upon the most fashionable view in London (you can see the Ritz from my apartment on Piccadilly), James will be similarly well versed on The Foreign Situation and prepared to discuss the exclusion of gnomes at the Chelsea Flower Show.

It was not so on that day.

"Yes, James," I said. "Sorry to impose, but I'm afraid I may need your help on this one."

"As you say, sir."

"You were a dashed good sport about helping me to get out of my engagement to that fairy princess. And I

107

certainly appreciate your assistance with the ghost of Lord Sandwich. Not to mention that you played an integral role in finding my periwinkle tie only yesterday. Stout yeoman's work all around, I say."

"You are too kind, sir. Perhaps, if you would inform me of the particulars of the situation."

"Ah, yes. Well. . . " I took a large sip of tea to fortify the inner Brubaker. "It started last night at my club. Ox Cartman was having his stag night. He's marrying the daughter of Judge Bowles. You remember Bowles, James? The one who dunned me a fiver for jaywalking on Drury Lane."

"Ah, yes," said James. "'The Hanging Judge.'"

"Exactly. In any case, Ox had downed a bottle of champagne and was taking on all comers at billiards. Well, that is my game, so I could not let the challenge go unmet. But, hark the sequel. He won. Twice in a row, in fact. Thus completely emptying my pockets of all available brass. After meeting such a Waterloo, I decamped to the club library."

James nodded sagely, and I continued, "I am ashamed to admit, James, that I paced about, idly running my fingers along copies of Dickens and *Wisden*, muttering aspersions against the good name of Cartman, all the way back to those ancient forebears of his who were the first porters. I accused old Ox of having. . . well, the phrase I used was, 'the Devil's own luck.' And then, after some business with a brandy bottle, I said that I'd sell my soul for that kind of luck."

"Ah," said James. "The operative phrase, I believe."

"Quite so. I would have sworn that I was alone in the library, but no sooner had I spoken that o.p. when I caught a whiff of sulfur. I turned around, thinking I had somehow missed some bloke there, and he had just lit up a cigarette. Well, there was someone there. Most definitely not an invitee to Ox's stag party."

"How so, sir?"

"To begin with, his clothes. All red velvet: jacket, trousers, waistcoat, and tie. Vermillion with black piping. Not the thing, James. Not at all. Clearly not from a Saville Row tailor. Oh, also, his skin was bright red, and he had horns and cloven hooves."

"*Indeed*, sir?"

"That's the second time, James. You're making me a bit nervous."

"My apologies, sir. Please go on."

"Well, he said his name was Mr. Nick, and he could provide me with exactly what I had requested."

"I believe I can see the rest clearly, sir. In your. . . impaired state—"

"I was not at my best, James, that much is so."

"You signed."

"In blood, James."

"*Indeed*, sir."

Third time. "Oh, is it that dire?"

"Infernally. What next, sir?"

"Well, then I went back and beat Ox for three straight games. Then I cleaned out Dicky's pockets in darts, and Flippy's at pitch penny. All told, I cleared ten bob. Not bad for a night at the club." I took another swig of tea. "But, in retrospect, I'd rather still be able to call my soul my own. My actions as a younger man, particularly during my college days, may not guarantee me admission into Heaven, but such uncertainty is preferable to reserved seating in Hell. But you have an idea, eh James? Surely, you can get me out of this."

"Possibly, sir. You did say, 'the Devil's own luck'? That was the exact phrase?"

"Yes. Important, is it?"

"Possibly. I may have an idea, sir. Give me half an hour."

…

109

Half an hour later, I had changed from my gray silk pajamas into gray flannels and the aforementioned periwinkle tie.

I met James in the sitting room.

He handed me a card. "If you will be so good as to read from this, sir."

I glanced at it. "What's all this, James?"

"My assumption is that you wish to break the contract."

"Yes."

"Then we shall have to open negotiations."

I read from the card. "'Beelzebub, Prince of Demons, Lord of the Flies, and Prince of Darkness, I call upon you to appear—'"

There was the whiff of sulfur, and Mr. Nick stepped out from behind the left side of my Chinese silk screen as if he were the Villain in a Christmas panto on stage at the West End. He was still wearing the egregious red velvet outfit.

"Ah, Mr. Brubaker," said Mr. Nick, his voice silky like the skin of a snake. "What an unexpected pleasure to see you so soon."

I nodded. "Allow me to introduce my valet, James."

"Indeed," said James simply.

The Devil sniffed in James' direction. "Do I know you?" he asked. He squinted. "You seem vaguely familiar."

"I am unaware of any previous acquaintance," said James.

"Hmmm," muttered the P. of D. "Yes, vaguely. . . Oh, well. It is of no consequence." He turned to me. "Well, Mr. Brubaker, I imagine you've had second thoughts about our agreement. Seller's remorse?"

"Exactly," I said. Was he going to offer me a way out? Perhaps conversion to a lease with option to buy?

That's how my cousin Alfred came to own his cottage in the Cotswolds.

"Too bad," Mr. Nick said flatly. "Our contract is unbreakable."

Damn, I thought. Appropriately so, at least.

James coughed the cough of the perennially discreet.

"Yes?" I said.

"Yes?" said Mr. Nick.

"Perhaps I might offer a suggestion."

"I don't know why," said the Author of Sin. "I feel neither the inclination nor the compulsion to negotiate." He turned to me. "You've signed, Reggie—I may call you Reggie, mightn't I? I feel I know you so well. And we will be spending a great deal of time together in the future." I nodded weakly, and he continued: "Excellent. You have signed, and that is that. You did receive the luck you requested, didn't you?"

"Yes," I said.

"*Quid pro quo*," said Mr. Nick. "My half of the arrangement was satisfied, so now it's up to you. I'm in no hurry. Even if I say so myself, my terms are very generous. We didn't stipulate luck for last night only. You may continue to enjoy your wonderful luck until you die. Possibly decades from now, due to old age, in bed, surrounded by a loving family." He grinned a horrible grin, and I saw, for the first time, his teeth. (The light had been dim in the club library.) They were twisted needles of ivory, spirals that, clearly, once they clamped down into something, would be nearly impossible to pull out. "And then I'll take your soul."

James asked, "If you are not open to negotiation, then why are you here?"

"It amuses me to see mortals squirm."

James said, "Merely for the sake of thoroughness, allow me to ask the—"

111

"Oh, that's good," said Mr. Nick, clapping his hands together. "In how many fairy tales and short stories in *The Strand* has someone been undone with, 'You never asked for it' or 'You didn't say I couldn't'?"

James continued, "Will you, Satan, please cancel Mr. Brubaker's contract with you?"

"No."

"He offers to return the luck you gave him."

"No."

"I'll throw in the ten bob I made last night!" I added.

"No," was the Fallen Angel's steely reply. He turned back to James, "Why are you negotiating for Mr. Brubaker? Are you his barrister as well as his valet?"

"No. However, as a valet, I endeavor to give satisfaction."

"Well, go ahead then. I enjoy seeing valets squirm as well as mortals."

"Why do you need all these souls anyway?" I asked.

"Hell is endothermic," said Mr. Nick.

I turned to James. "It requires heat to function," he elucidated.

"Precisely," said Mr. Nick. "Why do you think dead bodies are cold? Your heat is in your soul. Have you ever been stuck in a lift with two or three other people? You know how hot it gets in there. Same principle applies to Hell. The more souls in Hell, the warmer it gets. Hell is very large, and I like it *hot*."

"Perhaps," said James, "Mr. Brubaker could give you something else in exchange for canceling the contract. You would not get his soul, but you would be remunerated for your time."

"Oooo," chortled Mr. Nick. "Are we talking about *your* soul?"

"No," said James.

"Not willing to give that much satisfaction, eh?" He turned to me. "It's so hard to find good help these days."

James said, "It is simply a case of you having nothing that I require."

"Nothing! You are a *servant*, James! You are at the beck and call of this imbecile." He turned to me, and, with a half-nod, added, "No offense intended."

"Quite all right, old man," I replied with a toss of a hand.

"You cook his meals, do his laundry, and, apparently, get him out of all the assorted scrapes he bumbles into. And from even what little I've seen of him, that part alone must be exhausting."

"I find that being in Mr. Brubaker's employment provides infinite diversion and amusement."

"That's right," I said. "Just last month, we went to Cannes."

Mr. Nick said, "How would you like to live in Cannes all the time, James? Or, better yet, be one of those American oil millionaires? Go anywhere you wish, any time you wish. Not be dependent on this one." He nodded towards me. "Wealth, James. I can't imagine that what he pays you goes very far. In exchange for your soul. . . " He straightened his back as if to salute. "I could make you King."

"'To be a king and wear a crown is a thing more glorious to them that see it than it is pleasant to them that bear it,'" said James.

"Good Queen Bess," said Mr. Nick. "Didn't have any luck with her either." He pointed at my dinner table with a scarlet hand. "Simpler tastes, eh? Then, how would you like a valet of your own? Have someone else bring you the filet mignon and fresh, warm bread."

"'The sky is the daily bread of the eyes,'" was James' retort.

"Reduced to quoting Transcendentalists like Emerson? That's truly pathetic. Fine, you like being a servant. I could help you with that too. I could send some of my lesser demons to be your underlings. Sous-chefs, things like that. I'm sure there's aspects of your position that even you find tedious. They could bring in the logs for the fireplaces. There's no need for you to get your feet dirty trudging about filthy London."

"'London, thou art the flower of Cities all,'" said James with an unabashed sincerity that deeply moved me.

"William Dunbar now. Of the Scottish poets, I much prefer. . . *Burns*. Okay, cut to the chase: How about women?" Mr. Nick looked around my flat. "I can't imagine there are very many of those flitting in and out."

"'Sufficient unto the day—'" began James.

"Enough quotes!" said the Devil with a snarl. "Even I can cite scripture for my purpose. Well, here is a quote for you: 'It is better to reign in Hell than serve in Heaven.'"

"No," said James. "I am quite satisfied with my present situation. Besides, I have always doubted the sagacity of that statement."

"Then we have no deal. Mr. Brubaker's soul remains mine."

I said, "I thought everything was negotiable. Or is R. J. Woolverhampton, the author of *The Thinking Man's Guide to Modern Business Practices*, mistaken?"

"Well, of course, there is cancellation and then there is nullification," said Mr. Nick. "The contract can always be *nullified*."

Bluebirds arose and filled the sky of my heart.

"But only if both parties agree."

Bluebirds dropped from the sky like damp socks.

Mr. Nick continued, "That is part of every contract. It will not be said that the Prince of Darkness cheats."

James said, "Mr. Brubaker was not in his usual state of mind at the time he signed. Is there a mental impairment clause that would nullify the contract?"

The Chief Deceiver smiled. "Well, true, anyone who would wear periwinkle with gray flannels. . . "

James said, "Gentlemen who pair red velvet with hoofs are hardly in a position to comment." Mr. Nick's eyes glowed white hot, but James added, "And who sport a tail that has clearly not been brushed in a week."

His tail whipped in front of him, Mr. Nick examined it, then pushed it away. "No such clause! The contract is unbreakable!" He snorted angrily. "Unless both parties agree. Standard details of null-and-void. I do *not* agree."

"Have you ever broken a contract?" James asked.

"Never."

"I think you may wish to in this case."

"Why?" asked Mr. Nick.

"To avoid the following: Would you care to shoot dice with Mr. Brubaker?"

"What do you mean?"

"To 'roll the bones,' I believe is the vernacular. If you win, things stay as they are. If Mr. Brubaker wins, you tear up the contract, and his soul is again his to do with as he sees fit."

The Devil smiled. "Counter-offer: If I win, I take Mr. Brubaker's soul now, and—Wait! Oh, wait, wait. Oh, you are a good and faithful servant, James." Mr. Nick spun around, his velvet jacket flapping and his hands clapping. "No, no. Mr. Brubaker is extra lucky. He has the Devil's own luck. He's guaranteed to win. A clever notion, though. Good try."

"Would he win?" asked James. "Even against you?"

"Well, I am, of course, preternaturally lucky."

"Hence the phrase, 'the Devil's own luck.'"

"Hence the phrase," the Devil agreed. "Hmm, an interesting question. I've never tested my luck against that of a client's. Perhaps the dice would land on their points, with no resolution. His enhanced luck and my supernatural luck might just cancel each other out."

James said, "Possibly, but I believe not. You see, I believe that you are now *less* preternaturally lucky. I believe that you are now *unlucky*. Any luck you had is now gone, transferred to Mr. Brubaker."

"What? Preposterous!"

"Yes, your agreement with Mr. Brubaker was for 'the Devil's own luck.' Your luck, specifically."

"That's a mere expression. What you suggest is impossible. I'd know."

"What else have you done since you saw Mr. Brubaker last night?"

"Just going to and fro in the earth, and walking up and down in it. It's early yet. I rarely get started looking for souls until after lunch."

"Then you have not yet had time to realize your mistake. Shall we test it?"

James pulled a pair of dice from one of his pockets and gave them a casual shake.

What I don't know about James' past would be enough to fill half the volumes of the British Library. Had he spent his youth as a riverboat gambler on the Mississippi? Was he able to roll seven the hard way at will?

"No," said Mephistopheles. "His luck versus my luck means that the odds are already fifty-fifty. That would prove nothing."

Visions of James in a seersucker suit and straw boater sipping a mint julep dissolved before my eyes.

Mr. Nick said, "We need something more random."

"I believe I have just the thing, then," said James, who produced from my sideboard a silver, dome-covered tray. He removed the cover to reveal one of my best Wedgwood bowls containing half a grapefruit. Beside it lay a serrated grapefruit spoon.

The Devil picked up the spoon (Hooves for feet, but hands like anyone else you've ever eaten breakfast with.). He circumspectly turned the bowl and then dug in to—

"Ow!"

He had been hit in the eye with a squirt of juice.

"Try again," said James, "just to be sure."

The Devil examined the pinkish-red fruit again, turned the bowl to a new configuration and—

"Ow!"

"Twice," said James. "I'd call that bad lu—"

"Don't say it," said the Devil, his face turning from bright cardinal to deep maroon.

"Oh, dear," said James, "and I do believe there is a loose thread on your jacket."

The Devil began to whip his head around rapidly. "Where? Where?"

"Behind you. Where your tail separates your jacket's center vent. Does your tail dress left or right?"

The Devil spun around trying to look behind himself, and he appeared for a moment like the family dog chasing its tail.

"This does not seem promising," said James. "I suspect you could not make it to the lobby of this building without something untoward befalling you."

"Oh, do you? Well, we'll see about that."

With a huff, Mr. Nick stormed out of the parlor, opened my front door, sashayed through and—

BUMP! CRASH! THUD!

"James, did the Devil just fall down our stairs?

"Only one flight, sir."

I shall not transcribe the curses and oaths that followed.

Suffice it to say that the Devil reappeared in my parlor, accompanied by his signature whiff of sulfur. His jacket looked rumpled, and I would swear that one of his horns was askew.

"What have you done to me?!" he demanded of James. "Are you some other Archangel in disguise?"

"No, just a man."

"Then how did you—"

"Nothing," said James. "You did it to yourself. You gave Mr. Brubaker the luck of the Devil."

"You're out of luck, Nick," I said.

The Dark One spun and scowled his ice pick grin at me.

"Um, *Mister* Nick?" I ventured timidly.

"What you say is both ridiculous and impossible," said the Devil to James. "Give me those dice!" James handed them to Mr. Nick, who looked at them carefully then jostled them in his scarlet palm. "These seem ordinary enough."

"They came from my Monopoly set," I said.

"Very well," said Mr. Nick. "We'll each roll one. Highest number wins. If I win, Reggie here dies and comes to Hell immediately. If he wins, the contract is null-and-void. I don't get his soul, and whatever luck I gave him returns to me." He threw me a die.

I rolled a five.

Mr. Nick rolled a four.

The Prince of Darkness held out a rolled-up piece of paper, and we three watched it glow from within, until it became a cylinder of embers, then a column of ash. It crumbled into a pile that singed my Afghan rug.

I felt a momentary tingle as my enhanced luck left me.

Mr. Nick held his tail close to his chest. "Never speak my name again. If either of you ever say something that draws my attention. . . Next time, I will not be so easily mollified."

With that, he turned and twisted into himself, disappearing with a whiff of sulfur.

"James," I said. "I need a whisky."

"Indeed, sir." He moved to the sideboard and poured me a tumbler.

I sat down in my armchair. "That," I said, "was remarkable."

James stood beside me and handed me the salver. "Not really, sir. He gave you luck, but it wasn't his own."

"I don't really follow you, James."

"Millions of people must have wished for 'the Devil's own luck,' and I'm sure he's given luck to more than one person in exchange for a soul. You had only that extra luck granted to you last night. Magical as it was, it was never all of his personal luck. At no point was he without all of his preternatural luck."

"But how do you explain the grapefruit?"

"A particularly juicy variety, just arrived at the greengrocers from Florida this morning."

"The loose thread?"

"I do not know if there was one or not. As you noted, sir, it was distinctly evident that he had not used a Saville Row tailor. That, combined with the showiness of his ensemble, told me that he was insecure in his choice of outfits. I played upon that insecurity. There *might* have been a loose thread, and he knew it."

"The stairs, then?"

"A liberal application of butter. Do watch your step, sir, until I am able to remove it."

"Wait, so then I wasn't preternaturally lucky myself?"

"None of those things had anything to do with you, sir. You still had your enhanced luck. In order to trick him into nullifying the contract, I did not need to convince him of your good luck, just him of his bad luck. And that was easy enough to manufacture."

119

"So you lied to the Devil?"

"I am sure that is not counted a sin, sir."

"But the dice? How did you know they wouldn't, um, land on their points?"

"Oh, sir. Have you ever known dice to do that?"

"No," I said. "Ah, so my luck was stronger than his there at least. I was guaranteed to win, eh?"

"No, sir, they might have still fallen in his favor. That was a calculated risk."

"A calculated risk!"

"I am not a theologian, sir."

"Fair enough. James, it may be better to reign in Hell than to serve in Heaven, but it is decidedly best to holiday in the south of France. If you take my meaning."

"I believe I do, sir. I shall arrange for tickets to Cannes immediately."

I raised my glass. "Here's to a place that is warm—but not *too* warm."

About the Author

Kevin Lauderdale has written essays and articles for the *Los Angeles Times, The Dictionary of American Biography,* mcsweeneys.net, and teevee.org. His short fiction has appeared in several of Pocket Books' Star Trek anthologies as well as various small press publications. This story is a sequel to "James and the Dark Grimoire," which made Ellen Datlow's Honorable Mention list for the best horror of 2009 and was nominated for a Washington Area Science Fiction Association Small Press Award for Best Short Story. He hosts the Old Time Radio podcast, "Presenting the Transcription Feature," and co-hosts "Mighty Movie's Temple of Bad," the podcast about movies that are so bad, they're practically a religious experience, both on The Chronic Rift Network. He is a member of SFWA. Find out more at KevinLauderdale.Livejournal.com

*****~~~~~*****

Spellcasting

by Gerri Leen

The pen she uses is sleek and glides across the paper, leaving no smudges, no empty spots where ink has not flowed evenly. It is a thing of beauty, this pen, with its black onyx body and silver accents. The ink is a thick blue—indigo, really. The color of the night sky before the moon has risen. The color of love when it is mature and strong.

The color of the moments before death, when blue turns to black. Black: the mixing of all colors. Strange that black is seen as pejorative in so many ways, when it is the most inclusive of the colors. Nothing like white, the absence of color.

Candles burn around Darya as she writes out her spell and puts it in the box she keeps all her magical workings in. In her lap lies a folded piece of paper, an old spell, one she no longer wants to keep in effect.

She unfolds it and holds it up. The writing is in English, but her script is so intricate it looks like another language, one that is beautiful when written out, like Arabic or Sanskrit.

She can feel the power pulsing from the spell, and she almost feels guilty that she ever did the spell in the first place.

Almost.

"Darya?" Daniel is at the door, peering into the room she has asked him not to enter. His feet are on the outside, but he leans across the threshold. The spell in her hands keeps him from coming all the way in.

She studies him, all the wonderful ways his face and body come together to add up to handsome.

"Did you miss me?" She gives him the smile she never used much with her other lovers. This much trust—

this much love. It is headier than the magic, and there was a time she thought magic was all she would ever need. Calling a lover here and a lover there, no man out of reach. And never staying around long. By her choice, not theirs.

"I did." His smile is beautiful, but it is false. It is coerced from him, and she wants more than anything for him to be free now. Free to show her that this love is real, that he feels the way she does. That there is no need for special ink and beautiful paper and sacred circles. "I always miss you."

The words mean less each time he says it; she feels more a captor and less a lover. Isn't it true love to want to let someone go? To want to give them back their right of choice?

She remembers the first time she saw him and how she wanted him. Flushed with desire, she'd approached him with her magic tamped down.

Even then she'd wanted him to want her for her.

But he didn't, and she's never been sure if it was hurt or anger that made her write out the spell, their future sealed in the scratches of her pen on the lovely parchment she buys just for magic. The smell of the rich ink as it sank into the paper gave way to the feeling of power rising as she bound this man to her.

The next time she saw him, he looked up as she walked into the bar. His smile was luminous. His voice pitched low as he said, "I was an ass."

"Yes, you were." She enjoys it, the power. She always did in the past, too. This feeling of guilt is new. "But you can make it up to me."

And he had.

The spell seems to be pulsing with power, as if it knows it might die and is resisting. She folds it and smiles up at him, "I'll be out in a minute, darling."

He beams at her. He loves it when she calls him that.

124

Spellcasting

She waits for him to walk away, then holds his spell to the candle, letting the fire flick at it, then devour it. She holds it as long as she can, then drops it in the copper bowl that sits on the floor before her.

He is free. He deserves to love whoever he wants, even if she hopes more than she ever has hoped for anything that he chooses to stay with her. But she barely knows him—the real him. What she has lived with for a year is a construct of the spell. She knows full well their happiness is false, since she controls it. It is a bitter thought for this new Darya that she could ask Daniel to die for her, but she doesn't know who he really is, other than the handsome combination of features, the strong muscles, and tanned skin.

It is wrong to be so intimately connected to someone and to never have let the real person come out. Wrong, and she is sorry.

She waits, the sound of guttering flame all around her. The smell of paper burning fills the room: it is the scent of love dying, and it's comforting.

She is doing something good. For once in her life.

He shows up at the door again. "Darya, we're going to be late for dinner. I made reservations at your favorite place."

His voice is not as warm as it used to be. His eyes shine with something closer to malice than the adoration she has grown bored with.

But he is still here? He is himself again; he could leave if he wanted, but he does not. She feels a thrill in that.

But then he puts a foot over the threshold, his expression daring her to say something about it. She cannot read him.

"I'm not hungry," she says. It is a lie; she is starving. Her kind of magic is best worked after fasting.

"They're expecting us. Get a move on." He sounds annoyed with her, and in his eyes there is an anticipation that rivals how he used to look before sex.

"I'm not hungry." She tries to load her words with power; the candles flare up around her. She'll say them again if she has to. Over and over, until he really hears her.

Until he strides into the room and through the perimeter of her circle, breaking the lines of power she has set up. "I don't care, *darling*." There is a world of spite in the way he says the word. And the expression on his face is ugly.

The candles go out as one. The burning smell turns into something rancid.

His hand connects with her face, a hard slap that knocks her backwards, crushing one of the candles as she lands on it. Hot wax goes through her thin t-shirt, burning through the fabric, into skin. He balls his fist, and she can tell that the next hit will be much harder.

"Daniel, what are you doing?"

His smile is chilling. "Finishing what you started. Poor little mouse of a girl. Coming into the bar, expecting me to notice you. I was hunting, you little fool, and a woman like you would never be my target. It's been a long time since I've hunted. Why? How did you do that to me?"

She holds a hand up, trying to calm him, but he isn't really upset. His seeming serenity is more chilling than being hit.

He hunts. And hunt, that could mean kill, couldn't it? He might like to hurt women. Not all monsters are ugly.

She has never known the real Daniel. Is this who he is? This angry, violent man? And how long has he been artificially kept down? How much does he need to come out to play?

Spellcasting

She gave him no choice in loving her. She looks up, her ears ringing from the slap, and thinks he knows what she's done. On some level, he understands.

He probably admires the power that it took to hold him captive. But she thinks he is sneering at the weakness that made her let him go.

"Your special room," he says, looking around. "Always keeping me out. What do you do in here anyway?" He leans down and wipes his finger through blood trickling from the corner of her mouth. He rubs his finger and thumb together, smearing the blood, and whispers, "Too long, my old friend."

Her magic relies on the pen, on the paper, on the flames, on the power she raises outside of herself. She cannot stop him like this, cringing on the floor.

As he leans in, there is nothing she can do to prevent him from lifting her up, from squeezing her throat. It hurts, more than she can believe, and the world starts to blur and go dark around the edges of her vision. She can see his face enough to know he is smiling. A smile of pure delight.

She abandons magic, stops trying to make him let go, and instead pulls the cap off her beautiful pen. Then she jams it into his throat as hard as she can.

She's not ready for the abrupt way he lets go, isn't able to right herself as she falls, crushing another candle.

He holds his throat, blood coursing around his fingers. She wonders if she is as happy to see that blood as he was hers. If he's scared or only angry.

She scuttles away, her arm scraping the corner of the box, the box that contains the new spell.

The spell that says, "A chance to start over with Daniel. To know the real man."

He falls at her feet. In his eyes, hatred burns. That then is her answer. Even bleeding out this man will not show fear.

127

She imagines the powers that fuel her magic are laughing at her—at the hubris of the little human who thinks to control them. She got her wish; she is meeting the real Daniel. She just forgot to say she wanted to survive the encounter.

Stupid of her. And if she hadn't been blinded by love, she might not have made that mistake.

She sits, trying to come up with stories to tell the police. But in reality, all she can think is that next time, she will have to be more careful.

About the Author

Gerri Leen lives in Northern Virginia and originally hails from Seattle. She has stories and poems published by *Daily Science Fiction, Escape Pod, Grimdark, Athena's Daughters 2,* and others. She is editing an anthology, *A Quiet Shelter There*, which will benefit homeless animals and is due out in 2015 from Hadley Rille Books. See more at http://www.gerrileen.com

*****~~~~~*****

What Is Sacred to Dogs

by A. P. Sessler

"Blood and fire, and billows of smoke!" shouted Reverend Foster as he gripped the podium.

The minister, not even thirty years old, had preached fiery sermons before—brimstone and all—but never this real. Even in times past, when the Horseman of War reared his ugly head in the Middle East, Reverend Foster was never able to fully communicate the impending judgment of God.

But this sermon was different.

Streaks of fire trailed behind the falling meteoroids. Like blazing missiles, they pummeled the parking lot outside. The church shook, and dust as old as the building itself fell from the rafters, peppering the preacher's pitch-black hair. His own words, and the weight they clearly bore, terrified him. His booming voice cracked beneath that weight, and like his listeners, he soon found himself pleading for salvation.

"Have mercy upon us, Lord—upon me. For we are all sinners, weak and frail, and all our righteousness is as filthy rags. So please, remember we are but dust," he implored on bended knees.

His parishioners hid beneath pews; their clasped hands over their heads to shield them from the falling heavens. They prayed, confessed, promised, until the firestorm passed. Slowly the banging upon the roof ceased, and the hammering in the parking lot stopped.

"Is it safe, Deacon?" asked Sister Charlotte, still crouched behind the pew, holding the brim of her straw bonnet with both hands.

The fine-dressed middle-aged man cautiously approached the tall windows that lined the front entrance of the church. He cupped a hand over his eyes and gazed at the sky, now a calm gray, no longer angry and black.

"It's clearing up," said Deacon Tate, still surveying the scene.

"Does that mean it's safe?" asked John Dean.

The disheveled young man's gray suit was slightly larger than his lean form.

"I think we're okay," answered Deacon Tate.

John came out of his pew and assisted Sister Charlotte to her feet. Slowly the parishioners came from their pews, and looking over each shoulder every other step, they made it to the front entrance, where they, too, peered outside to ensure the hellstorm was over.

Reverend Foster was the last to join them. "Let me," he said, to their many objections, but with a raised hand, they parted like the Red Sea.

Deacon Tate held the door for Reverend Foster to exit. The minister stepped outside and beheld the apocalyptic panorama, until he was certain it was safe.

"You can come out now," he said, and with many sighs of relief, the Caucasian congregation followed him into the parking lot.

Outside the shelter of sanctuary, a heap of dented metal and smashed glass awaited. Some vehicles escaped the onslaught. Among those that hadn't, few would start. After several phone calls, the tow trucks came and left, and gradually the parking lot was cleared, except for the debris.

When everyone had left, Reverend Foster circled the church property to evaluate the damages. The monkey bars, merry go round, and spiraling slide of the small playground were unscathed. He nodded his head. "Their angels do always behold the face of my Father," he said to himself.

It was then a sound, like a child crying, caught his attention. He followed the noise to the back entrance of the church, where he found the thing huddled and trembling beneath the awning. It hid there instead of the wide, covered double-door entrance. He smiled. *It chose the narrow gate,* he thought.

He couldn't make out its breed, but the black dog was clearly malnourished.

"Hello, there. What's your name?" he asked the dog.

It whimpered inside the thin man's shadow as he stooped over.

"Don't be afraid. I'm not going to hurt you."

Whether his voice, his eyes, or his smile communicated his intent, the dog ceased from its trembling. Reverend Foster held out a hand for the dog to sniff. Hesitantly, it craned its neck forward and stuck out its tongue to lick the stranger's hand.

"See. You can trust me."

And it did. The dog timidly followed him into the church, whimpering at any sound the old building made. He took it to the kitchen, and in the fridge he found a bit of leftover steak, rare, still red with blood.

"Here you go, boy," he said as he put the meat on a plate and laid it on the floor. "You are a boy, right?"

A frenzied wag of the dog's erect tail revealed a pair of large testicles visible from behind.

"Yep, you're a boy."

In a few gulps the bloody steak was gone.

"You have quite the appetite, don't you?"

The dog licked his muzzle and began to pant.

"I'll get you some water," said Reverend Foster.

He took a bowl from the cupboard and filled it with water from the sink faucet, then placed it beside the plate, which he picked up and placed in the sink.

As the dog drank from the bowl, Reverend Foster cautiously stroked the dog's head.

"I suppose I should give you a name," he said and looked up as his imagination went to work. "I found you at the back door. And when I did, I thought of the narrow gate. For wide is the gate and broad is the way that leads to destruction. But narrow is the gate that leads to salvation. What do you think, boy? Mind if I call you Narrow?"

The way the dog looked at him, Reverend Foster would have sworn (if it wasn't a sin) that he was smiling.

...

In the weeks that followed, the man and beast formed an inseparable bond. Narrow slept by his bed, ate beneath his table, followed him on walks, and attended him on errands—the hound was ever at his side.

But while Narrow grew strong, the congregation slowly shrank. It was at the local diner on a particular Sunday after church, when speculations began to surface.

"I think it was that crazy storm," said Dwight Burke, who sipped iced water from a clear glass. Through the bottom of his glass he observed a black man and white woman dining at a table across from him. "Did you ever see anything so unnatural?"

"It's his soft sermons," said Deacon Tate, shaking his fork. "He doesn't preach on sin anymore. He's watered down the Word, right Jim?"

Jim glanced at Genie, his girlfriend, then silently nodded.

"Not like that one message. That was a *real* sermon," said John Dean, his mouth full of meatloaf.

Sister Charlotte eyed him with disdain. A well-endowed female server sporting a black, v-neck tee stooped over and refilled her unsweet tea. Sister Charlotte stared at the young woman's cleavage before looking away with disgust. When the server left, Sister Charlotte took several packs of artificial sweetener and emptied them into her tea.

"I think it's that dog," said Genie, wiping her mouth with a napkin. "Why's it always there beside the pulpit? It makes me uncomfortable, being that close."

Jim nodded.

"No one said you had to sit on the front row," suggested Sister Charlotte and took a sip of tea.

Genie's eyes grew wide as she leaned back in her chair. She stared at Sister Charlotte's overly rosy cheeks and red lipstick that didn't stay within the lines. Genie was about to speak, when Jim placed his hand on her thigh. She took a deep breath and bit her lip.

"I swear it's eyeing me every time he gives the altar call," John insisted, his face just inches from his plate.

Sister Charlotte looked away from him. "Did you see it drooling? Licking its lips? It's a disgraceful mess is what it is."

Jim swallowed a bit of chocolate cake and wiped his mouth with a napkin. "What do you think we should do, Deacon?"

The deacon finished a bite of banana pudding before answering. "There's not a whole lot we can do at the moment. At next month's meeting I could suggest that having a dog in the sanctuary is against church policy, or at least common decorum."

"You think he would know that," said Sister Charlotte.

"The question is, if I propose an amendment to have the dog removed from the premises, would you all offer your support?"

As he looked around the table, each nodded their approval.

"Good," he said. "It's unanimous. At the next meeting, I'll propose the dog be removed and we'll vote on it. Problem solved."

"To problems solved," said John and raised a glass in toast.

"To problems solved," they each affirmed with a clink of touching glasses and insincere smiles.

…

The dog lay sleeping at Reverend Foster's feet when an afternoon breeze blew over the parsonage porch. Narrow woke up and sniffed at the air. Reverend Foster placed his leather-bound King James Bible on the small, round table beside the porch swing he slowly rocked himself on.

"What is it, boy? You smell something?"

Indeed the dog did, but he wasn't just a dog. Narrow was a Hellhound, and he only needed the scent. Not blood or sweat. Sin. Once he had that, there was only the running and a simple matter of time. He stood tall, the muscles of his legs aglow in the afternoon sun.

"Is it a rabbit?" Reverend Foster teased him. "Go get that rabbit!"

And without hesitation, as he had several times in the past weeks, Narrow bolted from the porch like a bat out of hell in search of some far-off prey.

That night it would be John Dean, the drug-dealing fisherman and generous tither. He was a strong runner, too. He made it from the boat docks to the post office. Narrow worked hard for that score.

A few days later, it was Deacon Tate—the car-dealer and head of the deacon's board. The fat man had just sold his last lemon to a first-time buyer when the hound came sniffing at his office door. Narrow worked the groveling liar into the corner then sealed the deal.

That Friday night it was Sister Charlotte, the gossip who led the prayer meeting. She was standing at her kitchen window when death came calling. She had just hung up the landline after sharing Sister So-and-So's marital problems with another busybody. When Narrow grew tired of her shrieking, he tore her throat out. That shut her up.

Sunday after church it was Jim and Genie, the fornicators who always had some testimony of God's favor on their business and finances. Genie's ecstatic praises drew the Hellhound to their defiled bed, where he

134

caught them mid-act. Narrow couldn't eat for a week after snuffing those two out.

When he regained his appetite, he went after Dwight Burke, the pharmacist and self-appointed eugenicist. The closet supremacist had just filled his last birth control prescription with something to aid the White race when the black dog made a colored man out of him—it seemed his genes contained a lot more red than he thought.

One thing. For a bloodthirsty dog, he sure didn't leave any mess. Perhaps it had to do with the fact that after a Hellhound has his fill, the very bowels of Hell open up to receive the bodily remains into an everlasting fire that consumes nothing but the clothes one wears, so no one knew where the missing congregants had went.

They just stopped coming: to church, to work, the grocery store. While Reverend Foster lamented their unannounced departure, he took comfort in the company of his best friend and the congregation's sudden passion to serve God and love their neighbor.

For anyone who dared entertain an impure thought in his church service immediately felt the burning stare of the Hellhound, and if they were wise, they adjusted their thinking accordingly.

...

It was a bright, sunny morn. Reverend Foster sat the glass of orange juice next to the stack of unopened mail. On top of the pile lay a letter from the Church of the First Born Association. He took a swig of OJ and opened the envelope, then skimmed through the introductions to the last paragraph, which he read aloud:

Without showing a significant increase in church attendance and tithes to meet your membership dues, the Association cannot justify further financial assistance. We see no alternative but to withdraw our support until you are able to satisfy the Association's requirements for membership. You may re-apply for enrollment the first

135

week of Spring. If you are successful, you are welcome to attend our annual conference that weekend.

> *Signed,*
> *The Right Reverend Alton Lewis,*
> *President*
> *CFB Association*

He stared at the paragraph in dumbfounded disbelief, until realization sank in. He crumbled the letter and tossed it in the trashcan. He sat at the table to eat his breakfast, but the first two bites were utterly tasteless. He slammed his fork on the table and fumed in silence, until he felt a comforting lick upon his hand.

"You know, don't you boy?" he asked his faithful friend.

Narrow's eyes darted to the side then back.

"Who are they to judge? Sure, offerings are down and times are tight, but you're well-fed, aren't you? *A righteous man regardeth the life of his beast.* Right?"

If Narrow could have offered verbal condolence, he would. Reverend Foster patted his head.

"Yet there they sit on their high horses, living in their six-bedroom houses, riding in their sports cars, taking three vacations a year, *and* their kids attend the finest schools and universities.

"They got their megachurches and big overseas missions. What do I have to show? I'll tell you what I got to show," he said and took the sharp knife in his hand, shaking it as he spoke. "My congregation may be shrinking, but I'll be damned if they aren't true converts. Let the Association try and find a more devoted flock—ha!"

His appetite began to return. He sliced the sausage in half and took a bite—a tasty morsel it was.

"Maybe we *will* reapply in the Spring," he said with his mouth full. "Who knows, maybe we'll even go down to Jacksonville and apply in person, then we'll crash that conference wide open. How would you like that, boy?

Think you would like those self-righteous pharisees and their trophy wives?"

The Hellhound licked his muzzle as saliva pooled at his feet. He would like that very much.

About the Author

A resident of North Carolina's Outer Banks, A.P searches for that unique element that twists the everyday commonplace into the weird. When he's not writing fiction, he composes music, dabbles in animation, and muses about theology and mind-hacking, all while watching way too many online movies.

His short stories have appeared online at *Human Echoes Podcast* and *Acidic Fiction*, as well as print anthologies such as *Zippered Flesh 2, Dandelions of Mars, Star Quake 2,* and *Cranial Leakage.*

*****~~~~~*****

The Apple Falls Upward

by Andrew Kozma

The one thing John was sure of was that Sir Isaac Newton was a lying bastard. He didn't have proof, but what more proof do you need other than the story everyone bandies about? You know the one. The apple and the tree. Nothing like that ever happens in real life. Nothing that pat, that necessary.

Newton made up the apple, came up with a cute tale about how he was out reading, or writing, or having a picnic, whatever it was, and suddenly, while leaning against a tree, he was konked on the head. Likely story. Too likely.

"Or not likely enough," John argued for the sake of argument.

"What?" Carver eventually asked. He sat outside in a folding chair by the front door.

"What what?" John stood at the far end of the entrance hall with a cold Lone Star in his hand. From where he was, leaned up against the beige wall, he could see the small front lawn, haphazardly mown, and the ill-looking sidewalk bordering it.

"You know what," Carver said.

"No. What?" John hated when Carver did this. It was some twisted version of the Socratic method he had learned in college as a philosophy major. And now, with all that higher education under his belt, he cut meat for a living.

Carver upended his own beer and finished it with a long swallow. He turned to stare at John, thick eyebrows raised. He dropped the bottle. It clattered on the wooden porch and slowly stopped moving.

"I know," John said and he did, now. They were out of alcohol, which meant that John had to call Wee Delivery to get his groceries and, more importantly, more beer. "I'll get the phone."

The fridge was empty and the cupboards bare. There was nothing left to drink but unfiltered water. With Carver, having beer around was a necessity. John picked up the phone, and there was silence. No dial tone. No nothing.

"It's dead," John said.

"What?"

"It's dead!"

"Fuck."

John walked back to the front porch. Carver was leaning over the right-hand railing looking around at the side of the house.

"You're going to have to get my groceries," John said.

"Looks like a rat bit through the wire," Carver said, and pointed. He leaned out so far the railing creaked. "Right there you can see the frayed edges. Looks just like when squirrels dug up my cable."

"I'll take your word for it."

Carver shook his head. "Tough luck, man."

"You're going to have to—"

"No way."

"I can't go myself." The sun burned the grass. The sky was a badly washed sheet, threadbare and thin. No birds or planes to focus on, just a wide field of blue. The blue changed intensity, sometimes nearing white and other times shadowing its own surface. John knew it was space leaking through.

"I don't have any money," Carver said.

"I'll give you my credit card," John said and took out his wallet.

"Uh uh. The last time we tried that I got arrested."

"How was I supposed to know you still had it?"

"You called the cops on me?"

"You were gone for two weeks." John held out the credit card delicately, between his fore and middle fingers.

"Well, I'm definitely not going to do it now," Carver said. He sat back into his chair with a loud thump, all six-and-a-half feet of him collapsing at once. "And, I warn you, I'm not sticking around if there's nothing to drink."

"Here," John said and handed Carver what remained of his beer.

"This might last fifteen minutes, if I drink slow."

John walked to the edge of the porch, directly under the rim of the overhang. It wasn't even two o'clock yet.

"I never told you I called the cops on you?"

"You did," said Carver. "But I'm still bitter."

"Well, you could always refuse my hospitality and give the beer back."

"Not that bitter."

Carver was never *that* bitter. Not even after John ran over his leg with a car, back when he had a car. John had just learned his parents had died in a plane crash, and didn't even notice Carver was waiting for him in the driveway. He'd been in shock, and then Carver was in shock from the broken leg, and both of them shared a beer while waiting for the ambulance. Afterwards, thoughtfully, Carver didn't even ask John to pay for the medical bills. He convinced the butcher shop the broken leg was an on-site injury.

"If you're not going to get groceries for me, could you at least go to the neighbors and use their phone to call the phone company?"

"What for?"

"To let them know that my phone line has been chewed through," John said.

Carver shrugged, took another drink from the beer, and walked over to the house on the left. On the other side

141

of the street builders were just beginning to tear down some abandoned houses, but nobody'd worked on the house for days. John could see into the living room and half of a bathroom. The construction people were unnaturally tidy, stowing all the rubbish in a giant green trash bin. The house looked like a cutaway diagram in an architecture book.

Without a phone line, John couldn't even do work. All of his web design information was on the web, and, though he could work on projects, e-mails came in several times a day relaying changes he was supposed to implement. The books on freelancing never talked about a downed phone line. Phone lines were supposed to be indestructible in the modern age, like plastic grocery bags.

Carver walked slowly back from the house. The beer can was gone, but he had two new bottles in his hand.

"I got us some beer," he said.

"What did the phone company say?"

"I couldn't make the call." Carver took a bottle opener from his pocket and opened the bottles.

"Why not?"

Carver offered John a bottle, and so he reluctantly took it. He needed a drink on a day like this.

"They weren't home."

"Then where did you get the beer?"

"Their fridge," Carver said, and took a drink. At the look John gave him, he shrugged. "I knocked, but no one answered. The back door was unlocked, though, so I went in to ask if I could use their phone. While looking around for your neighbors I checked to make sure the fridge door was closed, because sometimes, you know, people leave them open, and then all the food spoils. I found these, then came back to share."

"Can you go back and make the phone call now?"

"I can't. I locked the door on my way out," Carver said. "To be nice."

John sipped the beer. It was horrible. He took a second drink.

The walkway beyond his porch was seductive. Every so often John would sit on the porch and stare at the uncovered outside. It would be so easy to step out onto the cracked concrete and jump. The open sky would swallow him up, and that would be it.

"Your porch is infested, man," Carver said. He was gesturing with his bottle toward a large spider spinning itself down from the porch ceiling. It moved fitfully. "I think it knows we're here. You spending all your time in your house, I would've figured you'd killed every bug."

"Spiders kill other bugs," John said. "I had one as a pet, once."

"Doesn't seem like they'd be easy to domesticate." Carver leaned forward until he was only a few inches from the spider. His breath moved the web back and forth, so the spider became the weight on a pendulum.

"A tarantula," John said. "It was friendly enough. As long as I made no sudden moves, it wouldn't bite me. It was as big as my hand." Carver nodded. The spider was an inch from his nose. "In Brazil, where it was from, it would've spun webs between trees and caught birds."

"Really?"

"It was called a bird-eating spider. I fed it crickets."

"Can I see your beer?" Carver asked. John handed it to him. "So what happened to it?"

"I dropped it, and it burst on the kitchen floor." Carver put the mouth of John's bottle directly under the descending spider.

"What are you doing?"

"Just watch."

The spider spun itself into the neck of the bottle, but then Carver must have moved, since the spider rapidly climbed back up its line. Carver muttered, "fuck," and raised the bottle with it. He missed catching it twice and then it stopped, like a roach when the lights go on, and the bottle's mouth swallowed it. Carver jerked the bottle up until the spider reached the beer and was stuck, soaked, to the glass side.

"Now watch," Carver said and held out the bottle. The spider's limbs twitched. He swirled the beer until the spider was dislodged and floated free, its limbs flailing in a Duchamp doggie paddle.

"That was my beer," John said.

"And this spider is you," Carver said.

"Has anyone ever told you your symbolism sucks?"

"You stay in your house. This spider stays in the beer. It drowns. You do what?" Carver smirked.

"I don't drink the beer."

"You can't stay in here your whole life."

The spider was moving more slowly now.

"It's not a matter of wanting to. It's that I'll die if I leave. And you're fucking cruel."

"Don't give me that shit," Carver said. "You used to feed ants to spiders."

"But the ants died quickly."

"Not the second and third ones. They got trussed up and stored, paralyzed."

John snatched the bottle from Carver and threw it at the concrete walkway, shattering it into a jagged puddle. The bits of bottle glinted green like the idea of grass.

"That wasn't the best way to save it," Carver said and relaxed back into his chair.

"Think it's still alive?"

"No, but you could go out and check to make sure."

"I'm not drunk enough," John said.

"You never will be if you don't get to the store."

144

"I'm not going to the store," John said. "This is all your fault, anyway, so why don't you try my other neighbors?"

"John, no one has ever lived in that house."

"There's something moving in the puddle."

"How about this. To let you check on the spider in perfect safety, I'll take off my belt, and you can hold on to one end. I'll anchor you to the ground. That way if you fall up I can pull you back down." Carver took off his belt.

"You won't let go?" John took hold of the buckle end and the notch dug into his palm. He stepped to the edge of the porch.

"Even if I do, you'll be so close you can catch the edge of the roof."

"I should be fine as long as I don't trip."

"That's right."

John stepped from under the protection of the roof, walking down the stairs one at a time. He entered the sunlight like an amateur swimmer entering a cold pool. His skin glowed like paper brightened by a candle flame moments before burning. Carver didn't move from his chair, and eventually the belt was tight between them.

The broken bottle was a blur. John's eyes adjusted slowly to the immersion in light. Spots clouded his eyes. The spider was splayed at the edge of the puddle like an asterisk.

"It's dead," John said.

Carver yanked the belt from John's hand. John tipped forward but caught himself by slamming his hands on the broken glass.

"You didn't fall."

"Go into the bathroom and get me some band-aids," John said. Blood started to rivulet into the spilled beer.

"You don't have any. I stole them all last week. Notice, again, that you didn't fall off the earth."

John slowly stood up, pushing off the concrete with his wounded hands. The pain created a cottony distance between his thoughts and actions, sort of like the way his dad had explained his premonitions of migraines.

There was nothing above him and not even a tree close by to grab onto, assuming he was still able to grip. He raised his head so the sky was all he could see. He kept looking up until he felt like he was falling, like the earth was moving with him, closing up the distance to the sky.

"Here," Carver said, and John turned in time to catch Carver's t-shirt. He wrapped his hands in it. "Ready to go?"

"This must be what suicide feels like."

They walked to where the concrete path from John's house reached the sidewalk. John took every step with exaggerated care.

"Looks like I'll be doing everything for you after all, your hands like that," Carver said, then tripped.

John reached out to catch him, but his hands were tangled in the shirt, so that he pushed Carver farther up in the air instead of holding him down. Carver didn't say anything as he ascended, twirling like an astronaut cut loose from the space shuttle. Carver's face showed just mild confusion, as though he was trying to figure out the answer to a simple math problem he knew he should know.

John watched Carver until he disappeared in the empty blue. Then, very careful to avoid cracks and uneven edges, he walked on down the sidewalk to the store for bandages and beer.

About the Author

This is Andrew Kozma's second appearance in a Third Flatiron anthology. His fiction has been or will be

The Apple Falls Upward

published in *Albedo One, Daily Science Fiction, Stupefying Stories,* and *Drabblecast.*

*****~~~~~*****

Sam, Sam, and the Demoness

by K. T. Katzmann

Rabbi Sam Rabinowitz arrived five minutes early. His late grandfather had told Sam about the importance of punctuality to his dying day, and still wouldn't shut up about it fifteen years afterwards.

As Sam walked up the well-tended lawn, the glowing older gentleman hovering next to him peppered him with questions. "So, is she a looker, that one?"

Tall, bearded, and with what his mother described as "a boyish face," Sam sighed as he pushed in the doorbell. "Grandpa Samuel, she's married. We're here about a case."

Samuel, skinny, balding, and slightly luminescent, rolled his nonexistent eyes. "Like that matters. Married isn't the same as dead, trust me. If I had let a thing like that stop me, we wouldn't have your cousin Deborah."

The door opened, and Sam stared into eyes framed by disheveled hair and running mascara. He knew Miriam Williamson *née* Posner as the girl at the Friday night after-service snack table with the boisterous voice and quiet husband. He'd have imagined peace in the Middle East before she broke down.

"She is a looker!" His grandfather declared with a whistle and a feminist sensibility older than President Truman's tax returns. Sam was grateful once again that no one else could see his spiritual albatross. Still, he sighed. This was going to be a long night.

"Rabbi Rabinowitz!" Miriam mustered a smile. "Oh, thank God. I warn you, this, uh, may sound a little weird."

Sam looked sideways at the hovering specter in Bermuda shorts and sandals. "I'm accustomed to things of that nature. Can I come in?"

149

Ain't Superstitious

Once inside the living room, Sam couldn't help but notice the large statue of the Virgin Mary staring at him with disapproval from the mantle. "Mixed marriage, I assume?"

"Yes, she replied, passing him a cup of coffee.

He scanned the room. "And the husband in question is. . . ?"

"Robert's with the police right now, trying to prove that he isn't crazy. I had my turn earlier." Her shaking hand hovered over a glass of cold coffee before retracting. "Look, Rabbi, I've heard that you have a. . . spiritual advantage."

"I'll even prove it." Sam reached inside his pocket and dropped a deck of cards onto the coffee table.

"What?" Miriam giggled. "You can't be serious."

Sam breathed in and out slowly. "I absolutely am. Look, someone convinced you to call me, but I can see you're not quite convinced enough to take me seriously." He slid the deck of cards across the table. "Pick a card."

She obliged, showing her first smile in hours. "Okay."

Sam stood up and covered his eyes with a magician's flourish. "Dead Grandpa Samuel," he intoned, "I send you off to find the knowledge I seek." After a second, he add, "Wait a minute, Miriam. He walks slowly after his operation."

She paused. "I thought you said he was dead."

"I did. He's also pretty set in his ways. Hold on, he's trying to tell me."

Sam snorted.

"Really, Grandpa? This again?"

Miriam waited in the suspenseful silence before the Rabbi uncovered his eyes and sat down, hands up in surrender.

"Fine. Who am I to question the diplomatic skills of the divorce king of Miami Beach?" He shook his head.

"And the answer is?"

Sam shuddered. "Red, lacy, and size thirty. Second drawer down." At her stunned gasp, he rubbed the bridge of his nose. Sorry, he's incorrigible."

She carefully replaced the card. "I'm a believer. So, is this ghost thing, well, common for rabbis?"

"It's a long story."

…

It was all his parents' fault. After all, they had defied Jewish tradition to name him after a living relative. His grandfather Samuel swelled with pride, while the Rabinowitz family assured everyone that they were just ignoring a quaint folk superstition.

That all changed the night of his Bar Mitzvah celebration. Relative after relative had been called up by the DJ to give a rushed speech. When the DJ mentioned Sam's then-dead grandfather, Sam's mother had uttered the unfortunate toast.

"And though he is not here to join us, may the wisdom of your grandfather Samuel follow you all the days of your life!"

Sam didn't know whether it was the questionable naming, the toast, the Bar Mitzvah, or all three working in conjunction. Regardless, when his grandfather spectrally appeared in his bathroom that night, he had nearly simultaneously choked to death and strangled himself on floss. Fifteen years later, Sam had accepted that Grandpa Samuel was here to stay.

"Tell me about your problem," Sam said after spilling his tale of familial woe.

Tears reappeared on Miriam's face. "My baby was kidnapped last night. By all rights, the police should be trampling all over this place, looking for clues. They think we're crazy, though. The only cops they spared are the ones keeping watch on me from the car across the street!" She tried to lift the coffee cup and only succeeded in spilling half the cup across the table.

Sam exchanged a look with his grandfather before asking, "Why do they think your husband's crazy?"

"Because he said he saw our baby taken by a naked woman with red glowing eyes!"

His mouth opened and shut several times, but all Sam could manage was, "Great." With reflection, he continued. "*Oy vey. Oy gevault!*" He tapped the table, bobbing his head back and forth in thought, while Miriam held her breath. Finally, he broke the silence by asking, "Did you break a glass when you got married?"

"W-well, Robert wanted to, but his parents are really Catholic."

"Okay. So the spirits weren't warned off, then. And there's no amulets hanging in the nursery for the same reason, I assume?" At her blank look, he added, "Hands. Downwards pointing hands with eyes on them."

Miriam shrugged weakly, and he blew out an exasperated breath. "Okay. She got in, then. Look, Ma'am, you got salt?"

She blinked. "Yes."

Sam leaned forward, brow furrowed, strictly business in his demeanor. "Kosher salt?"

"Uh. . ."

"It's lower in sodium, you know."

"Now he tells me," Samuel said with an exaggerated clutch to his chest.

Sam leapt to his feet. "Spread salt over every doorway in the house. We'll go get your baby, Ma'am."

Miriam rose and nearly fell onto Sam, clutching his jacket. "Really? Do you really know what took her?"

"Oh, yes." Sam swallowed. "I do, Ma'am. She's quite a singular individual. Her name is Lilith." With that pronouncement, Sam spit into his coffee cup three times.

Miriam blinked. "You want decaf?"

...

"How long do we have to walk in circles, Sam? I'm not following you for my health, you know."

Sam, Sam, and the Demoness

Sam ignored his grandfather, focusing on the smartphone in his hand. From Miriam's door, the pair had canvassed the neighborhood by moonlight, Samuel floating after Sam while the younger, livelier man had turned down street corners seemingly at random. Sam suddenly stopped at his latest intersection, looking up in confusion.

"Why do you sound out of breath, Grandpa?"

Samuel wobbled in the air, hand on his chest as he breathed out. "We've been walking on this *schlep* for hours."

Rubbing the bridge of his nose, Sam kept rushing down the street. "It's been twenty minutes, Grandpa, and you don't even have lungs. Stop being so dramatic." Sam's attention returned to scanning the rows of stores laid out in the endless suburban sprawl. Samuel floated in front of his face.

"'Dramatic,' he says! How else am I supposed to make you notice me! I've been basically following a lanky mime with bad grooming for twenty minutes. It's not fun, you know." He frowned. "Cough it up, kid. You only get quiet when you're worried."

Sam checked the local street signs before pocketing his phone and sighing, slowing to a walk. "Fine. We're almost there anyway. I think I know where she is."

"She?"

"Lilith." Sam rolled the name around in his tongue before spitting on the ground three times. "Do that if you say her name, Grandpa. Otherwise, she'll hear you."

Samuel folded his arms as he hung in the air and kept pace with his grandson. "Feh. Tell the guy without lungs to spit."

"So pretend!" As Sam gritted his teeth and waved his arms at his grandfather, a car sped by, silhouetting him in the headlights. *Great*, he thought. *Driver probably thinks I'm crazy. I'm screaming in public and waving at nothing. For this, I went to yeshiva?* Sighing, Sam said,

"Fine. Look, we're dealing with. . . You know what, my mouth is dry, so I'll just say 'Her.' She was Adam's ex-wife. When she was kicked out of Eden, she became jealous of Adam's children. She vowed that her family would torment us forever. She still wants a baby, though."

"Of, course," Samuel said, smirking. "Her biological clock's been ringing for six thousand years. Hold on. 'Her family?' If you rule out Adam's kids, who'd she shack up with?"

Sam breathed in as he walked into a deserted plaza, his eyes darting at shadows. "Satan, Grandpa."

"Oh." Neither of them spoke for a moment. "Well, she beats my ex-wives in terms of crazy. So, how are we going to find her? Divination? Necromancy?"

Sam whipped his phone out with a smile. "Internet search. She may be an ancient ex-human demon, but she's still Jewish, Grandpa. Where's she going to go after getting a new infant?"

He pointed across the deserted parking lot to the only store in the plaza with lights on. The Baby Emporium's glass front doors had been shattered completely.

"She's going shopping," Sam declared with a smile.

As he dashed through the shadows towards the violated store, something inside gave a long mournful howl that nothing with a single throat should have been able to produce. Sam stopped, eyes wide, and Samuel put a hand on his grandson's shoulder. It didn't actually touch him, but Sam still felt cold at the touch.

"Grandson of mine, let's take this nice and slow."

With a shiver, Sam shook his head. "We don't have time, Grandpa."

The roaring started up again, and something else answered back.

Samuel whispered into Sam's ear, "Why? She's in there, and the baby's in there. We're almost done. She's not

154

going to hurt the little tyke, right? You said she raises them."

Sam carefully ducked behind the newspaper dispensers along the sidewalk, glancing inside the glass walls of the Baby Emporium with distrust. He saw only shelves, but something was screaming. "They didn't exactly have baby books in her time, Grandpa."

"Okay, right. First woman. I get it."

Ancient demons and unknown monsters abounded, but Sam Rabinowitz was still a rabbi. True to his calling, he paused within ten feet of the door and raised a lecturing finger. "Second," he whispered, "after the nameless one but before Eve."

Samuel nodded. "Third time's the charm."

Crouching outside the Baby Emporium, the odors of a zoo wafted out to Sam's nose. He could hear things stalking inside, their claws scratching the floor of the shop. With a muttered prayer and raised eyes, Sam sprinted inside the store. He was greeted by nothing but torn "Sale" signs and displays that had been knocked over. Staying low to the ground, he crept along the aisles, hiding amongst the gigantic piles of pastel-colored baby toys.

The barely controlled terror on Sam's face confused Samuel. "Sammy boy, what are you so worried about? Bad feeding leading to indigestion? She'll use the wrong diaper lotion?"

Sam gave a start as something spilled toys onto the floor in the next aisle over. A dozen dolls screamed for their mothers simultaneously. "Two things, Grandpa. One, she'll hold the baby so tightly that it suffocates."

"Wonderful. And the other piece of good news?"

Into Sam's path walked something covered in shaggy hair, crowned by horns, and gifted with more sharp teeth than anyone could use in a lifetime. It blinked beady eyes as a two-foot tongue lolled out of its mouth.

"She gives birth to a thousand demons a day," Sam whispered, turning pale.

The hairy freak roared, throwing lopping arms forward in a knuckle-dragging run.

As Sam ran with all the athleticism someone who studies for six hours a day could muster, Samuel gritted his teeth.

"I hate this part," he muttered as he stepped into the path of the demon. It blew right through him before pausing and shivering. Its mental train of thought being more like a pushcart, it wandered off in confusion.

Samuel found his grandson three aisles over, hiding inside a small pink plastic house. "Now what?" He asked as the demon started wandering down the nearby aisle.

"Look," Sam replied in a whisper, "this is not that bad. She gives birth to a thousand demons a day—"

"I like my cigar, but I take it out every once in a while. Heh. You know who—"

"Yes, Grandpa, it was Groucho, now be quiet. She gives birth to a thousand demons a day, but God's angels kill a thousand of her children a day. So. . . "

Specks of brilliant light exploded into existence in front of the beast before shooting through its body and winking out. The demon clutched its chest and dropped to the floor.

Samuel blinked. "Yeah, buddy. I know how that feels. Kid, do we just wait until they drop dead?"

Sam crawled out of his pink shelter and shook his head. "That muppety *schmuck* might have lived for hours. We got lucky. I'm going to need you to hover higher and play lookout."

"All right." Samuel began rising in the air. "None of them can see or hear me, right?"

"Oh, no."

"Oh. Good."

"She can," Sam said before jogging off.

Sam, Sam, and the Demoness

"Ah! Okay." Samuel peered down at the aisles. "Sam! Sam, turn left at the diaper aisle. There's a vulture-bear kinda thing there!" Flying forward to keep an eye on his grandson, Samuel's eyes widened in horror. "Not the bottle aisle! There's a snake-girly-waspy something. Wait, she just died. Okay, bottle aisle it is."

Sam crouched between two displays of formulas and beckoned his grandfather down. When Samuel reached the floor, Sam pointed across an open area filled with cribs and playpens. In a plastic reconstruction of Noah's ark, a baby was crying. Standing over it, whispering, was Her.

Fingers with nails grown into filthy claws rocked the ark, shaking it back and forth. They belonged to a naked woman, shapely once but emaciated now, with wild hair and wilder eyes. As she paced around the crib, her tail became visible, as wide as a man's thigh and tipped on the end like a scorpion.

"All right, Grandpa," Sam whispered. "If she hears the names of three angels, she has to leave. That's the deal."

"Whose deal?"

"God's."

"Why do I keep asking?" Samuel wondered aloud. "She'll be powerless to hurt you, right?"

Sam shook his head. "That's why you need to memorize the names. I'm getting something from the toddler aisles."

"Perfect." Samuel rubbed his forehead. "I waltz right up to the crazy *meshuggeneh* demon who can see me. What are their names?"

"Um, Senoy." Sam chewed his forefinger. "Sansenoy, that's the second one. I think."

Samuel clapped. "Wonderful. To think I helped pay your *yeshiva* tuition."

Eyes closed, Sam punched himself in the head. "Damn! What was the third name?"

157

"Curly!"

"No, Grandpa."

"Oh." His eyes dropped for a moment before a smile crawled across his face. "Shemp?"

"You're doing this on purpose." Sam snapped his fingers. "Semangelof!"

Lilith looked up in his direction for a second, scanning the area with teeth barred. Missing Sam's hiding place, she picked up the baby and clutched it to her chest.

Sucking in his breath, Sam began crawling away. "Come on, Grandpa. We gotta work fast."

"Wait a second. I have to talk to the demon. Uh, isn't lying a sin?"

"Oh, great, Grandpa," Sam whispered angrily. "Now, of all times, you decide to be a holy man."

Barely five minutes later found Samuel nervously levitating out onto the display floor, drawing a glowing red glare from Lilith.

"Behold!" He proclaimed like a medieval used-car salesman. "I am an angel of the Lord! I come in the name of Senoy, Sansenoy, and Semangelof!"

She looked up, crimson light flaring from her eyes. "And which are you, come to steal a mother's child?"

"Oh." Samuel scratched his head. "You wouldn't have heard of me. I'm, uh, Shemp."

Her fanged mouth opened and closed wordlessly. "Shemp?"

He shrugged. "I replaced Curly. Look, call off the demons, leave the child on the table, and you shall receive another baby. One who won't die on you, I might add."

She breathed in slowly. "Truly? After all this time?"

He threw his arms out. "What do you think I am, some plain old *schmuck*? I am an angel of the Lord, toots! You better believe it!"

"I," she spat out, "am no man's 'toots.' Adam learned that."

"My fault, sorry. Look, put the baby back in the crib, and a new one's yours."

A thump from a distant aisle drew her attention.

"And pay no attention," Samuel said with a wave, "to the scuttling sounds nearby! You need only be concerned with—"

"Momma," said a squeaky voice. "Momma."

Lilith nearly dropped the baby into the crib as she sprung towards the faint words, running on all fours. She pounced, reached in, and picked up the vocal little bundle, caressing its cheek as a ring of fire sprung up around her on the floor. With a flash, Lilith, the fire, and the other baby had vanished.

Standing up from behind a play pen, Sam walked over to the now-crying baby Lilith had left behind and picked her up with a smile.

"Good work, kid." Samuel said as he flew over. "How long is that going to work?"

Thinking about the "baby" he had given Lilith, Sam laughed. "Until the batteries wear out, Grandpa. Believe me, you'll be glad you're not Shemp when she notices the difference."

About the Author

Author K. T. Katzmann lives and teaches in Florida.

*****~~~~~*****

Ambrose's Eight-plus-Oneth

by Judith Field

If a bad rehearsal makes for a good performance, the Macclesfield Simfonietta was set for a five-star show. Pat and Mark sat alone in the front row of the empty auditorium. The conductor raised his baton. 'Go from letter J.'

Mark jumped. 'What on earth is that? He put his hands over his ears. 'Are they still tuning up?'

Pat pulled his hands down. 'Shh! They've started. Ambrose's Eight-plus-Oneth Symphony.'

'Can't Ambrose count?'

Pat shook her head. 'It's "the curse of the ninth." A ninth symphony is destined to be a composer's last, so he'll die after writing it.'

The conductor dropped his hands and turned to Pat and Mark. 'Quiet! We asked you here to find the missing musicians, not hinder the ones still around. Three of them—just vanished.'

Pat squeezed Mark's hand. Her engagement ring dug into his finger. Stainless steel, containing enough iron to ward off evil spirits. A blue eye-shaped amulet instead of a diamond. Their wedding rings were pure cold iron. Mark touched the jacket pocket in which, like a reminder that it was not some dream, he carried the one he would put on Pat's finger.

Finley, the Operations Manager, crept down the aisle and beckoned from the end of the row. Mark hefted the strap of his kit bag onto his shoulder. Pat picked up a holdall, and they followed Finley to the back of the hall.

Mark whistled. 'What a racket.'

'No!' A sheen of sweat covered Finlay's forehead. 'It's bad luck to whistle in a theatre.' His hands flapped. 'We need all the luck we can get. Two flautists and a

161

timpanist vanished into thin air in the last two weeks. We're starting on our summer tour the day after tomorrow. At this rate, all we'll be able to play will be Haydn's Farewell Symphony.' It was the one where most of the orchestra leaves, one by one, during the last movement.

'You've called us very late,' Mark said. 'Didn't you tell the police?'

'Didn't want to know. "It's a free country, people can go where they like." Private detective? Complete rip-off. Come outside.'

They stood in the foyer. 'I can't just hire replacement musicians,' Finley said. 'My niece was, er, is, engaged to the timpanist. She wants him back.'

Mark imagined how he would feel if there was no Pat. 'Say no more,' he said. 'We'll take a look round and report back.'

Finley went inside the auditorium, leaving the door ajar.

'Well?' Mark heard the conductor snarl at the brass section. The woodwind players, sitting in front of them, ducked. He peered round the door.

A trombonist nodded towards the empty chair to his left. 'Tuba's gone. I called his digs. Nobody knows where he is.'

The conductor threw down his baton. 'Take a break.' He stamped down the steps and out of the hall, shoving past Mark as he went.

'Four missing, now,' Pat said. 'We'd better hurry.' She picked up the holdall and turned towards the other end of the foyer.

...

Mark unplugged the leads and switched off the phasmometer, which detected magical entities. 'Nothing.'

Pat frowned. 'In a building this age, there's always some sort of entity. A revenant, at the very least. We'd better give the detector a boost.'

She knelt down and unzipped her bag. She pulled out a black velvet box from which she took a ball of grey fluff. It would have looked like the stuff that collects under beds, had it not had red eyes and been wriggling.

Pat straightened up. 'This is a fae. A little bit of nothing, but full of power. How do you think they get into bedrooms?

'Cheek!' A squeaky voice came from the fluff.

'Sorry,' Pat said, through gritted teeth.

Mark dropped the phasmometer into her other hand. 'No gossamer wings, then? Shame.'

Pat flipped a switch, and a metallic, spoon-shaped object popped out of the end. She draped the fluff over it, and the phasmometer emitted the sound of a violin playing a discordant chord.

'Something's here,' Pat said. 'At this frequency, I'd say it was made of wood.'

'Glad to help, lady, squire.' the fae squeaked. 'Now, what do you say?'

Mark turned towards it. 'Tha—'

Pat clapped her hand over his mouth. 'Never thank the fae. Puts you in their debt. You wouldn't want to be enslaved forever to an object that belongs inside a vacuum cleaner. Better to pay them some sort of compliment.' She turned towards the fae. 'You are very kind. Now go to sleep.'

The red eyes closed.

'Put it away for me, I want to check the reading again.' Pat stared at the detector.

Mark picked the fae off the spoon and put it in the palm of his hand. Poor creature, stuffed in a tiny box. Nothing to do all day. No wonder they got up to mischief. He remembered reading that they couldn't resist shiny objects. Perhaps coins would amuse it. He rolled it into a ball and put it into his pocket. 'Thanks, squire. Whoops!' came a muffled squeak, followed by a metallic rattle and another squeak. 'Shiny!'

163

Mark pressed his hand over his pocket and turned to Pat. 'Wood, you said. A door?'

She shook her head. 'Too big. More likely an instrument.'

'But we didn't spot anything while we were watching them.'

'No. The only way we're going to find anything is to join the orchestra. Just as well I came prepared.' She reached inside the bag again and pulled out a stringed instrument.

'I didn't know you played the violin,' Mark said.

'It's a viola. And I don't really play. My uncle left it to me when I was 16. I wanted to flog it, but Mum believed you should never get rid of a legacy. Unfortunately for me, she also believed if you had a stringed instrument that nobody could play, the house would be sad and gloomy. So I had to have lessons.'

'Couldn't she have?'

'Mum? Gave a whole new meaning to the term "tone deaf." No, it had to be me. I hated it.'

'Anyway, you're glad now that you learned, aren't you? Yet another one of your many skills.' He stroked her hand.

She shook her head. 'After a week or two Mum decided she'd rather have sadness and gloom than put up with the noise. But she was right about not getting rid of it, so I didn't.'

There was no viola part in Ambrose's Eighth plus Oneth, but Finley agreed to allow Pat to play any of the violins' notes that she could manage.

…

The rehearsal ended. Pat came down from the stage and sat next to Mark in the front row.

'I saw you looking at the phasmometer,' he said. 'Find anything?'

'There's a sensation coming from the direction of the violins. When one of them—Rob—bowed his instrument, the others vibrated in unison.'

Rob walked down the steps at the edge of the stage. Pat grabbed his sleeve. 'I like your violin. Mind if I have a look?'

He handed it over. The violin was made of dark wood. It gave off a dark brown glow as though lit from inside, and there were shapes in the grain of the wood on the back. 'A beauty, isn't she? My brother Shane made her, in school.'

'Gorgeous,' Pat said. 'What's it made of? I've never seen anything like it.'

'Dunno. School ran out of wood, but an undertaker donated some leftovers. Shane got hold of a bit. The weird thing is that, after that, he never managed more than a coat hook.'

'Could I borrow it for a while, take it home?' Pat said. 'Just for an hour.'

Rob's face shrivelled and wrinkled, and his mouth narrowed. 'Give-it-back,' he growled in so low a pitch that, in the split second before he shoved his hand at Pat, Mark wondered where the voice came from.

Pat's hand shook as she passed it over. Rob's eyes looked blank for a moment. He shook his head and walked away.

'What's the matter with you?' Mark asked. 'Muscle fatigue?'

Pat rubbed her wrist. 'No, I was fine before I held that violin. It's alive.'

Finley came bustling up. 'Get a move on. I don't want this to end up like it did when the other exorcist, Pittenworm, was here.'

Pat scowled. 'Reggie Pittenweem. You never told me you'd tried someone else. Yet again, we have to sort out his mess. What happened?'

Finley's face reddened. 'I don't know. He was OK one day, then the next he was off sick, for good. Just get on with it. Please.'

'That's about as much as I've got the energy for today.' Pat took Mark's arm, and they left the building. 'I'll call Pittenweem and see what he can tell us.

...

Mark arrived at the auditorium the following morning, just as the orchestra started a break. Pat took his hand.

Mark frowned and bit his lip. 'I went to see the undertaker. I put a bit of a glamour on him, and he believed I was from a magazine, *Better Funerals*. The wood he gave the school was left over from an old lady's coffin. A violin teacher.'

Pat went pale. 'This is bad. I'd hoped that those musicians had just wandered off, but now, I think some sort of entity's involved. You need to understand something. M-theory has it that there's a separation between our world, called the W duality and the land of the other, the O duality.'

'What does M stand for? Magic, I suppose?'

'Yes.'

Mark rolled his eyes.

'Don't blame me.' Pat scowled. 'I didn't name it. Something has breached the separation between the dualities. That violin is a bridge between the two.'

'Why did people disappear on this side but nothing come through from theirs?'

'I don't know that it hasn't, but we haven't got time to hunt it. We have to get those musicians back, then close the gap. It'll take a huge amount of magical energy. We have to get hold of that violin.'

'I don't know how; you said Rob never puts it down.'

'It ties in with what Pittenweem's mother said—he couldn't come to the phone. He's lost his memory. Things are starting to come back, but he doesn't know what's true. Like, he thinks he remembers seeing a violin playing itself.'

'We've got to act now,' Mark said. 'Before they leave on tour.'

Pat thought for a moment. 'There is a spell I can use, and I need to start now. I've left my phone in my bag, on the stage. Come up with me and help me set the kit up so that when Rob comes back it'll start working.'

As they headed up the steps beside the stage, Mark heard a dry, creaking voice. 'Why are a violist's fingers like lightning? They never strike the same spot twice.' He looked round. Nobody was there. 'How do you stop a violist falling downstairs? You *don't*.'

As the last word sounded, Pat jerked forwards and fell down the steps, pulling him after her. His head smashed onto the floor. As he lost consciousness he saw her white face, and her arm twisted underneath her.

...

Pat and Mark sat at their kitchen table. It was ten in the evening.

'A fine set of wedding photos we're going to get,' Pat said. 'You with a surgical collar and me with my arm in a sling. Pass the tramadol; I'm ready for another dose.' He slid the box to her across the table. 'This stuff knocks me out,' she said. She put a capsule into her mouth and tried to lift a teacup with the wrong hand.

'We're lucky nothing's broken,' he said. 'What are we going to do about that violin?'

'As we were waiting for the ambulance, I heard the conductor telling them to leave their instruments in the theatre, to be packed up ready to go first thing. He told them to sleep with their music under their pillows, for luck.' She stifled a yawn. 'We could have gone back in tonight. But not now.'

'I still can. Tell me what to do.'

'You can't do this on your own. M-theory is high-level stuff. I'm coming with you.'

Her eyelids drooped. 'Get the big bag from upstairs and pack all the gear up, you've got more hands than I have. I'll just have a little rest.' She leaned back in her chair. Her eyes closed.

Mark hauled himself downstairs, holding the bag in one hand, clutching the banisters with the other. He tiptoed across the hall and peered into the kitchen.

Pat had leaned back in her chair, her eyes still closed. 'Sweep the hearth towards the fire every morning, Mark,' she muttered, 'in case pixies came down the chimney during the night while the fire burned low.' Her head dropped to one side, and her breath was slow and even.

Mark took off the collar, and stepped outside, closing the front door so that the lock made only the faintest click. He put the bag into the boot, got inside the car, shut the door as quietly as he could, and let off the handbrake. He waited until it had freewheeled down the hill before starting the engine.

The auditorium was locked, with alarms set on all doors. Mark walked round the back of the building and set the bag down in front of a filthy sash window, level with his feet. In the distance a church clock chimed eleven. He shivered despite the warmth of the summer night.

A dog barked at the front of the building, growing nearer. He froze, but the sound grew fainter again, and he heard the dog's owner telling it to hurry. He breathed out, took the high-energy wand, rowan wood bound with red, from the bag. He pointed it at the window. A crimson spark flew from the end, hitting the window and lighting the pane. With a creak the sash slid up. Mark eased himself inside what seemed to be a broom cupboard.

The instruments were not in the basement. Mark walked up the back stairs to the ground floor, holding his wand in front of him. In the auditorium, the 'ghost light' that burned on the stage day and night glimmered. Some said it was to stop spirits getting up to mischief because they realised the theatre was empty, others that it was to reduce the risk of fumbling around on a cluttered stage in the dark. Mark was glad of it as he stepped inside and walked down the central aisle.

He reached the middle. A violin began to play a tune more captivating than any he had heard in his life. The song came from his left, next from the right. He walked up and down searching the rows of seats. He saw nothing on the stage. A dream-like numbness washed over him, and he leaned against a pillar, eyes closed.

The same, cracked voice that he had heard before they were pushed down the stairs called his name. 'Who's there?' he shouted. He heard his own voice echoing in the empty theatre, and the sound of the violin. He looked at the stage. A grey mist covered the floor, and the light grew brighter, shining on a glowing violin hanging in mid-air. His eyes would not turn away. He felt sick. His heart pounded.

'What's the difference between a viola and a coffin?' the voice said. 'The coffin has a dead person on the inside. I tried to put your little violist in hers. My coffin, my violin. But, no matter. You are mine.' The violin fell silent.

He dropped the bag and turned to run. His feet felt glued to the spot.

'Come to me,' the voice said. He felt himself walk up the steps and onto the stage. The violin floated towards him.

'Those young musicians were ignorant. I collected them and devoured them. I need an older, wiser man. Pittenweem was old, but a fool. Once I had emptied his mind, I did not care to collect him.'

Mark pointed the wand at the violin. The crimson spark flew from the end, enveloping the violin in flame, but it did not burn. It came closer.

'You know that death is inevitable. For everyone,' the voice said.

Mark aimed the wand again, but no spark came. He grasped it, ready to use it as a club if the violin came closer.

'A man about to be married is the greatest prize.'

Mark's arm fell to his side. The wand fell from his open fingers.

'Die and be with me.'

If he reached out, he was sure he could touch the violin. As his hand moved, his fingers brushed against his pocket, and he heard another voice, squeaky and muffled. 'Here, squire. Take this!' He felt fluff against his fingertips as the fae pushed Pat's wedding ring into his trembling hand. He slipped it onto the tip of his ring finger.

The song of the violin grew sweeter, imploring him to listen, filling his mind. He shook his head and raised his hand to his ear. He heard Pat's voice, telling him of the love and the years they would have together. She sounded faint, and the violin grew louder. His feet began to move, propelling him forward.

His hand shook. He could not keep it raised. Pat's voice swelled, telling him that she had waited for him all her life. The violin made faltering, harsh scrapes. 'And I for you, Pat,' Mark said. The mist that had gathered around his feet blew away. The violin shattered to powder, covering the floor, and Mark in dust.

He looked up at a window. It was growing light outside. Outside, a bird began singing. A shaft of early morning sunlight shone onto the empty stage.

###

About the Author

Judith Field was born in Liverpool, England, and lives in London. She is the daughter of writers, and learned how to agonise over fiction submissions at her mother's (and father's) knee. She has two daughters, a son, a granddaughter, and a grandson. Her fiction, mainly speculative, has appeared in a variety of publications in the USA and UK.

*****~~~~~*****

The Annual Scarecrow Festival

by John Paul Davies

Caroline saw the scarecrow first, the sight eliciting a strange warbling sound from her throat. Over the reception desk, the scarecrow's boots slowly turned as the noose twisted, the sewn features of its sackcloth head a child's caricature crudely brought to life.

"Are you even sure this is the right place?" Caroline asked, flapping her hands about her face in a vain attempt to banish the image.

"Corn Rigs Guest House," Joe read from his crumpled printout, looking up to confirm the number. "This is the one."

"Then why's the door locked and no bastard answering?"

Joe removed his finger from the archaic bell-push, leaving a not-quite silence resonating inside the house.

Through the breakfast room window, more scarecrows could be seen patiently awaiting service, the stalks from their sleeves soaking into murky teacups.

Each window of the slumbering house brought to Caroline's mind mannequins contorted in a shop display, the scarecrows facing each other as though in deep conversation. No effort spared by the festival organisers, the house rivalled the macabre celebrations of previous years, as the villagers attempted to outdo their predecessors' efforts.

"Maybe the old dear who runs this joint has stepped out for a minute," Joe speculated. "Why don't we go for a wander until she gets back?"

Away from Corn Rigs, they followed the narrow lane on its downward slope, soon descending into dense woodland. A canopy of foliage overhead denied the mid-morning sun, while the wind-goaded leaves sounded like

173

waves extinguishing on a shore, before being instantly reborn. Somewhere a stream gurgled.

Glimpses of cottages could be seen through the trees, with moss-draped stone walls concealing evidence of existence. Foreign birdsong filled the woods on either side of the path, while lower down, rootier animals shuffled through the fallen leaves. Something rattled along the branches, shaking the leaves, keeping time with the tourists as Caroline clung to Joe's arm.

The verdant orchestra stilled as the woods drew back to reveal a decrepit churchyard. The outline of a removed clock was visible on the church steeple, the crumbling turret tapering to a rusted crucifix. A contained sound pervaded, like the whispers of children running through string, threaded between tin cans.

Near the church, scarecrows draped over the weather-rinsed gravestones, as though they had flung themselves over the monuments in dramatic mourning. Others adorned the entrances to family crypts, standing sentry: almonds for eyes, barleycorn ears, the torn hay of gaping mouths.

"Slightly distasteful," said Caroline.

"Oh, I don't know," Joe said, producing his camera. "A Kodak moment, I'd say."

A carved, mirthful sun grinned back from the church door, its cartoon flames shooting like compass points from its centre. The useless bell stood still in its tower. Clouds sped overhead, decimating blue sky.

"Well, I'm going inside to light a candle," Caroline said.

Joe grunted a response, looking longingly at the pub opposite the church. The illustrated sign for 'The Landlord's Daughter' flapped on its hinges, beckoning him inside, though he knew Caroline would not permit a mid-morning pint.

"All that every good village needs," Joe said. "A church and a pub. Come on then, let's enter your dreary, beerless place."

A draught followed them in, hurrying debris along the cracked mosaic floor of the church. As their eyes slowly adjusted to the gloom, Caroline sought out the prayer chapel, leaving Joe to wander the empty aisles.

The high stained glass windows afforded thin light, their depictions of New Testament highlights almost unintelligible with grime. The wooden beams of the roof met like an inverted ship deck, and in the gloom of the rafters, Joe tried to make out the birds he could hear fluttering in the shadows.

"A classic church interior," Joe said, unable to conceal his boredom.

Fumbling for a coin for the donation box, Caroline placed a new candle onto a vacant brass holder. The surrounding burnt-out wicks seemed countless souls snuffed out, disparate lives that had ended all too suddenly. The candles were no more than stubs; their molten prayers had congealed along the dimmed shrine.

"Have you got a light, Joe? None of these candles have been lit for ages."

"Joe?"

Standing amongst the splintered pews, Joe was gazing up at the altar, where the effigy Christ should have been. In its place, a scarecrow had been nailed, ankle and wrist, to a crude wooden crucifix. Even the detail of a crown of thorns had been added, adorning its burlap head. The Scarecrow Christ displayed like some forgotten martyr, overseeing its paltry congregation.

A white tunic contained the bristling cadaver, a hernia of straw gashing its side. Paint had been applied to the stalks of its face to represent a beard, while pressed deep into its head, twin tawdry lights glowed red for the eyes.

"If *that* doesn't bring people flocking back to church," Joe said.

"Well, I refuse to look at it any longer. Now hand me your sodding lighter, please. Let's go to your pub. Think I've seen enough." Caroline's solitary candle sweated its wax, the small flame contorting in the breeze, refusing to die.

In the jaundiced light of The Landlord's Daughter, scarecrows clustered at the round tables, nursing grab-handle tankards. The scarecrow barman's hay-fist was twined around a cask pump, poised mid-pour. No one serving the no one drinking.

"We've committed a night to this place?" Caroline asked, studying the pub's clientele. "Hardly jumping, is it?"

"We're too early, that's all," Joe explained. "Probably doesn't get going until the afternoon. Now, what are the chances of getting a pint around here?"

A band of scarecrows were set up on what passed for the pub's stage, complete with banjo and fiddle players. A straw hat was offered up at a side table, "All Tips Gratefully Received" ambitiously scrawled on a piece of cardboard.

"We could go for that bike ride I saw advertised, kill an hour or two?" Joe suggested.

"To a village called Slaughter?" Caroline asked. "Think they need to rebrand that tourist route. Can't have them flocking in, can it? The Slaughter Trail?"

"*We're* here, aren't we?" Joe said. "I fail to see what could be putting you off."

"Well you mull that over, love, while I go to the loo. Sure you'll be okay on your own for two minutes?"

Joe looked around at the inert pub patrons. "Don't worry about me," he beamed broadly. "I'll be bonding with the locals."

It was not yet midday, and any slight enthusiasm Caroline felt for the trip had long evaporated. They could have driven to the Lake District in the time it had taken to find this dreary dump. Trudging upstairs, she visualised spa treatments followed by poolside cocktails, the fantasy dampened only by the straw floating in her imaginary daiquiri.

Historic pictures of the village followed her up the staircase, interspersed with faded posters advertising obscure musical troupes. The framed photographs captured the same disheartening streets, but at least these were occupied by real, walking people. The earliest festival Caroline could see dated back to 1874, suggesting they liked to maintain tradition in Fairleap. Whoever *they* turned out to be.

Entering the Ladies, Caroline pushed open the toilet cubicle door and immediately began to apologise on finding it occupied.

Her words evolved into a newfound shriek as she saw the scarecrow perched on the toilet seat, trousers about its thatched ankles. The effigy stared unwaveringly at her with stuffed crows' eyes, as though waiting for Caroline to leave in order to complete its ablutions.

"Fuck this *place!*" Caroline spat, closing the stall door and rattling back down the stairs. Shock had rescinded the urgings of her bladder.

"Joe?" she shouted on re-entering the bar, voice hardened by her bathroom encounter. "Come on, we're leaving!"

Seeing no sign of him, Caroline reasoned the pillock must have also gone up to use the toilet. Listening for any outcry from upstairs, she slumped down at their table, studying the neighbouring scarecrows. Each straw hand was entwined in another's, making it difficult to see where one scarecrow ended and the next began. What she wouldn't have given for a match.

Disturbing Caroline from her bitter musings, a noise began to emanate from behind the bar, as though something was scrabbling across the floorboards.

177

Groaning, and what sounded like a coughing fit swiftly followed these ruminations.

"Joe? Is that you?"

She was only answered by further coughing.

"Joe?" Getting to her feet, Caroline saw her hapless boyfriend's moccasins jutting out from behind the bar.

"Down here!" Joe managed to say.

Rushing over, Caroline found Joe lying prone on his back; his mouth still raised to the offending ale tap, which had recently spat out its dry contents over his eager face.

"Let's at least find somewhere for lunch before heading back," Joe pleaded.

"No chance. If we leave now we might just beat the traffic," Caroline said.

"You just wait for the big rush," Joe said. "You'll be thanking me I made that dinner reservation at The Landlord's."

As they walked, scarecrows were buckled at regular intervals to lampposts, telegraph poles—any vertical structure used to backbone them. Most were clad in dungarees or gingham dresses, presumably what passed for the 'His and Hers' summer collection in Fairleap.

They soon came to what Caroline recognised from the pub photographs as the market square. Four buildings of identical grey stone squatted at each corner of the deserted crossroads; monoliths dredged from the Fairleap quarry, flung up to the heavens in the villagers' devotion to their unseen demagogue.

A gallows was the focal point of the square. A solitary crow watched them from it, seemingly the last to be banished by the villagers' efforts. The vacant noose hung uselessly.

Next to the gallows stood a set of stocks, once used to publicly humiliate petty thieves and providing Fairleap its weekend entertainment. The main stock was locked into place, with the holes for the wrists and head presently unoccupied.

"Want to get in for a photograph?" Joe asked and did not receive a response.

Off the square, alleyways led to stark courtyards, presumably where stagecoaches would have rested overnight. Scarecrows loitered in the shadows, leering around corners and looking down on the gallows from dust-filled windows of vacant shops.

Joe had wandered over to look at the old schoolhouse, mindful of Caroline already heading back in the direction of Corn Rigs. The building dated back to 1874, according to the Roman numerals etched into its brickwork.

"Come and look at this, Caroline!" Joe called, squinting through the classroom windows. "Worth your while, I promise!"

The scarecrow children sat in rows of ink-welled desks, oozing through the backs of wooden chairs; their undivided attention given over to the scarecrow teacher at the blackboard.

"You can't see what's holding them up," remarked Joe as Caroline joined him, marginally preferring to look on this new horror than be left alone at the gallows.

The children sat in tattered uniforms, striped ties hanging loosely around the twisted stalks of their necks. The more studious had arms raised to answer the teacher's silent question; straw presumably twined along wire, poking out of ragged cuffs. A mathematical puzzle had been chalked out on the board, to remain unsolved until the end of time.

"I'm going back to the car," Caroline growled. "It's not like we've paid for the room, is it? If anyone sees us, we'll apologise for wasting their time, then get out of this adorable hellhole!"

"Don't be so defeatist. Why don't we just head into the tourist office over there and take the guesswork out of

179

the situation?" Joe walked through the shadow of the gallows, with Caroline following close at his heels.

"If there's nothing happening here today, we're on the road to Windermere," Joe said. "You've got my word."

Decapitated lions greeted them at the doors, the knockers large enough to accommodate their heads between their bronze dripping jaws. A faded sign declaring 'Information' filled an adjacent window.

"I would say, at this very juncture, that's the one thing we need," Joe said.

"Can we just get inside?" hissed Caroline, looking around nervously at the uninhabited street. Wind twitched the hanging rope.

The heavy doors finally gave enough to allow them to slip through the gap, and they passed through into the gloom of the hallway. Oil portraits immortalising long-gone village elders occupied the oak-lined walls. Greeting them from the top of the wide staircase, a customary scarecrow clung onto a broken-bulbed chandelier like the final reveller of some debauched masquerade.

Caroline nuzzled into Joe's back, nudging him forwards through the open door of the tourist office.

A scarecrow manned the reception desk, waiting on its swivel chair to answer their queries. Broken furniture, filing cabinets, and boxes of yellowing documents littered the room—a thinly stocked archive of all things maudlin.

"Joe, I don't think you should—"

Failing to heed his girlfriend's advice, Joe lifted the latch of the counter and ducked into the cluttered room.

"Well, who's going to give me a bollocking?" Joe asked. "This character?" As he spun the scarecrow on its chair, detached straw drifted to the grotty carpet.

Caroline sneezed once, praying Joe wouldn't make some idle remark about hay fever.

"Bloody hell, look at this!" Joe turned a large wooden sign towards Caroline. Originally declaring 'Annual Scarecrow Festival' in uneven black lettering, a red diagonal banner had been plastered over it: 'Cancelled.'

"Fucksake!"

"That's it, then," Caroline said, still eyeing the swivelling scarecrow. "I'm gone."

"How can it be cancelled? No one had the common decency to tell her!" Joe gestured towards the scarecrow receptionist. His words dangled in the musty air as Caroline abandoned the office.

Joe heard her scream moments later, the sound carrying through the nailed-down sash windows. After staring disgustedly at the sign again, he went outside to see what had so perturbed his love this time.

The wind sought out any exposed flesh as they trudged uphill past The Landlord's Daughter, the pub still failing to attract any breathing patrons. The guesthouse seemed further away than ever.

"We just didn't notice them before, that's all," Joe attempted to ration. "Don't get yourself upset over it."

"Bullshit, Joe! There was no scarecrow in the stocks before, and you know it! And definitely not one hanging from the bloody gallows!"

Joe searched for a reasonable explanation, and once again came up short.

"The wind wasn't even shaking it! Are you seriously telling me a sack of straw would weigh that much?"

Silence ensued as Caroline maintained a two-yard advantage, refusing to let Joe get any closer as they tackled the hill through the woods. Finally arriving at Corn Rigs, Joe sighed, "Windermere it is, then."

Patting his pockets for car keys, Joe stopped abruptly, his heels digging loudly into gravel. At first glance, it looked as though a tin of paint had been thrown across the car's windscreen. A garish orange smeared the glass, presumably the work of listless, local kids. They would doubtlessly be hiding close by, sniggering in anticipation of their victims' reaction.

As they neared the car, however, Caroline saw exactly what was occupying the driver's seat; even though the windows and doors were still locked, just as they had left them.

The first scarecrow was slumped over the steering wheel, an arc of pulp from its pumpkin head covering the windscreen in an obscene spray. The passenger seat scarecrow leaned backwards, its sackcloth head slit at the throat, bleeding straw. Joe looked back at the guesthouse and saw others at the windows, watching.

An early dusk seemed to fall in the shadow of Corn Rigs. The wind became an alive thing, tugging at their clothes as they huddled together, Joe struggling to hear Caroline's panicked words over it.

There were more of them in the car park now, some even holding scythes, as though depicting a rural tradition. Threshing season, Caroline vaguely recalled from the pub photographs.

The acrid air thick with them, overpowering the senses; the sight of the scarecrows doubling, trebling through their watering eyes. Caroline imagined she could feel straw in her mouth, bristling the back of the throat, clogging the lungs until there was no more room for breath.

There were more scarecrows wherever they looked. The front door of the guesthouse now stood open, as Joe held Caroline uselessly and the wind became louder than their temple-blood, drowning out all.

...

"Can you be entirely sure they arrived here?" Hodgkins asked. "Fairleap has never been much of a tourist hotspot."

"That's the report their friends made," explained Tyler. "All we've got to go on. Said they were stopping by 'for the scarecrows' on their way to the Lakes."

"Weird to just abandon the car like that," said Hodgkins.

The signs of forced entry were unmistakeable. Following a trail of straw leading in to the derelict funeral chapel, the policemen opened up the first coffin.

"Some work went in to nailing this bastard shut. Give you the willies, Hodgkins?"

"No, sir, it's the mentality that frightens me. Who would do this?"

"Christ wept!" The lid prised open, Tyler turned his head away, as though something more putrid than a scarecrow had just been disinterred.

"Another one!" said Hodgkins.

"The festival was cancelled years ago," Tyler said, attacking the next coffin with the hammer's claw. "Any bloody fool knows that. Got to be too popular, didn't it? All the attention the village was getting. Strangers trampling flowerbeds."

"Can't have that," said Hodgkins.

Side by side, the coffins displayed their scarecrows, straw hands crossed at what passed for their laps. Judging by the threadbare outfits, the effigies of the latest two were meant to depict a scarecrow of either sex. Clumps of straw decomposed to a mulch. Dull buttons for eyes, the scarecrows stared ahead into their shared eternity.

"Bloody blow-ins, sniffing around," Tyler said. "Ruining everything, I suspect."

###

About the Author

John Davies is a member of the Poised Pen writers (thepoisedpen.co.uk). Originally from Liverpool, UK, he now lives in County Meath, Ireland.

His work has previously appeared in *The Fog Horn, Pseudopod, Ares Magazine, Rosebud, Unsung Stories, Third Flatiron Anthologies,* and *The Pedestal.* He was nominated for a Pushcart Prize in 2012 and 2013, and longlisted for the Penguin Ireland Short Story Prize in 2013.

*****~~~~~*****

Nine Ways to Communicate With the Living

by Sarina Dorie

Whether you're new to haunting or an old spook looking for new tricks, remember to make your messages to the living meaningful. If you're going to go to all the trouble of speaking with your hauntee and you want to be taken seriously, your words should be something other than a cliché, "Wooooooo!" or phrases that no longer scare people such as, "Red Rum."

1. Write in fogged-up mirrors. This never fails to make an impression on the receiver. Especially if you write the words, "GET OUT, GET OUT, GET OUT OF MY HOUSE!"

2. Leave notes written in blood. Whose blood is your discretion, as you no longer have any.

3. Ouija boards. If the living makes an attempt to contact you, it isn't an appropriate time to mention that your hauntee plays music you dislike, even if it is country. Instead, wait until later to use your kinetic energy to throw his radio down a stairwell as it's playing Garth Brooks.

4. The ghost in the machine. Several "nerd" ghosts with tech know-how from before they were deceased specialize in possessing computers, cell phones, and even blenders in order to communicate. You're never too old— or too dead—to learn to use a computer.

5. Morse code. Even dim hauntees can come up with one knock for yes, two knocks for no. Imagine how disturbing this will be if you knock every time your hauntee asks a question out loud. "Should I make an angel food cake for dessert?" Knock-knock. "What's that noise? Is it my neighbors having sex again?" Knock-knock. "Is

there a little gremlin in the walls haunting this house and intending to eat my brain?" KNOCK.

6. Mediums. Most psychics are not very good at what they do. If they were, they would have won the lottery long ago. That means you may have to perfect your possession skills so that you can speak through any old quack.

7. Animals and children. It's common knowledge that dogs and children are more receptive to paranormal energies than adults. Become the imaginary friend of a lonely child and give him messages that will scare the shit out of the adults around him.

8. Automatic writing. This only requires possessing one body part, such as the receiver's hand. Humans' minds are most receptive when they are distracted or in a relaxed state. Use opportunities while they are watching TV and writing a report, or scribbling down a grocery list as they listen to music. Won't your hauntee be surprised when she sees her grocery list has: milk, eggs, bread, and JOHN KILLED ME, JOHN KILLED ME, JOHN KILLED ME.

9. Infiltrate a recording studio. If you speak while a musician is recording her music, your voice will be heard when someone plays the music backward. Because your target audience of listeners will most likely be Satan worshipers and nerdy hipsters who prefer vinyl, make sure you target your message to your audience.

...

And remember, when you do make contact with your living neighbors, be professional, be yourself, and have fun!

###

About the Author

Sarina Dorie is the author of RWA award-winning, YA paranormal romance novel, *Silent Moon*. Her Puritan and alien love story, "Dawn of the Morning Star," is due to come out this year with Wolfsinger Publications. Sarina has sold over eighty short stories to markets like *Daily Science Fiction, Magazine of Fantasy and Science Fiction, Orson Scott Card's IGMS, Cosmos,* and *Sword and Laser.*

By day, Sarina is a public school art teacher, artist, belly dance performer and instructor, copy editor, fashion designer, event organizer, and probably a few other things. By night, she writes. As you might imagine, this leaves little time for sleep.

You can find info about her short stories and novels on her website: www.sarinadorie.com

*****~~~~~~*****

Schrödinger's Schrödinger

by Benjamin Jacobson

Amadi Yakubu petted his cat, Pemba, one last time, or perhaps not, before lowering the lead box into place. He couldn't help but crack a smile at his own ingenuity. The empty lab held no witnesses for this momentous event. Even scientists tended to take Sunday evenings off. Soon enough, everyone would know what happened here this night.

Ever since his first year at university, Amadi had been obsessed with the Schrödinger's Cat thought experiment. The experiment said, in short, that since observation results in determination on a quantum level, if one could tie a macro-level event, such as the life of a cat, to a quantum level event, you could create an impossible condition. In the case of the experiment, that condition was a cat that was neither alive nor dead, until it was observed to be so.

Of course, no one ever conducted this experiment. There would be no point. As soon as one observed the cat, the quantum uncertainty would collapse, and the cat would just be dead or alive, with no evidence to point to any other result. Still, Amadi couldn't escape the beauty of it. To recreate such an elegant example of life's mystery on a large scale would be an honor. When he had bought Pemba that first day, a glimmer in the back of his mind urged him to do so.

Now, here, eight years later Amadi had built a diabolical mechanism to fulfill the requirements. He hadn't told anyone, though he couldn't wait to be able to do so. He thought that most of his friends would not approve of Pemba dying for a pointless experiment. Amadi could think of no better purpose for his beloved cat, no higher honor. He knew that when he told the story

189

they would all laugh and applaud his ingenuity, that in retrospect colleagues and undergraduates alike would hail him a hero. But now was the time for risks best taken alone. It was always better to ask forgiveness than permission.

Inside the box, the experiment unfolded. A cat sat confused in the dark next to a Geiger counter, a vial of hydrocyanic acid, and a hammer. The hammer stood ready to break the vial should the unseen radioactive particle decide to decay, which it had about even odds of doing.

Outside the box, Amadi waited. Eventually, the cat would be both alive and dead, at least mathematically. The excitement of this idea sent Amadi's heart a-flutter in a way that his love life had never managed. He imagined future conversations in which his peers would stand in awe of his willingness to take ideas to the next level. This reverie kept him from noticing the half-dead cat walking out of the box and sitting perched in front of him.

"Amadi," the cat ventured, in a voice biology said it couldn't possibly possess. Amadi looked down and froze. He looked away and then back again. As the saliva drained from his throat, he stepped backward and rubbed his eyes.

"Pemba?" he ventured.

"Not really, no." the half-cat said. Amadi watched as the death state traversed over the cat's twitching body. Its eye would glass over and close. Its leg would give up and then reposition. Death approached the animal but then retreated like a nervous boy at the end of a first date, hopeful of confirmation but fearful of rejection. The word odd did not cover it.

"What's. . . what's going on?"

"I'll tell you," said the half-cat. "You guys are just pushing my buttons lately." The cat attempted to rise and walk, which proved both gruesome and comedic, as its 50% deadness smeared around the body. "Look, I'm not your cat. If I were your cat, I would be stuck underneath that hideous contraption you concocted, hoping not to die. No, I'm something else. I just took the form of your cat, as it is right this moment. It's a favor, if you like, for you, Amadi."

Amadi began to suspect a trick, but his logical mind couldn't accept it. The magic in front of him was too bizarre to be real but too mundane to be fake. It must be happening. The cat's forepaws gave out and it tumbled off the counter, landing on the floor. It disproved the axiom that cats always land on their feet.

"Oh, forget this," the convulsing pile of fur said. The form began to shake and quiver and fold in on itself. Soon the cat pile vanished and a little cat-sized man stood in its place. Amadi recognized him instantly, Erwin Schrödinger. The living action figure had all the features of the departed scientist, down to his bow tie and tiny John Lennon glasses. He didn't, however, have an Austrian accent.

"Listen, Amadi. You have got to stop this. I mean, seriously, white flag. We give. Let's talk."

"Um. . . I don't quite know what you mean." Amadi found it very odd to talk to a miniature man. In his mind, he compared the size of his head to common objects. Finally he decided that it lay somewhere between a large grape and a small plum.

"Exactly! And if I could just get you guys to commit to that on a more regular basis, we wouldn't be having this problem."

"I'm trying to understand you, but I'm afraid I'm confused. Could you explain it to me?"

"There it is, right there. That's what I'm talking about. Always questioning and probing. Got to know the answer. Got to find the 'truth.'" He air-quoted the last word with toothpick-width fingers. "Alright, well, I surrender. We lost the war. You win. I submit to your terms."

191

With this, the tiny Schrödinger folded his arms behind him and began to pace in a way that professors do. Amadi imagined punting the little man across the room. Not that he wanted to, but he didn't exactly not want to either.

"I am a nescionist. It's my job to keep the mystery in life. The mystery your lot keeps stripping away like a banana peel." At this, he paused, composing himself.

"Look. I'm good at my job. Really good. I've been doing this for a long time. When you guys cracked the four elements, whom do you think came up with the periodic table? That was me. But every time you nail down some new physical law, you limit our ability to do the job. It's not like we haven't been trying. Light as both a particle and a wave, 90% of the mass of the universe missing, the freaking PLATYPUS! I mean, seriously, take a clue. Some things are not meant to be solved." The red-faced mini-man took a deep breath and stared up at Amadi.

"Of course, it's too late for that, isn't it? I mean, here you are poking holes in quantum physics. Quantum Physics. You know how long it took us to come up with that stuff? So, you win. I'm just asking for some quarter, leave us something. A little reservation of ignorance to ply our trade. It doesn't have to be much, just enough to keep us busy." Amadi took a deep breath in preparation for his response and then discovered that he had none. He stood there, mouth agape, as the lecture continued.

"Anyway, spread the word. The war is over. You are victorious. But I hope you will remember this. When you are done, when you have solved every mystery and understand every particle in the universe, what then? What will you do with no more questions to answer? I mean, that's what gets you up in the morning, right? The mysteries. Can you really live without them? Think it over."

Schrödinger's Schrödinger

The little man's bowtie began to spin and sent him flying into the air and toward the lead box. When his body intersected the edge, it bent and distorted and then disappeared through the wall.

Amadi blinked twice. He stared at the box and the spot where the little man had so recently stood. He blinked again. He grabbed the lead box and hefted it suddenly. Pemba shot out and into the corner of the lab. The vial was unbroken. The device had never sprung. Amadi replaced the materials and collected his pet. As he walked out the door, he switched off the light and stared back at the dark room. He couldn't help but wonder who or what might be hiding in the darkness. In his mind, he was designing the experiment to find out.

About the Author

Benjamin Jacobson has published previously in *Cricket, Wisdom Crieth Without, Crossed Genres,* and *AE.*

*****~~~~*****

A Little Mischief

by Ken Altabef

Jester was not content. She should have been, so comfortable and well fed, but she wasn't.

It was one of those early autumn nights, when warm memories of a playful summer still lingered, challenged now by the cozy lure of the fireplace. Jester licked the last scraps of canned tuna from her plate and, with a satisfyingly swollen feeling in her belly, curled up before the fire. She kept a safe distance, of course—the grating occasionally shot out a stray spark to singe fur or whisker.

As the Hendersons cuddled together on the couch, making little love noises, Jester pushed a rubber squeeze toy back and forth across the warm brickwork in front of the grate.

Well fed, cozy, yet by no means content.

Outside, with a voice the humans couldn't possibly hear even if they had been paying attention, the night was calling. The night and the Moon and the other cats. And something else too, something that spoke in a wordless whisper, a nudge from that dark place deep inside. Jester was hungry for something much more than minced tuna and warm milk. And it was out there. Tonight she was in the mood for a little mischief.

She let out a long, annoying whine. Her plea, lost in the tortured strains of Pagliacci setting the Hendersons' love mood, did not disturb their amorous fumblings.

Undaunted, she circled coyly around the edge of the carpet. Up onto the dresser, tighten and release; the stereo cabinet, coil and spring. It felt good. The melancholy tones of Pagliacci at her back, uneasy, nightmarish, like the wailing of near-dead cats crying out in deserted alleys. Jester waited for just the right moment, a break in the toccata just a few beats before the crashing entrance of the strings, and leapt down onto Henderson's lap, mid-smooch. She punctuated the movement with a suitably shocking screech and the gentle poke of a claw.

"Damn it, Jester!"

She allowed the man to knock her off the couch with an angry slap, but landed deftly on the quilted Mandarin rug. She headed straight for the back door, the little bells on her hindpaws jangling softly as she went.

Henderson followed. What other choice did he have? When Jester wanted out, she got it, or else there wasn't going to be peace for anyone, no sleep for the baby and definitely no late-night action on the couch. His hand lingered on the doorknob as he caught sight of a nasty thunderhead rolling in from the south, dark clouds cutting sharply against the brilliant half-moon.

Jester squeezed through the cracked screen door, little bells jangling as she went.

...

It was a silvery, cool, and curious night. The chill air caressed her fur, tingling and waking the flesh beneath.

Jester quickly made her rounds, circling the fence, sniffing eagerly for scent of Shadow or Ginger, but finding only sharp dog piss, the bulldog's freshly laid marker. She turned quickly away.

The newly mowed grass shone gray in the moonlight. Jester let out a long caterwaul that split the darkness, but her call went unanswered. She must find her friends. Where were all the other cats?

A practiced flurry of fur and muscle. Over the fence and down into the schoolyard. A blanket of fine mist rolled slowly across the baseball diamond, sinewy and mysterious like the night. She rolled playfully on her back, pivoting lazily in the wet grass. So typical and boring. Tonight was different, and she wanted something more. She headed for the other side of the street.

A Little Mischief

Watching and waiting. Speeding headlights quickened her heart's beat. Leaping forward, hair on edge, ears up, eyes wide. Bright lights bearing down. Two-way traffic. A horn. She panicked, spewed urine, but kept moving, lean and quick, and was across.

She darted into a hidden, shadowed alley. Hardly a chance to catch her breath before something new teased her questing nose, demanding investigation. Rust and rotting cabbage, wet newspaper, and week-old banana. Apple core and soiled underpants. Jester launched from garbage can to garbage can, each a wild foray into the unknown. The lids clattered magnificently in the alley, a rival to any fever dream Verdi could have devised.

Just off to the side, a hint of movement. Bells jangling, she spun as quickly as thought itself; for this she need not think. She darted left, leaving the glorious glut of garbage behind, to cut the mouse off. Flick left, flick right. A forepaw flashed like lightning. The mouse skidded and careened into the wall. Jester was in front of it and behind it and to either side. What fun!

Suddenly she smelled something else, behind the cans, a Dead Thing.

She let the mouse get away. Dead Things had a way of tweaking the curiosity, and this smelled like a big one, freshly killed. She sniffed and sniffed. There was Death all right, and Evil, not too far away. And something else—was it lavender? Perfume?

Jester harkened carefully to the voices of the night. Water drip off standpipe; car splash puddle. No cats. The smell of blood was strong. So hard to see, even with keen night-eyes. A dead girl stuffed between the garbage cans, a tattered dress, a crescent of half-congealed blood.

She called out again, perhaps with a shade less bravado than before, and circled away. There were strange things afoot, mischievous, marvelous, and she wanted to be sure to get her fill. She decided to go to the park.

...

Ain't Superstitious

At the park, everything was alive. Oaks and willows looming sentries, thorny bushes swaying breeze, whisper of welcome. Long grass rustled back and forth, offering glimpses of concealed treats scampering, crawling, buzzing things. And there were people. A jogger crashed past, startling cautious cat. Jester darted into the safety of the azaleas just below a stone bench.

Two figures sat on the bench. One was a human being, the other clearly not. Jester felt suddenly nauseous, fur standing on end, rumble stomach, a deep ache in her bones.

They were talking softly, the demon and the girl.

"Okay, forget about getting high," he said, offering a boyish smile and a pair of empty, upturned palms. "I don't really like that stuff anyway. Honest."

The schoolgirl stared dreamily back at him. She couldn't have been more than fifteen. He appeared at least twice her age, dressed in a dark pea coat and black jeans, clean-shaven, hair cut neat, perfectly scented and combed.

His eyes, the girl said, reminded her of the exact color of the water in Cancun. Family vacation, two years ago.

He laughed, expelling breath scrubbed too-clean by a handful of mints. The girl did not notice the fetid stench lurking just below that sugary mask. Jester did. Thoughts of Henderson's snug fireplace loomed enticingly right about then, and she supposed there just might be a bowl of milk waiting beneath the fridge. She fought the urge to run. She would wait a bit longer and see. It was her night out, after all.

The girl shared an ear-bud with her new friend.

"You like? The way they layer the synths? Intense, right?"

He nodded. "Hell, yeah. Dubstep rocks. Sounds like a couple of Transformers having rough sex."

The girl laughed.

"Or souls screaming in torment," he added softly.

198

A Little Mischief

One of his slick-shined dress shoes shuffled backward along the salty dirt. Jester leapt to the side, bells jangling.

"What's that?" he said, demon eyes blazing down at the cat.

"It's just a cat," said the girl.

"Just a cat," he repeated, leveraging the foot for a proper strike but finding the angle under the bench too awkward. Jester scampered away, little bells jangling.

"You know," said the girl, "people used to believe that black cats were witches in disguise."

"I know," he said. "Let's go for a walk. It's such a beautiful night for a walk." The girl flashed a self-satisfied smile, mistaking the little tremor in his voice for nervous excitement, which it was not. Whiskers a-twitch, Jester smelled the demon's confidence and wicked anticipation. He fingered a long shaving razor in the pocket of his coat. Jester could scent the fresh blood on it.

"I know a better place," he said.

From the safety of the bushes, Jester watched them move away. The demon draped a hand loosely around the girl's shoulder. She pushed it off playfully. The demon laughed.

Jester followed along behind, unwilling to miss anything. She swished her jangling paws against the wet grass to dampen their noise. As they rounded the fountain, she nosed the familiar, repugnant scent of a decrepit bag lady, liniment and onions and unwashed sweat, who prowled the neighborhood by night and always had a dreadful one-eyed black tabby with her.

The withered old bag lady moved in the same direction as the strolling couple, pushing a small cart brimming with junk. No sign of the black tabby. Jester crinkled her nose, scenting rubbing oils and damp toadstools, sour-mash whiskey, and old time.

Ain't Superstitious

The strolling couple paused in front of the fountain at the far side of the park. Jester, now grown tired and thirsty, longed for a taste of its cool, brackish water.

The demon ran his fingers along the girl's golden-blonde hair. She let him do it. "You know," he said, "I think I'm falling in love with you."

The girl laughed.

"And love deserves pain," he mumbled softly, so very softly. The girl didn't hear.

Jester's gaze was drawn skyward. The Moon had grown inexplicably full. More than full, it was swollen, bloated, bulging and about to burst. A gigantic luminous womb, fully pregnant.

Beyond the fountain, the muttering bag lady stood hunched in the sharp moonlight, her crooked fingers working a charm in her withered hand. Jester felt the pull of it, felt its weird imperative build and strengthen. She tried to shake it off, fur rippling along her arched back, electricity crackling along her spine.

Out of the corner of his eye, the demon caught sight of the bag lady. His face convulsed, immediately suspicious. "Maiden and crone," he muttered. His eyes cast warily about. "Maiden and crone, but no other. . . "

"What?" asked the girl.

His eyes flashed shyly away. "Kiss the girl and make her cry."

He was still confident. Without all three, he did not think the old witch's spellcasting could hurt him. He had not noticed the mother; he had not counted the Moon.

He leaned in. Just before their lips touched, the girl got a fair sampling of his nightmare breath.

The shaving razor flashed upward.

A familiar screech split the night. The old woman's black tabby careened along the side of the fountain, leapt high, and struck.

It was all too much for Jester. The old woman's magic was strong. She felt the tension rise to a breaking point, her blood boiling. She leapt forward, bells jangling, claws at the ready.

And the cats came. They fell screeching from the trees, surging out from behind the fountain, leaping up from the grass. Even before the blade came down, the demon found himself staggering backward amid a sea of tawny fur, dozens of rending claws and pointed teeth. A riot of hissing, screeching, and yowling infected the night. Shadow was there, digging in between the demon's shoulders, the Jones' kitty clawing wildly at the demon's face, and Ginger and Sammy, and tens of wild cats, cats with no names, whose song was a savage *a cappella* of heady music, not entirely unlike the whining strains of Pagliacci Jester had enjoyed earlier.

"Just a bunch of cats. . . " hissed the dark man desperately.

Yes, thought Jester, and you are just a mouse.

She couldn't help herself. She dove in, happy to rend and tear, joining the others in their merry little game, her bells singing along. Slash, jangle. Slash. Jangle.

###

About the Author

Ken Altabef lives and works on Long Island. His short fiction has appeared several times in *F&SF* as well as *Interzone, BuzzyMag, Abyss & Apex,* and various anthologies including Third Flatiron's *Astronomical Odds* anthology. His first short story collection, *FORTUNE'S FANTASY,* was released last year. ALAANA'S WAY is his epic fantasy series with an arctic twist. All five novels in the series have been published by Cat's Cradle Press. You can preview this work and others at the author's website: www.KenAltabef.com

*****\~\~\~\~\~*****

Gualicho Days

by Gustavo Bondoni

In a hospital in Patagonia, an old woman lies dying. She knows the end is near. She can tell from the expressions on her doctor's face, and even by the young woman. She isn't completely certain who the young woman might be, but she can see a certain resemblance to her people, despite the much lighter skin and modern clothing. Something in the shape of the lips, or perhaps in the arch of the eyebrows. Or maybe something else— perhaps the spirit of the people shines through even wrong-colored eyes.

It occurs to her that the young woman is a member of her family. She can't quite recall. There are so many things she can't remember these days, and she just can't afford to waste the energy on them. The only important thing is the plea. Without the plea, life would not be worth living. She was proud to never have missed a day of the plea, not once, not since she was a little girl.

The old lady can't tell if the young woman is of her family, or if she is even of her people, but she will have to do. She takes hold of the girl's hand. "Listen well. I must tell you of Kóoch, and how he orders the world, and I must tell you of why he gave the Tehuelche people the responsibility of reminding him to do his work against the ravages of Gualicho. Listen now, my time is short. . . "

. . .

Dr. Alejandro Benetti hated this part of the job. "I'm sorry, Jimena, but your grandmother passed away early this morning."

Jimena nodded, a slight tightening of her lips the only sign that she was affected by the news. They'd been expecting this for a couple of days at least. "I'm not sure what I have to do now."

"Don't worry. Selena handles all the administrative side. She'll have the paperwork ready in a couple of hours, and we can also arrange the burial, if you want to bury her locally."

"I think that would be best. As far as anyone knows, she never moved more than walking distance from the house where she was born. Esquel is all she ever knew. My mother said that she always insisted that she would stay with her people. They've been gone for years, but she stayed anyway."

"Yes, you told me. The Tehuelche." Benetti paused. What he wanted to say next might not be what a recently bereaved family member wanted to hear, but he decided to risk it anyway. "It was actually an honor to be here, in a sad kind of way. It reminds you that there are bigger things than what we think about every day. I can't imagine a whole civilization just dying out."

She shrugged. "I guess. But they're not really dead. They had children, and those children are just regular Argentines. They're not actually gone."

"But the language. What she was speaking yesterday was Tehuelche, wasn't it?"

"I guess. She was the last known speaker, so only she would really be able to tell us. It did sound like what she used to speak with the other women, back before she quarreled with my mother, so it must have been."

"Do you know what she said?"

"Not at all. I never learned the language."

Alejandro felt the blood run to his head, felt his cheeks grow warm. "I recorded some of it. It just seemed important to get it on audio. It might be the last time in history that those words will be heard. I hope you don't mind."

"I don't mind." And now she hesitated. "Do you think I could see her?"

"Oh, yes. I'm sorry. But are you sure? We'd have to see her in the morgue. . . wouldn't you prefer to wait until the funeral?"

"Just let me see her."

With that, Dr. Benetti was all business again. He led her through the small hospital to the morgue, and stood beside her as she said her final farewells. Then a group of tourists out rock climbing had stumbled down an incline, and he had contusions and a broken femur to deal with, and the day picked up speed. It would be quite a while before he thought about lost languages again.

. . .

A few days after the old lady was buried, the deaths began. No one noticed, and most people just shrugged them off. It was understandable.

Ten block's worth of street signs suddenly indicated that the one-way street they signaled had changed directions. People who'd been going down that street for years ignored the signs—most of them didn't even notice them. A stranger driving an SUV, however, took it literally, and—just as he was turning in—encountered a number 5 bus full of children on their way to school. The driver and three of the children died in the accident.

Gas leaks abounded. Electric wires fell into convenient puddles. People died, and no one, macroscopically speaking, really cared. It was just life.

But someone was eventually bound to notice. This role—perhaps understandably—fell to a young woman in Buenos Aires called Vanesa Federini. She was a journalist's assistant at a newspaper called Crónica, a sensationalist rag whose associated TV channel had become fleetingly famous worldwide for a headline that that said "Multiple dead in accident: two people and a Bolivian."

She was desperately looking for better employment, but, in the meantime, she did her job, and did it well. Her job was to investigate the death of a man in a suburb who'd died when a car driven by the owner of a local dry cleaner had accelerated in a multi-story parking facility and burst through the retaining wall, dropping on his head. The woman driving the car had been pulled out of the wreckage, unconscious, and wasn't expected to recover. It was a bizarre enough occurrence that it merited a trip to the local police station—but not important enough to send a fully accredited journalist.

The police station in Merlo was about what one would expect. Surrounded by rundown light-industrial buildings in one of Buenos Aires' less-fashionable areas, it was manned by a single overweight woman with sergeant's stripes on her shoulder. She sat under a 100-watt bulb in a small office and chewed gum as she gave Vanesa a quick once-over.

"How can I help you?" she asked, bored, but evidently not bored enough to bother concealing her contempt at the other woman's fashionable clothing, completely out of place anywhere near where they were.

Vanesa outlined the situation, expecting to be tossed out on her ear. To the journalist's surprise, the woman's demeanor changed completely.

"Oh, yes. It's the strangest thing. Did you know they knew each other?"

...

". . .so it turns out that she actually had some of his clothes at the dry cleaner. He was walking over there to get them when the accident happened."

A single editorial eyebrow raised. "So?"

"It doesn't end there. It seems that the dry-cleaning lady was on the way to her son's kindergarten, where another little boy had been hit by a bus. The driver claims that he was distracted, thinking about an accident he'd heard of that morning."

...

"Where are you going with this?"

Vanesa paused. "I'm not really sure. The policewoman was convinced that there was a chain of strange little connections to each of the deaths we've seen over the last few days. And that each was slightly related to the last. Looks like all the cops are comparing notes, building a chain."

The editor sighed. "And I suppose she told you all of this before you told her you worked for Crónica?"

"If you'd looked into her eyes, you'd believe me."

"And if I had a coin for every time some journo used that overused phrase, I'd be a rich, rich man."

"Look, they mean it. And the police are actually doing it. Won't you let me look into it? They're adamant that there's a connection, just that it's never an obvious one. Never the husband or the brother." She smiled. "Heck, you're the editor of the girl who went to Merlo to look into it. You could be next."

"If I let you look into it, will you go away?"

…

"It's actually a huge opportunity for me. Having actual journalism work on my résumé means that I might be able to get a job at a real news outlet."

Ernesto laughed. "Yeah, as long as you don't tell them what you actually did."

"Can't you be supportive, just once? I don't spend all my time throwing mud all over your dreams."

"All right, I'm sorry. Tell me."

"Anyway, the cop lady is looking at me like she's telling me the secrets of the universe, and she whispers that anyone could be next. She says that none of the officers want to work on the case, because they're afraid that it might just be enough to set the curse on them."

"The curse. . . Sorry, go ahead."

"That's what she said. Even when the story runs out of steam, we can run an article on the lack of professionalism in the police force. They believe in malicious spirits who kill people. Not really the kind of people I'd want guarding my security in this city."

"What kind of spirits?"

"They say it's something called a *gualicho*."

"I thought that was some kind of spell. Anyway, no one would believe that the cops are really that stupid."

The conversation was interrupted by a loud buzzing. "I'll get it," Ernesto said. He walked to the door, looked through the peephole, then shrugged and opened it.

A huge bang sounded, and Ernesto fell to the floor. From the hallway, Vanesa heard voices. "That wasn't Luciano, man, you shot the wrong guy." This was followed by silence, then a single word. "Shit." And then footsteps running down the hall and into the stairwell.

Vanesa ran to her fallen husband, and looked at the bloody mass of entrails that came from the gaping wound in his abdomen. She'd been a journalist's assistant long enough that she could recognize a shotgun wound, and she also knew that pressing her hands to his stomach would do no good.

She did it anyway, crying as she did, watching bubbling blood ooze from between her fingers and out of Ernesto's open mouth. His eyes stared emotionlessly at the wall beside which he'd fallen.

. . .

Alejandro hugged her, not letting go, allowing Vanesa to cry herself out. It took quite a while, but eventually his brother's young widow managed to get herself under control. Even through her tears, she was an amazingly pretty woman, and he'd always been amazed that Ernesto, the quiet, unassuming one, had managed to convince her to marry him.

"I can't believe he's gone. . . "

And she broke down again, unable to hold it in.

It was midnight on the night of the funeral when she finally ran out of tears. Alejandro just kept her company, holding her when she needed it, and bringing her occasional cups of coffee. Even when Ernesto and Alejandro's mother begged off to get some sleep, he stood by the widow.

"It's my fault, you know."

"Don't be silly. It was random. An accident. You know it as well as I do."

"No. I know it was the gualicho. I just know it."

"Vanesa, you really need to relax. Maybe you should get some rest." The funeral home was a good one, and had plenty of room for family to lie down.

And yet. . . and yet the word gualicho nagged at him, left him with the strange feeling that he'd heard it before somewhere, and the fact that it didn't come immediately to mind irritated him. Where had it been? He set it aside, drawing her closer, intending to lead her to one of the couches.

She pushed him away. "I know you don't believe me. I laughed at the policewoman as well, but now look at me. There's something going on, and if you don't believe me, you'll be crying over someone you love one of these days as well."

That was unfair, Alejandro thought, and yet he said nothing. He would have time to tell her about the endless summer afternoons he'd spent playing football with Ernesto on deserted sidewalks, or riding bicycles across the park, or just playing video games inside and fighting about whose turn it was to be "Player 1." The memories he had of his brother were no less important than the ones she had of her husband, and neither was the gaping hole torn in his life.

He held his tongue, trying to think of something helpful to say, but his mind had other ideas, and kept circling around and around that single alien word.

Gualicho.

Gualicho.

Gualicho.

Ain't Superstitious

Unexpectedly, it clicked, and Alejandro found himself remembering a dying old lady in a Patagonian hospital speaking what the doctor knew were her final words—and the final words that would ever be spoken in a language about to disappear from the face of the Earth.

"I recorded her," he said.

Vanesa looked into his eyes, clearly not knowing where he was going with this, clearly expecting to have to reproach him for bringing up a subject both banal and unrelated to her suffering. But he explained anyway.

...

They were scheduled to meet the linguist five days after the funeral, and on the morning of the appointment, Vanesa showered, dressed, and sat down to breakfast. For the first time since the murder, she opened up the paper—not the one she worked for, but a serious national sheet—and proceeded to ignore the difficulties in Europe and the violence in the Middle East. Local news was not much better, and she was about to push it away in disgust when one article caught her eye.

A cab driver in one of Buenos Aires' endless suburbs had, against all logic, managed to run over himself with his own cab, dying in the process. It was printed as more of a curiosity than as actual news, but the strange nature of the accident chilled her to the bone. She left her half-finished cup of tea on the table and walked out of her apartment to meet Alejandro.

They drove to the University in silence, broken only by Alejandro's soft cursing at the inevitable aggressive drivers cutting in front of him. Vanesa wondered if that would be the way the gualicho did away with her: an anonymous car crash, far from notice. But no. . . That wouldn't be its way. It was playful, wanting not just to kill, but to kill in such a way as to satisfy a sadistic need.

The linguist turned out to be a middle-aged woman in a large, wood-paneled office that looked like something left over from a more bureaucratic era. Stacks of paper in faded yellow and pastel-green folders littered every available surface. The sign on her door said Prof. Serena.

"So, tell me," Serena said. She didn't sound like she was in any hurry to get rid of them, but she didn't sound particularly interested, either.

"I'm a doctor, and I made a recording of a woman speaking in what they say is Tehuelche, and we were wondering if you could help us understand it. We think it might be important." He pressed play and let her listen to the old woman's rasps and gurgles, until they faded to silence.

Serena suddenly looked animated. "When did you record this?"

"Maybe two months ago, in Esquel."

"And who is that woman? She's speaking the lower-base Tehuelche tongue. We thought that was extinct years ago. We might be able to decipher a few things that have been bothering us for ages—or at the very least get the words on record for the archives. Tehuelche is a very endangered language, you know."

"Oh, you don't understand. The woman died right at the end of the recording. I thought that was clear. I'm sorry."

The light went out of the Professor's eyes. "Then why did you even bother recording it? Why bring it to me?"

"I recorded it, because I thought it might be the last time that Tehuelche was heard on the face of the Earth, and I thought it would be important to keep some record of it. As to why I brought it to you, I wanted you to tell us about the use of the word 'gualicho,' and what the woman was saying."

Serena shrugged. "Oh, that. Nothing important. The old woman was just telling someone that it was important to say the invocation to Kóoch. Standard stuff. The Tehuelche religion believes that if their main deity,

Kóoch, isn't reminded, at least once a night, to keep the world in balance, the spirit called Gualicho will take over, sending the world spinning into chaos and ending human life. All the indigenous people in South America have something like it in their lore."

"And do you know the invocation?" Vanesa blurted.

Another shrug. "There may be some versions, incomplete versions, at the sound library, but you'll have to wait until next week if you want to hear it. Gómez is on vacation, and he's the only one who knows where everything is. A lot of it's still on tape, you know. Old native languages aren't really a high priority for the government."

Alejandro and Vanesa listened to her diatribe and then politely excused themselves.

...

That night, Vanesa watched the news, waiting for a sign that she was right. Just when she thought nothing would come of it, at the very end of the program, a short piece about an accident in a styling salon aired. It seemed that a very well known hairdresser had, most uncharacteristically, stabbed a client through the eye with a sharp scissor, sending it all the way into the brain with fatal results.

Vanesa managed to stay calm when she heard that the incident had occurred a mere twenty blocks from her apartment, but when the woman's name was mentioned. . .

She called Alejandro. "I tell you it's getting closer. The gualicho is coming for me."

"Calm down. Why do you think that?" Alejandro asked.

"Because she had the same last name as the driver from this morning. And because it was right here, just a few miles away. She must have been a cousin or something, and now the curse is in my neighborhood. How long do you think it will take to get here?"

"Listen. . ."

"No, you listen. I'm going to the archive on Monday, and I'm going to learn that prayer. I know you think it's stupid, but I know what I'm doing. I'll barricade myself in my room, I'll make sure the gas is off. It won't get me. I'll—"

"Look, I have to go. My family is waiting at the table, and I've been away too long. If you have something to calm your nerves in the house, take some—and that's a professional order, by the way. I'll call you, to see how you're doing after dinner." Alejandro hung up.

. . .

Through a huge effort of will, Vanesa managed to convince Alejandro not to send one of his friends from the psychiatric wing of the hospital to see her. She apologized for sounding insane, and she promised to seek professional help.

But that had been a front. She barricaded herself in her room with nothing but a few supplies and a computer, and spent the next four days on Facebook, as insulated from the real world as any human could be, just waiting for Monday to come around. She ignored all incoming calls, especially those that seemed to come from her colleagues.

Isolation did not breed tranquility. Vanesa jumped at every sound, squealed every time the wind blew against her shutters. The days dragged by at a snail's pace.

Eventually, Monday morning rolled around, and Vanesa showered, making certain to step carefully into the tub, and to hold on to the handle—a nice fall in the shower might just be banal enough to satisfy the spirit. She survived the bath and had a quick breakfast, scanning the Facebook updates that had been her constant companions over the course of her withdrawal from society.

There were an unusual number of them, and most from her old high-school classmates. It seemed that a girl

213

in her graduating class had slipped and rolled down a staircase, breaking her neck.

The consensus was that it was an awful thing to have happened to the family, at the funeral of her cousin, no less. Another comment said that, yes, having two young women in the family die in accidents so close together was truly unfortunate. A more curious classmate wondered what had happened to the cousin.

"Didn't you hear? She was the woman killed in the styling place last week."

Vanesa ran out the door, muttering under her breath. "You won't get me. You won't get me. You bastard. I'll beat you. I'll get Kóoch to send you back to wherever you came from."

A chill came over her as she reached the elevator hall.

Are you so sure about that?

Vanesa froze. She wondered if she might be going insane, wondered if the stress had finally gotten to her. There was no way that voice could have been real. Why would an ancient native spirit care about her? And even if it did, why would it be able to talk to her in a language she understood? It was ridiculous.

Still, she pressed the elevator button repeatedly. She would get to the archive and repeat whatever the prayer said. "You'll be gone this evening, you little piece of shit." She knew there was no one, and nothing, there, but she had to get the fear out of her system.

Now that isn't very nice, is it?

"Where are you? What are you? Leave me alone!"

I think you know who I am. As to where. . . Maybe above, maybe below. Maybe right next to you.

Frantically, Vanesa looked all around, but saw nothing. She pressed the elevator button again and again, until, finally, the door opened. Still looking around, trying to make sure that nothing could enter with her, she rushed in.

214

As she fell down the empty shaft, all she heard was a dry chuckle, but the echo of her screams soon drowned it out.

###

About the Author

Gustavo Bondoni was born in Argentina, which, he believes, makes him one of the few—if not the only—Argentinean fiction writers writing primarily in English. He moved to the US at the age of three, because his father worked for a multinational company that bounced him around the world every three years. Miami, Zurich, Cincinnati. He only made it back to Buenos Aires at the age of twelve, by which time he was not quite an American kid, not quite a European kid, and definitely not Argentinean! His fiction spans the range from science fiction to mainstream stories, passing through sword & sorcery and magic realism along the way, and it has been published in fourteen countries and seven languages to date. Apart from over a hundred short stories, he has published two collections, a short novel, and a novella, with a third collection coming in 2015. His website is at gustavobondoni.com

*****~~~~~*****

Wolf Call

by Adele Gardner

Saturday's my big night down at Diamond Bob's. The King never died for some folks, and believe me, there's nothing finer than belting out "It's Now or Never," while foxy women swoon. I love that gasp they take when they see me for the first time. Eight feet tall in a white sequined suit, the dark curls atop my crown slicked back into one flowing wave. And that strut. It feels so natural that sometimes I swagger when I'm only a wolf, and not in costume.

Naturally, a costume is all some people think I'm wearing—from a distance. But the women know. They stretch their arms toward me, straining for one touch of my fur, their hot little hands petting me. Sometimes the wolf comes out in them as well, and I go home with my gold lamé in tatters.

This Saturday was special: January 8, the King's birthday. We had a big party planned. The underworld adores Elvis, but we'd heard rumors that the demons who owned Hell's Barbells would try to stop tonight's festivities. They couldn't handle the competition—claimed we were burying them. It was their own fault: the demons made food so hot it burned through human stomachs. Diamond Bob's appealed to both humans and supernaturals, so the only ones who came to their dingy bar were those who'd just clawed their way out of hell.

So there I was, doing my number, sweating like blazes with the jumpsuit and all that fur. The place was packed so tight I could barely see the tables. When I squinted, I could see demons drifting between the humans, wearing their people suits. Well, they were paying customers. Malice, Don Carlo, and Porter waited in the

217

wings for the first sign of trouble, but the demons were dancing and swaying like everyone else.

I'd just finished "Suspicious Minds," when Greta—excuse me, Bob—started waving from the bar.

Now, I'm not one to disrupt a concert. Give the audience what they paid for, even if half of them are demons. As Bob gestured, I sang "Hard Headed Woman" and "Surrender" to be sure she got the message.

Bob waved the bar rag furiously. Well, that looked enough like a white flag. Plus, Bob's my boss. It doesn't pay to make her mad.

I fixed the audience with a soulful look, letting a lock fall over one eye. "Looks like it's time for a break. Would y'all excuse me for a moment?"

I waded through their cheers and clutching hands, nodding and smiling as I slid behind the bar. "This had better be good, Bob," I said. Once I started performing, it felt like pulling out fur to leave them.

"Why do you keep calling me that?" She flung the rag on the bar.

"That's what the sign says, isn't it?" I asked innocently. "Bob's always tended bar. Diamonds or no diamonds, without Bob, they're going to want their money back."

She sighed and threw up her hands. "Fine! Just follow me, okay? We have a situation."

We walked deep into the storeroom. Behind two cans of canola oil and a cask of Amontillado, a hole gaped in the stone floor. There wasn't any rubble. Some hungry beastie had gnawed its way up from the underworld while Bob wasn't looking.

A demon sprawled by the hole, its head flattened. A shattered bottle of Tequila mixed with the green goo.

"Guess he wasn't planning to use the front door," I said. "How many more, you reckon?" Gob demons never came in single drops. My tail puffed out. My reflection in the canisters looked like a sequined porcupine. "I knew we should have rented more seats."

"You think they're here to see you?" She eyed me critically. Other bars had animal heads tacked on the walls. Diamond Bob's was the only one that boasted a live werewolf.

I went out and got Malice and the gang. Malice looks like a cross between the Jolly Green Giant and the Purple People Eater. Something resembling a stalk of broccoli tops his neck, and his pear-shaped body is a lovely shade of violet. No one knows what he is, and everyone's afraid to ask.

"What's up, Red?" Malice asked.

"You know I prefer to be called Elvis." I raised my brows significantly, waggling the tufts and inclining my pompadour. "Red" was so out of date. My fur was brown, and my red human hair had already been falling out by the time I'd conjured the wolf-skin from that medieval manuscript.

Malice rolled his eyes.

Don Carlo, my mummy friend, groaned and tugged frantically at the bandages flying out from beneath his Armani suit and tangling in his bling. "Stop him now," Don Carlo groaned. "I can't afford to lose what's left of my stomach. Where's the sushi?"

"That will only make him worse," observed Malice.

I said, "Actually, I think a little sushi could solve all our problems."

Bob stared angrily from me to that hole. There was a cold breeze blowing out of the floor . . . or was it Bob's eyes? "You and your sushi. The world could be ending, and you'd still want sushi! Sometimes I think you lose your mind when you put on that wolf suit."

I shook my head violently. Curls flew into my eyes. Hang it all, she'd got me so upset I was mussing my hair. "I told you never to mention that!"

219

"Why not? It's not like anyone wants to see what you look like without it."

I decided to ignore her. Right now, there were more important things to worry about. I turned to Malice. He was a good—whatever. He'd halt their nefarious plot. I outlined my plan.

"What good is hot sauce going to do? They're demons!"

"Exactly. Hot and spicy—just the way they like it." I moved fast, collecting food and condiments. They'd go for the hot stuff first. It was our best chance to contain them, before they wreaked so much carnage no amount of crooning would bring the humans back. "We need more tequila. They love that devil worm. And don't forget the demon rum. We got any garlic buds? A bite of fellowship might do them good."

"You did *not* just make a joke about garlic." Porter the vampire spat involuntarily, then turned his back with great dignity. But he couldn't fool me: I could see his shoulders shaking under that cloak.

Malice said, "Go easy, Red. You know how sensitive he is."

I snorted. I knew, all right. Porter had scared away some of our best customers—like the giantess and her tiny twin—by making soulful eyes at them. Porter had a lot of class, but when people see a vampire, certain assumptions just come naturally.

I said, "How about some hot and spicy frog legs?"

"I resent that," said Malice. "My grandfather was a frog."

Bob helped me set up a table near the hole, where they'd smell it first thing. If I knew anything about the underworld, they were going to be hungry when they climbed out. Bob didn't look happy about the extra chairs, but Malice insisted the demons had a right to get off their feet.

"They'll go for that hot stuff first. We can lure them to the sushi with a little wasabi—"

"Red, I think you've got a sushi problem." Bob folded her arms across her chest.

"Is that what they call it these days?" Malice mused.

"Oh, good, an intervention." Porter's fangs gleamed.

I'd had enough of being insulted. My public was waiting for me. "I've got to get back out there. You have fun holding down the demons."

Malice grabbed my arm. "Come on, Red—"

"That's Elvis to you, son."

"Greta, you talk to him."

"What's the point?"

Two demons poked elongated oval heads through the hole, waving their sixteen scrawny arms like tentacles, in an attempt to scare us with lack of elbows. I'll admit, the teeth were horrifying. You can't chomp stone without chipping a few canines.

I could see their nostrils working—two wide slits on either side of their heads. They'd caught the scent, all right. But they surprised me. They bypassed the hot sauce and tequila altogether. "Soooo-shiiiii," they moaned, in unison.

They had better taste than I'd thought.

I'd been off the stage for a few minutes now. The crowd was getting restless. I left the devils in Bob's competent hands and took the stage. Camouflaged demons milled with other paying customers. Maybe they were in cahoots with the gob demons—or maybe they'd come to enjoy the show. Either way, until they started acting up, I wasn't going to deprive them of their favorite songs.

I fixed my eyes on them and sang "Devil in Disguise."

Bob kept disappearing into the storeroom. I sang louder to cover up demonic moans. But a man at a booth

221

drowned me out. After his first shriek, his wife took up the caterwaul, while he clutched his throat. Bob rushed over with a pitcher of milk.

Everywhere, folks were gasping, their eyes bugging out. As I dropped from the stage and rushed to the victims, I discovered the cause: the demons had brought their own Tabasco and jalapeños, their habañero peppers. Some of those clutching their stomachs were zombies and mummies, who'd downed glasses of the demons' Everclear thinking it was water. One vampire who'd been nibbling through the crowd actually burst into flame.

Well, two could play that game.

I called for the sushi and wasabi. Don Carlo and Porter helped me with the trays.

I have to admit, I got a little distracted. I had to fight hard, passing around that sushi plate. My arms shook. I wanted to pop rice rolls and balls into my mouth like candy. The platter shivered—my hand was in the sushi—I stuffed pieces into screaming mouths. It was the only way to keep from gobbling up the goods.

Sushi has a certain—how can I put this? It's a mystical experience. For every supernatural creature, it seems similarly. . . enlightening. The sushi eater enters a dreamy state in which the underworld seems beautiful, and supernaturals and humans are brothers. Ever wonder how a werewolf bar could be so peaceful? Nothing calms a crowd like a good California roll.

I couldn't resist. For every piece I put in someone's mouth, I hid one in my own. While patrons screamed, I was soon snorting and giggling, caught in a wave of sushi euphoria. Darn it all. The fool was definitely I.

Malice shook me. I swayed dizzily, looking up at his green and purple height. He stuck an onion under my nose, and I came up spluttering.

"We're out of sushi," he muttered.

All around us, brawls broke out, patrons punching each other, scrabbling for scraps. This was no party. It was a madhouse.

I strode back to the stage. Time to distract them. But while I'd been busy in the crowd, the demons had wormed their way onstage. They'd broken the mikes and instruments. Even the house musicians had joined the melee.

But I'd been waiting for an opportunity like this. While the room shrieked, I used my wolfish baritone to get their attention. It was now or never: what better time to try my new repertoire?

"Why did the werewolf cross the road? To get to the sushi bar! Two guys walk into a bar. How do you know which one is the werewolf? Watch who orders the sushi!"

A demon rolled on the floor, groaning and wheezing, "Make him stop!"

Unfortunately, the jokes had the same effect on the humans. Those who could still stand were screaming insults and hurling silverware. A fork lodged in my pompadour.

"You stink!"

"Get off the stage!"

"Who ever heard of a hirsute Elvis?" That was unfair, from a long-hair with gold specs. Furry bat-wings hovered over his tweeds.

"Hairy back!" a woman screamed.

That stung. I looked around for support. Behind the bar, Don Carlo and Porter held a shaggy werewolf's shoulders, while Bob mixed something in a tub, pouring in bottle after bottle of clear alcohol. Malice was bashing demon heads with an empty sushi tray.

There was only one thing to do. Even if they hated me, I knew someone they still loved.

A werewolf's voice booms over any crowd. I howled as the King had done, giving them that old "Wolf Call."

I won't say they calmed down. But they were listening.

I took a deep breath, ran my hand through my hair, and plucked out that gosh-darned fork.

And then I squeezed the hurt they'd dealt me into tears as I crooned "Love Me Tender." As the silence spread, demons clutched one another and began slow dancing. A few dreamy humans traded partners by mistake. As they danced with the devils, tiny flames burst from their hair, but they didn't seem to notice.

Bob and my friends were quietly circulating through the crowd with shot glasses of the witches' brew they'd been mixing behind the bar. At last the moaning stopped. With streaming eyes, the patrons gradually recovered.

Porter brought out his old Gibson from its hiding place in the storeroom. While he played lead guitar, I sang "Don't Be Cruel." But it was "Hound Dog" that really brought down the house.

The last patrons finally filed out, sobbing and touching my hand. Women planted kisses on my cheek.

As we stood outside, Bob brought me a shot of whatever they'd made. I held it to the moon and eyed it dubiously.

"Buffalo punch," she explained with a tired but mischievous grin. "Stirred by the hairiest werewolf legs we could find. It's the only thing that might strip the hair off a demon's back."

I smiled back at her. "Bob, you really take the cake." I downed the mixture. Dear Lord.

Malice loomed beside me, his great eyes shining like twin moons in that stalk of a head. "You know, Red, calling her Bob is kind of insulting. I mean, I know you're a monster, but you could at least be civil to the ladies."

Wolf Call

I sighed. "Why can't you just call me Elvis?"

Greta said, "What's the matter, *Elvis*? Don't you know we love you for who you are?"

I hugged her. I'm afraid my eyes misted over. But that was all right. The King had a right to be emotional on his birthday.

We walked through the bar arm in arm. We'd have a lot to clean up before tomorrow night. Once word got around, we'd be busier than ever. My jokes had flopped, but I had my eye on a better gimmick: naked sushi.

The thought of Greta as the platter had my mouth watering already.

###

About the Author

Currently cataloging librarian for a public library, Adele Gardner loved being editor for The Mariners' Museum and projectionist for AMC Theatres. Home wouldn't be complete without five cats, four birds, a kit harpsichord, and two friendly guitars. A graduate of the Clarion West Writers Workshop and an active member of SFWA, Adele is also literary executor for her father, her mentor and namesake, Delbert R. Gardner. Adele's first poetry collection, *Dreaming of Days in Astophel*, appeared in 2011. With one long and one short poem winning third place in the Rhysling Awards, she's had over 300 works of short fiction, poetry, art/photography, and nonfiction published in venues such as the Third Flatiron Anthologies *Playing with Fire* and *Astronomical Odds, Strange Horizons, Daily Science Fiction, The Doom of Camelot, Legends of the Pendragon, Challenging Destiny, Arcane II, PodCastle, New Myths, Heroic Fantasy Quarterly, Liquid Imagination, Silver Blade, Goblin Fruit, Mythic Delirium, Tales of the Talisman*, and *Songs of Eretz Poetry E-Zine* (including two Father &

Ain't Superstitious

Daughter Special Features). Two stories and a poem earned honorable mention in *The Year's Best Fantasy and Horror*. Learn more at www.gardnercastle.com

*****~~~~*****

The Candlestick

by Will Morton

Dennis Patterson lay drenched in the bottom of the rocking lifeboat, head aching, shoulder burning with pain. The moon lightened the surrounding fog, which swirled ghostlike.

Rescuing Linda had been the whole reason for tonight's adventures. He and Bub had slipped aboard her new husband's yacht. He'd taken a bullet in his shoulder, and Bub had started a fire.

He still clutched the candlestick.

…

Dennis had peeped over the yacht rail near the bow, across a barely illuminated twenty-foot deck. The Caribbean seawater, so warm while he and Bub swam over from the stolen sailboat, now felt chilly in the evening breeze. It was dark this far from shore, but his eyes had adjusted.

An aroma of food teased his nose. Two men in white uniforms cleared dishes from an elegant table, in the center of which stood a large, heavy-looking ornate candlestick. The ensconced candle no longer burned.

Candlelight dinner. Linda and Antoine.

I'd like to kill them both.

Dennis shook his head and wiped his nose roughly with the back of his hand.

She's still my wife—I don't care what some judge says. Anyway, she's not used to this snazzy kind of life. She'll thank me for this.

Ten feet away, Bub, whom he had recruited that afternoon in a bar in Key West, eased over the rail. The big guy crept up behind one waiter, slipped his hands around the man's neck, and the two stood unmoving. Then the waiter slumped, and Bub let him fall to the deck.

227

I specifically told Bub: no killing. They'll think I did it.

Before the other waiter could cry out, Bub seized the candlestick and clubbed him over the head. This victim fell face forward onto the table, then slipped backward, pulling the tablecloth and the remaining dishes with him. The candle stub rolled on the deck.

Bub knelt and extracted a gun from the first victim.

These guys have guns?

Then a bright light from the raised cabin in the stern flashed, and a man's voice shouted, "You, there! Put your hands up!"

Blinded, Dennis lifted his arms. Bub, silhouetted against the light, fired the newly acquired gun, fired in the direction of the voice.

Dennis lowered his arms, took a deep breath, and tried to stop shaking. *I've gotta see Linda—I've gotta talk to her.*

A shot sounded, and his shoulder exploded with pain like some invisible monster's claw ripping his soul out through the wound. His left arm fell useless at his side.

He fell to one knee as he heard more shots, and then the bright light disappeared.

Bub, holding a cigarette lighter in one hand and a flask in the other, came back but made no move to help him up. He looked at the flask, muttered, "Hate to waste good liquor," and abandoned him.

Dennis looked around, dizzy with pain, tried to get his bearings. The deck, the cabin, everything, vibrated. At any moment, he would keel over in a faint.

Antoine, you rich punk, you had no right to take Linda away from me! I hate you both!

The yacht lurched, toppling him forward. Screaming, he rolled on the wet deck until he bumped against something. God, my shoulder!

The Candlestick

His eyes adjusted to the fire and he saw that he lay against a lifeboat. Using it for support, Dennis tried to stand but fell inside and fainted.

"Yee-hah!" Bub shouted, as if from far away.

Splash! The impact tortured his shoulder, pushed him to semi-consciousness. The lifeboat must have hit the surface.

"They were loaded, pal!" Bub crowed, a pile of booty before him. He held a bottle of whiskey to his lips and upended it.

The lifeboat shook, and the metal trinkets clattered. In a daze, Dennis saw a face at the side of the lifeboat.

Someone from the yacht, must be.

"No, you don't!" Bub cried as he aimed the gun at the newcomer. Dennis heard a click.

Out of bullets. Or too wet.

Bub smashed the face with the butt of the gun. The face disappeared. Bub grinned at Dennis and said, "Dead men tell no—"

Then he cried, "Behind you!"

Numb, Dennis grabbed something from the loot and swung. A heavy candlestick connected with a jolt that seared his bad shoulder. Just before she sank away, Dennis realized it was Linda, saw the look on her face as she recognized him.

"No!" cried Dennis.

I just wanted to tell you I've changed, Linda.

Tears rolled down his face like blood from his wound.

Bub shouted, "I think that's all of 'em. We're home free!"

Maybe it wasn't her.

As if through heavy breakers, he pushed his suddenly aching head over the side to gaze at the water. Surface wavelets slapped the lifeboat, a sound like that of the candlestick as it cracked Linda's face.

229

Ain't Superstitious

Everything's gonna be different, Linda, I swear.
Come back!

He pushed with rubbery legs and tried to go in after her, but only collapsed and thumped his head against the gunwale.

...

It seemed as if years, not hours, had passed since he laid out his plan to Bub in that slum bar in Key West. "There's a yacht I want to chase. It just left—"

"We're gonna rob it?"

"No! We're gonna visit, is all."

Bub was silent, grinning. Finally he said, "A chick, huh?"

Dennis started.

Bub slapped his knee. "She don't wanna see you, pal. Not when she's on a yacht with some rich dude."

Furious, Dennis said nothing.

"So lemme get this straight," Bub continued, "You gonna kill her?"

"No!"

Out there on the ocean, nobody would know. . .

Bub shrugged. "You're kidnapping her, then. And you want me to do what? Kill the new boyfriend?"

"Husband," Dennis blurted.

"Oh ho! She's married to this yacht dude! I kill him, and you play the hero and save her!"

"Yes. . . no! We're just gonna scare them."

Bub threw back his head and laughed.

I should kill Antoine for taking Linda away from me. Linda too. She left me for him.

Dennis grabbed Bub's arm. "No killing!"

Bub stiffened, jerked, and pointed a knife at Dennis. Then he put it away and slapped on an insincere grin. "Just funnin' with you, pal."

With effort, Dennis released the breath he was holding. "As long as I can see Linda and tell her I don't run drugs in my boat anymore."

"Whatever you say, pal. It's your funeral."

…

From the bottom of the rocking lifeboat, Dennis stared at the place her face had appeared, now filled with swirling fog. Mesmerizing fog.

There's never fog in these waters.

He remembered the jolt of the candlestick as it made bone-crunching contact, how it had bounced back in his grip, seared his shoulder.

No, it couldn't have been—it was someone who looked like her. I would never have hit her.

The front of his head felt like it had split open.

Tears formed in Dennis's eyes. "I've never gotten a fair deal," he said to Bub. "Life's been against me from the very beginnin'."

Bub nodded, smiling skull-like. He seemed very drunk.

Dennis blinked back his tears. "Even when I try to get better, it always turns out worse."

"Thass true," Bub commiserated, slurring his words. "But keep moving, thass the way."

It's your fault, Linda, leaving me. I'm glad Antoine's yacht is burning. I hope Bub shot him.

"It doesn't seem real," Dennis slobbered. "If I could just go back and relive the last few minutes."

God, if you're there, make it okay. Please, God! Make Linda okay.

Dennis gasped as Linda hovered between him and Bub. He lifted his arms to embrace her, but she shrieked as her forehead caved in. Blood gushed down her face, looking in the fog like an old black-and-white movie.

"You were fun for a while," she said, "but deep down I knew you'd always be a loser. The stupidest thing I ever did was marry you. Just look at all the people you've hurt, whose lives you've ruined."

"No, Linda, that's what I want to tell you! I've changed—I really have! Since I got out of jail, I worked hard and I've stayed on the right track. All for you!"

But Linda went on as if he hadn't spoken. "The drinking, the fights, never having enough money, it got old fast, Dennis. I was happy when you got caught. Made it easier to move on with my life."

"It'll be good between us this time, I swear!"

But he was talking to Bub, who sprawled against the stern, his feet, crossed at the ankles, propped up on his pile of loot. He had a black patch over one eye, like a pirate. An odor of spoiled fish made Dennis gag.

Dennis blinked. No patch, just a shadow.

Dennis gulped and said, "She wouldn't see me, wouldn't talk, nothin'. Last time I called, her husband got on the line, threatenin' me."

Linda's face swirled again. "Daddy likes Antoine too, which is a relief after you."

"After I got out of jail, I got all straightened out. But you abandoned me. It's all your fault!"

"'Sall a bad dream," Bub slurred.

...

In the moonlit fog, a skeleton loomed over him; he felt bony fingers clenched around his throat.

Dennis awoke suddenly. No skeleton. He coughed, cleared his sore throat. His neck felt stiff.

Bub could easily strangle me, wounded like this. Who would know?

With rising panic he looked up. Bub was passed out in the stern, snoring like a foghorn.

Beyond, out on the water, he could just see an old-fashioned sailing ship, three-masted, all sails spread. And at the top of the center mast, was that a Jolly Roger?

The ship creaked as it drew closer, sending a whisper over the water, sounding vaguely German or Dutch: "If I must sail 'til Judgment Day. . . "

232

Not the slightest breeze blew, yet the black flag flapped.

I'm hallucinating.

The huge ship was about to run them down. Dennis searched frantically for oars.

From the deck of the three-masted ship, a man wearing a dark jacket with a white ruff at the neck, whose long hair whipped wildly behind him as if buffeted by a gale, cupped his hands around his mouth. He called, "Ahoy!"

A skeleton stood on the surface of the water, hovering in the roiling fog. One upraised bony arm held a boxy glass lantern. The light glowed ghostlike over the water.

Dennis blinked and squinted at the skeleton. It stood at the end of a long, rickety pier.

The fog grew so thick the three-masted ship was hidden.

In the stern, Bub, wearing a dark jacket with a white ruff at the neck, upended his bottle of whiskey. He lowered it, wiped his lips with the back of his hand, then stared at Dennis. Bub's eyes seemed to suck energy right out of Dennis.

...

Raindrops pelted his face. He lay in the bottom of the lifeboat, in shallow, stagnant-smelling water.

Dennis felt the candlestick in his fist and wanted to throw it overboard. But when he looked, his fingers grasped nothing.

Wincing, he pushed his back against the gunwale and inch by inch wriggled to a sitting position. His stomach rumbled, and his mouth felt gummy with thirst. Bub had abandoned him, taking his whiskey and booty with him.

He wriggled higher, his feet sloshing bilge water, looking left and right. The lifeboat had run aground on a sandy beach. No gulls. No seaweed washed up. No people. No real surf either.

The hazy outline of a shore curved on either side. A lagoon. Which explained the lack of waves.

Maybe this is a deserted island. I might never be found. I might starve to death.

Or worse, there might be natives. Weren't the original Caribbean Islanders cannibals?

Through the rain, he peered inland at the dense jungle. Several fierce island warriors emerged from the trees brandishing spears. He blinked. Nothing there.

I'm easy prey here. I need to hide in the trees.

He forced himself to stand, clothes sticky with dried salt water. His shoulder felt swollen and infected. A wave of dizziness made him sway and almost fall.

When he had somewhat balanced, he lifted one leg out of the lifeboat. The wet sand seemed to roll under him, but he gripped the gunwale and kept his balance. His head pounded.

The rain had ceased by the time he dragged himself to the trees. When he spied several mangoes on the ground, he staggered to them and collapsed to his knees. His hand trembled as he seized the nearest one and bit into it.

The mushy mouthful tasted putrid, and he was horrified to see writhing worms inside. A smell of vomit filled the still air. He spat out the mouthful and threw the fruit far away. He spat several times, but couldn't get the taste out of his mouth.

He tried another, tore into it with his fingers, then another, but all were wormy and rotten. He sighed, more hungry than ever.

Looking around, he saw a table with a fancy white tablecloth and two plates of rich food. He stood and started toward it. Linda sat, regarding him with a smirk.

"Fine dining. Life is so much better than when I was with you," she said. Her forehead crumpled in, and she collapsed under the table.

Antoine, seated with his back to Dennis, stood so fast he knocked his chair over. He turned and pointed at Dennis, face crimson with rage.

"You!" he said. "If you call her one more time, I'll bring in some of my, ahem, associates and they'll—" He grasped his shoulder and his hair erupted in flames. His face broiled darker and darker brown until completely charred. Then ashes crumpled and scattered.

But the table remained. And the food was untouched! Dennis lurched forward, stomach rumbling, eyes blurry. But he bumped into a tree trunk, hitting his head and tearing open several pus-filled blisters in his shoulder.

He screamed and saw through tears that the table was gone. Falling to his knees, he whimpered, "It's not my fault. I didn't mean to do it."

Laughter rang out. It sounded like Linda.

But Linda was dead.

I gotta get off this island and forget Linda!

He collapsed and pounded the fist of his good arm on the ground.

"Linda, I don't want you to be dead. I love you. Please come back! Linda!"

He was pounding the ground with the candlestick. He flung it away, but it did not go far.

…

He snapped open his eyes when a native warrior kicked his sore head. Dennis shrieked.

"Hey, sorry, pal," Bub said, sounding like he didn't care one bit. "Didn't see you there."

We scuttled the stolen sailboat. Everyone on board the yacht is dead. Once I'm out of the way, Bub can go back to Florida scot free.

"What're you chewin'?" Dennis said. His stomach rumbled.

"Food from the lifeboat. It's stocked, pal."

It is?

Not wanting to sound surprised, Dennis replied, "Not as fancy as what they ate on that yacht, I bet."

Bub shrugged and turned away.

Dennis tried to stand, and the trees seemed to flow and bend, so he crawled on his hands and knees toward the sound of waves, ignoring the agony in his shoulder. The undergrowth was dry, with sharp thorns that broke off as splinters under his skin.

The texture under him changed. He was crawling now on sand. Way down the beach, the lifeboat rested in the moonlight, occasionally lapped by small waves.

If I don't get there soon, the tide will carry it away.

Then he was clutching the gunwale, lifting himself to a kneeling position.

A receding wave tore it from his weak grasp. He watched in horror, kneeling in water that stung his knees, as the lifeboat raced away.

As he panted, sobbing, a light appeared down the beach. He squinted. It looked like a lantern held by a skeleton at the edge of a pier. It turned its skull face toward him, its bare teeth looking like an evil smile.

Then the lifeboat bumped his bad shoulder, and with a cry he struggled into it. He tore open every container looking for food and water but found none.

He found one oar and paddled, but the oar was the candlestick, and Dennis let go of it.

...

The smell of sausage and eggs and coffee awoke Dennis. Sunshine filled his eyes, causing his head to pound.

Then he saw the Coast Guard vessel! Someone threw a rope down to him, and his shoulder screamed with pain as he grabbed it.

The Candlestick

The Coast Guard vessel struck the lifeboat, cracking the hull. It filled with water and sank out from under him. Dennis was left dangling half-in and half-out of the water.

In small jerks, the rope was hauled up. A lurch, and Dennis' throbbing head banged against the hull. He cried out.

"Almost aboard," said the good-natured officer in a smart white uniform. "Bet you can't wait for some good old American grub!"

"You got that right," Dennis croaked. His throat felt sore—was he catching a cold?

"Sounds like you could use some nice cold water, too!"

Dennis looked up. His benefactor wore an old-fashioned jacket with a white ruff. And the warm, sunny day had become foggy night. He was being hauled aboard a three-masted sailing ship. The acrid smell of rancid fish choked him.

"Ya veren't a-tryin' to leave?" whispered the Dutch captain, his long hair whipping wildly behind him.

Beside him stood Bub, a patch over one eye, grinning.

The candlestick felt heavy enough to pull his arm from its socket. No matter how he shook his hand, he could not get rid of it.

From the captain he heard, ". . . not 'til Judgment Day. . . " in a voice that sounded like Linda's.

He dared not look.

###

About the Author

Born in West Virginia, Will Morton now lives in the Los Angeles area with his wife, Yvonne. His story, "Parallel Universe" was included in Third Flatiron's *Lost*

Worlds, Retraced anthology. His stories have also appeared in anthologies published by Pill Hill Press and Spencer Hill Press. Visit him at his website: www.willmorton.com.

*****~~~~~*****

Dead Men's Drinks

by Christina Bates

"If a dead man asks you to come in for drinks, politely decline." That's what my grandfather said, holding me on his knee. It was pouring sheets of rain, and grandfather sat stroking his mustache, banishing the storm with his own sheer strength. I asked why.

"Because," Grandfather said, "If you do come down and visit with him in his grave, you'll be old before you finish his cups."

Grandfather didn't know if it was the whole country that believed the story, or just his village. It sat where the river narrowed, where a cherry pit spat from the eastern bank would land in Ukraine. Not that there was a Ukraine then, or a Poland for that matter.

Babcia Hania lived beside the forest. Grandfather was very young then. She was very old. Some reckoned her a witch, and maybe she was. On St. Andrew's day everyone brought their keys and candles to her. She'd give them their futures in wax and call them fools for asking. And she was never wrong. This was why grandfather knew the story was true.

It all started in her own grandmother's time, when said grandmother was engaged to be wed to Mietek Skorupa. Mietek stopped the whole procession on the church stoop, for he had promised to call on his best friend when the happy day arrived. This friend had been kicked off his horse a week before and now lay quiet in the churchyard. A man is only worth his oath, so Mietek walked off into the churchyard. His shadow turned the corner, and he was gone. They waited till the sun came down, and then they left. In time, Mietek's beloved wed Babcia Hania's grandfather.

Ain't Superstitious

The story was old gossip by the time Babcia Hania was a small girl. Old gossip, told only by men deep within their own cups, and mothers warning children. One Sunday morning, as the mass ended, a man tumbled out of the graveyard. He was rag and bone and matted white hair, and he answered to the name of Mietek Skorupa. The pious ladies howled, and the men crossed themselves, and only the timely intervention of the priest kept the day from ending in disaster.

No one quite knew what to make of him, but his sister's children did their duty. They took care of him, and explained what they could. When Mietek had enough sense back in his head to talk, he claimed to have only been gone for a few hours. He and his friend had sat and spoke, pouring vodka, until a distant clock had struck. His friend had rushed him back into the living world. It was not his friend's fault, Mietek insisted. They'd just lost track of the time.

A month later Mietek Skorupa walked out of the house of his sister's son and through the village, to the edge of the old church. Where he went next, no one quite knew. The more pragmatic, who'd never quite believed in dead men drinking, decided he must have gone back to the city. Babcia Hania, whose family had always lived on the edge of the woods, knew otherwise. Seeing the world gone mad around him, he had turned back to the one place he might find welcome.

The day before he died, Grandfather made me swear that I would not look for him.

"I might not have the strength," he said, "to not ask you to join me. And you might not have the strength to decline."

I told him not to be silly. That the doctors said he was improving. He rolled his eyes and growled.

"Babcia Hania was better than any doctor that ever lived, and had the sense to let a body die in peace

240

besides." He closed his eyes, and the silence was rubbed raw by the whir of machines.

"My sister died in the war that gave us back our country. A poor trade. I saw her on my wedding day, waving from the graveyard, and I lost my mind." He smiled. "Jumped the fence to embrace her. Pissed her off when I asked her to let me in. She wouldn't let me join her then. Smart woman, my sister. But she says she will now."

"Grandfather?"

"So promise me, you won't go looking. Promise me you'll be content to wait, and let the dead lie."

I humored him, and I promised. I kissed him and told him I'd see him in the morning. He gave me a last smile. My Maggie was born the day of the funeral. I wish she had come earlier. He would have loved her.

When she grew old enough to talk, my Maggie begged for the graveyard story night after night, while her eyes went moon-wide. Her curls would bounce up and down as she crawled into my lap, her arms full of frogs or flowers or fudge. She swallowed every word, putting it away somewhere safe. She would later regurgitate it full out, to the horror of our neighbors and amusement of her father. Ten times a night, she asked for it, until she got school-aged; old enough to smirk at any stories her mother could tell. And yet I went on, giving her others. It was all I could do.

Unlike Grandfather, I had no language to try and give her. While I was growing up, the thought was that a second language only served to confuse and befuddle a young mind. My grandfather had been ordered to cease and desist. So he gave me stories and superstition, and these I gave to Maggie.

I tried to register her when they set up the bilingual school up in the west end; they didn't teach beginners. So I gave her stories, of the knights beyond the borders, the mermaid in the river, and the princess on the glassy hill. I gave her superstition, and she learned that spiders in the house are good luck, that a nun in the morning means a pleasant and safe journey, and that plants ought to be planted as the moon is growing, so they will come out of the ground.

We buried her father as the moon was growing. It didn't console Maggie. She got quieter and stayed in her room for months on end. When she finally came downstairs, she asked about the story. Did it really happen? Or was it just a story? I lied. I told her I didn't know. I humored her.

One All Saint's, she went missing. We had gone to lay flowers and candles. I'd gone off to visit my grandfather's grave, and left Maggie by her dad's. When I got back, Maggie was nowhere to be seen. I lost my mind. I ran over the whole length and breadth of the cemetery, screaming her name, only to find her sitting in the grass beside his grave. She swore she hadn't moved, that she'd been there the whole time, just chatting. According to her, only five minutes had passed. I showed her my watch, showed her that it had been a half hour. I asked her what the hell she'd been doing.

"I was chatting with Dad," she said. "Just like in your story, except he didn't ask me to come in."

I slapped her for a liar. I regretted it the moment it was done, of course. We didn't talk properly for a month. I never apologized either, but somehow we got to be almost human around each other again. She grew up tall and fine, and fond of parties. My Maggie loved dancing, especially late into the night. Curfew was never late enough for her, but she made a point of keeping it, grumbling and grousing all the while.

I let her break curfew, to go to that party. After all, she was almost grown. Responsible, competent in school, if not top of the class. Her friends were all good kids. Their designated driver drank water all night.

Maybe he should've had coffee instead.

Maybe he wouldn't have fallen asleep on a 3 am highway. The car might not have gone into the ditch. And maybe my Maggie. . .

I wish it had rained during the funeral. Instead I was half-blinded where the sun struck the spring snow. Hers was the last of the funerals, closed casket. It had been bad enough, going to identify the body. They'd let that boy out, in his shiny new wheelchair. I think he might have tried to apologize. I don't know, I walked past him.

I was too busy remembering. I remembered her soft little mouth, and the way she'd pause when I fed her, pause just long enough to look up and smile. Again she was learning to walk, tumbling over our carpet giggling. Even then she bounced and danced. And I could almost feel her crawling up my knees when I sat in the pew. I heard her voice. I heard her fount of questions asking about my grandfather, her own grandparents, the color of the sky, the color of the sea. I know I felt my hand stinging from my slap.

I had asked my grandfather once, if Mietek Skorupa was happy when he went back to his friend's grave.

He had shrugged, and stroked his mustache in silence.

"Maybe," he said, after the clock had ticked away an eternity. "After all, he never returned."

I haven't gone to see her since the funeral. I am afraid to. I promised Grandfather. Could I be less than my oath to him? Yet I grow sick of waiting.

I will go the graveyard. I will sit beside her grave.

And I will wait, however long it takes.

###

About the Author

Christina Bates is a Canadian writer of Polish descent, and a recent graduate of the University of Alberta. She lives in Edmonton, Alberta, with a cat and her two brothers. Her work has appeared in *Glass Buffalo Magazine*. Christina enjoys moonlit strolls through the graveyard and the occasional shot of vodka.

*****~~~~*****

Pantomimus

by Lyn Godfrey

There's a big show tonight. This just might be the one. Pantomimus must don his suit. Straight black pants. A crisp white shirt. Black suspenders. A black-and-white, horizontally striped blazer jacket. Glossy white shoes that curve upward to a point on the ends. White gloves with pointed fingertips. He also wears the obligatory beret atop his head.

The most important part of his attire is the mask. It's a Venetian style mask, inspired by the masks of comedy and tragedy. Its right side is comedy with a laughing smile. Its left side is tragedy with a scowling frown. Its base color is shiny and white, but the eyes are surrounded by the blackest of black. The comedy half has a twinkle over its eye, and the tragedy half has two delicate teardrops under the outside of its eye. The smile-frown forms a devious yet sideways "S" shape across the mask's lower half.

Pantomimus must attend a show every day, and every day he must await that fated sound. It doesn't happen often, but it always happens eventually. People have been warned or asked not to whistle inside a theater or inside a circus tent, but people often do the thing they are warned or asked not to do. Maybe that's why so many superstitions are born.

When someone does eventually whistle on the night of a show at a circus or theater, then Pantomimus must take three individuals for each whistle he hears. No more, no less. Accidents always happen in threes, after all. At least, that's what superstition says. Superstitions are a delicate thing. If not enforced, people stop believing. Belief is what fuels every supernatural thing.

The mime must respond if engaged by a person. He must pretend to be in a box, or pulling a rope, or eating an apple, and he must be good enough at his pantomime that no one suspects a thing. But he can never make a sound. He is not capable of making a sound.

He despises being a mime, but it is the easiest way to blend in while remaining hidden, until he gets what he needs. What he must have. What was taken from him by unnatural means. He used to speak, he used to whistle. Oh, how he'd loved to whistle. Until the damned curse. Now, it had been so long he couldn't recall what it felt like to have his throat dance with the vibration of a word or a song.

Pantomimus attends a show tonight and takes his seat in the back of the theater. Should a whistle occur, he needs to be positioned in the best place to determine where the sound came from. He will only have three chances to get it right. He can only take three. Those are the rules.

There it is! The sound he has waited so long to hear. A short but ever so sweet whistling tune. Where was it? Who did it? His head snakes side to side with anticipation. It must have been there. Over by that young man. No, there, that woman has her lips pursed. Or perhaps there, that man looks quite jovial.

With a few good options, it is time to start his work. He can only use his gifts once a whistle has occurred. His gifts are thrilling to use, but he'd still rather have a voice. When his voice, and likely his mind as well, had become corrupted by the curse, he knew he'd do anything to again feel the tickle of sound within his neck.

He decides to start with the woman. He waves his hand in front of him and stops abruptly with a point. Migraine. That should get her moving. The woman crumples over in her seat and lets out a weak cry. With her hand cradling the side of her head, she stands and excuses herself from the performance hall. Pantomimus follows behind her, nary a sound to betray him. Into the Ladies Room he goes, and before she has the chance to scream, he claws his left hand into her throat. The pointed-finger gloves sink in and open up her neck to him. Using his right hand, he removes a scalpel from his inside jacket pocket and proceeds to cut out her vocal chords.

Silently he begs for this woman's chords to be the ones, but there's no way to know for sure until he performs the ritual. Holding them up to the light of the bathroom, he inspects them as if he hoped to see the signs of a recent whistle. The woman clutches at her opened throat as she lies on the floor and watches wide-eyed and unable to scream as he places her vocal chords into a special pouch on the inside of his jacket.

He still has two more chances to find the whistler, and he intends to use them. There isn't much time, now that he's made his first attack. His now blood-soaked white gloves could give him away.

He stands outside the performance hall and peeks in. Knowing that he needs to formulate his plan of attack perfectly, he scans the theater for hidden opportunities. Perhaps he could have a simple glass bulb fall onto the jolly man's head. Or he could simulate the young man's phone ringtone so he will leave unattended. Pantomimus takes another second to look around the lobby. Whatever he decides to do, he must do it quickly.

Seeing that the concession stand is unattended, he gathers up a bag of popcorn and zips back to the door. With the door open just a sliver, he takes in a deep breath then sends an enchanting puff of popcorn scent with a dash of hunger towards his next target. The young man sniffs and looks around. Then, just as predicted, he rises from his seat and heads to the concession stand.

Pantomimus stands just outside the door, facing the wall, with his hands hidden in front of him. Within the instant the young man has exited and closed the door behind him, before he's even had time to wonder why a

mime is standing with his face to the wall, Pantomimus
has his hand inside the young man's neck. He makes quick
but delicate work of slicing out his vocal chords.

An attendant is coming down the hall. Pantomimus
would dispose of him, but he can only kill those whose
vocal chords he takes. However, he still has his abilities
until the time his ritual is performed. He zips into the hall
and stands in front of the jovial man. He raises a bloodied
hand, then claws downward at the man's throat. Without
even bothering with the scalpel, he snatches out the man's
vocal chords with his clawed glove, to the horror of the
nearby audience. He immediately flickers out of existence
to the theater and reappears at the ritual site inside an
abandoned circus train.

Inside the accursed train car, the mime pleads once
again that one of these sets of vocal chords belongs to the
whistler. He would live a thousand lives, or take a
thousand lives, in order to be able to speak his mind,
corrupt as it may be, or even to speak at all. At last, he
begins his ceremony.

He approaches the old bloodied dressing table and
marks a small straight line on the mirror before him with
the blood of his victims. His own image is barely visible
through the numerous dried bloody marks. There are
dozens of similar lines. One for every attempt at breaking
the curse. One for every three sets of vocal chords.
Wooden bowls stack up alongside the legs of the dressing
table. He picks up three of the bowls and sorts them into a
straight line in front of the mirror.

After adding a sprinkle of bone dust over the
bowls, he runs his hands down each set of vocal chords
and collects all the remaining blood onto his gloves. He
follows up by placing one set of vocal chords in each of
the three bowls. Then, he pleads with the chords again
before beginning the final part of his ritual.

He turns to the wall beside him, where he's written
his incantation so many times before. The blood is thick

and wet on his gloved hands. He traces over the written incantation once more with his bloodied hand. *Bring back my whistle to me.*

When his hand releases from the last word, the walls shake with a supernatural strength, and the sky rumbles along with them. The still-wet blood on the wall drips down from the incantation, forming hooks and teardrops underneath the letters. But the vocal chords are in the same place within their bowls. Nothing has changed. His voice is still gone.

The mime falls to his knees and slouches over to the floor. Tomorrow night, there will be another big show. Once again, Pantomimus will don his suit. He will attend. You never know where, and you never know when. But, now, you know for certain that you should never whistle at a show.

About the Author

Lyn Godfrey is a freelancer writer of speculative fiction. She is also a small-town, American southwestern, book-hoarding, animal-loving kind of girl. She writes in most "genre" genres (including science fiction, fantasy, urban fantasy, horror, YA) and is a self-described Geek of All Trades. Video games, superheroes, steampunk, aliens, dinosaurs, zombies, and so on and so forth. If it's nerdy, she loves it. Yes, that includes Star Wars AND Star Trek.

Lyn began writing her first book (a Star Wars sequel) at age eleven. She has been making plans to write ever since but is often distracted by reading or looking for shiny things, like spaceships and robots. Her short stories will be appearing in various upcoming anthologies to be published this year, including *Ain't Superstitious, Sproutlings,* and *In Memory: A Tribute to Terry Pratchett.*

*****~~~~~*****

O Shades, My Woe

by Eric J. Guignard

The night wanes darker in absence of gods, darker still in light of ill-penance. It is a darkness tinged with enchantment, with sorcery, a darkness men must flee should any regard linger for the continuance of their life, the preservation of their soul.

I flee no more.

The night is dark, yet I see things in it, things that move, that approach. For black is the sky, though mists of amethyst slither across, hiding, then revealing, occasional diamond-shaped stars, glimpses of a moon so full its bloated belly should burst, and the sad, squinty-eyed faces of pale babes that bob upon unseen waves.

The infants mewl with the despair of abandoned kittens, their soft sweet notes as plaintive as those from a shepherd's curved gemshorn.

They come for me, and I know upon their waves I'm soon to be taken. . .

. . .

I am a soldier in King Arthur's army, a man-at-arms crusading under the red dragon of his banner. I fought with Arthur at the fortress of Leodegran, where ten thousand men died in battle, and I travelled in his retinue to far-off realms, where golden unicorns rule and castles are built of glass.

I, who was born the same year as Arthur, was even present the day in Westminster when he, a boy, pulled the heir's sword from its stone-mounted anvil. O! How I dreamt it to be me raising that ancient blade in exaltation, how I thought of fate's vagaries and that I could have been anything. . .

251

But I contented myself, at least, to have witnessed such wonder. And when we came of age, and Arthur marched to campaign against Lot Luwddoc and his eleven armies, I joined, pledging my fealty forever to the boy-king.

And such victories were ours to be had! Death's cold hand but grazed our warriors, whilst it sought our enemies like a beggar scrabbling upon lost coins. Arthur's banners raised on every defeated field high above the slain. His trumpeters called for victory so frequently that their lungs swelled and voices broke. Arthur's song was grand, his daring renowned.

And Arthur was mighty. Arthur was fair. Arthur was triumphant and wise and beloved by all of Britannia, a king who kept his peoples unknown to the strifes our land suffered whilst leaderless. Famine, disease, sedition, poverty: It is Arthur we praise for their eradication. It is Arthur we worship as heir-divine.

It's true he kills many, many men, but Arthur is a warrior. It is expected to slay thy enemy. It is also true he fornicates with lasses in every town, but this too is expected. Tales of Arthur's lusts are heralded as exultantly as the sonnets of his battles. When one speaks of our king's conquests, damsels and dragons may be commutable. And because of his loins' unrestraint, it was whispered he took to bed his own half-sister, Morgause.

I knew not the veracity of such musings; hearsay is as prevalent as the nits slumbering in our wool. But one does not discount idle reports either, as disquieting acts have ways to make themselves known, and not even Merlin can always shroud their secrets. Children in the shadows, talking horses, soothsayers, there is always someone—*something*—that is aware of wrongdoing. There are times even blades of grass pass along through rustles the implications of looming peril.

It takes only tuned ears to hear their message. My raven-haired wife, Roisia, dabbles in dark magik herself (though few would suspect such a thing), and she expressed those implications would have dire effects far-reaching even to us, though when or how she could not presage.

I worried not long at her augury, for certain events were soon dragged woefully from the mucous pits whence they stewed. *May Day. . .* That is when the rustles of grass grew loudest. And thereafter did Roisia glimpse what Merlin saw in his flames: That Arthur had made child with Morgause, wicked she who by seduction avenged her husband, the defeated Lot Luwddoc. Wicked she who bore most terrible enmity toward our beloved King Arthur. Wicked she who poisoned Arthur's dreams and his seed before taking flight.

Merlin foretold that this son of Arthur would himself begin the fall of Camelot, and at any cost the infant must be found. The child was born on May Day, Merlin ciphered, but the location was not known. As with all sorcerous ways, only certain shadows may be seen and not others.

King Arthur ordered all boys thus born that year on the first of May be brought before him. Mothers and fathers rejoiced that their sons were perhaps *significant* and willingly delivered their children to Arthur for blessing in providence of some great destiny foretold. It *was* destiny indeed foretold, yet, alas, not in fortuity. . .

So too were there parents who mistrusted the king's decree—regardless of his trumpeted rectitude—and sought to hide their such-born sons. But Merlin's finger found them all. One-by-one we soldiers were pointed to hiding nooks beneath straw-filled beds or in small chests or behind false walls, mothers angry with fright and tears as we tore babes from their homes.

No reason was given them, no comfort provided, no word spoke further of the matter. The May Day-born sons of farmers, merchants, nobles, and beggars alike were taken and set to nurse at a secretive *hof* of clay floors and low ceiling. There they remained until decided upon. Roisia, through her 'sight,' told me the child Merlin and Arthur sought had been collected, though they could not determine which of the infants he was.

And so, two nights passed 'til I found myself on a secret mission. On Arthur's order, I and a dozen others, led by the knight, Anguselus, were ordered to the hof, to retrieve those babes.

Though weather had long been fair, the night turned unaccountably stormy, and the infants cried loud at our arrival, whether from gale or nascent foreboding, I cannot say. The soldier, Hawais, drove a covered wood cart, and his normally taciturn face evinced more dread than I've seen him show in a hundred battles. We took the babes, and we loaded them in stacks like fleshy logs, and at this, even mighty Symounde trembled.

The cart filled—thirty, forty—I dared not count, for fear of weeping. The babies punched and kicked the air with tiny limbs and wailed in tongues none but their own mothers might cipher, calling for these very same mothers who were absent, and the children knowing not why.

Anguselus gave the command, and we departed thence for the seashore. Perhaps more enchantments filled the air, as we encountered no one on that midnight road. 'Tis a strange thing, is it not, that the cries of so many infants streaming across the countryside like wafting fumes should not draw the inquiry of a righteous man? But 'twas true. Though if Merlin wove a spell of secrecy o'er us, why, I ask, could he not have silenced those May babes? Or perhaps many *did* hear the wails, but sensing the malevolence of our charge, chose rightly to hide in the deepest of cellars or 'neath the thickest of blankets, praying such ill-omens never to find them. For evil such as this must always leave a linger, a residue of char and hideous smoke.

O Shades, My Woe

After some hours we reached a spit none could name that stabbed out into the great, frothing ocean. A small ship there awaited us, a flat-bottomed cog with single mast. Its sail was set. There was no rudder. Ierimiah, the noted jouster, whispered desperately for forgiveness, even as he took the first of the infants and laid him within the ship. If cries were knives, we should all have been sliced asunder by the child's desperate wails, pleading in dribble-specked bleats.

We worked with the haste of furies stacking the others into the boat. The wind howled malisons upon us, and hastening rain drove nettles into our eyes and hands, but still we obliged our oaths of duty to Arthur. For if our king decrees this for the good of the realm, then it must be so, regardless of its despicability. And when its terrible cargo made ready, Ranulf pushed the ship into the angry, storming sea. Like mewlings of terrified kittens thrown out and drowning in a well, so too were the babes' cries—Arthur's cursed son among them—drowning under the waves of the great brine. The boat sped away, caught by the wind, and gray crests rose up like mountain slabs and fell over its bow, and the mewling worsened. . .

Our orders completed, we fled. The cries fell silent as we galloped away, and I pledged to never bethink upon those events again, believing that for the greater good, the realm had been saved.

And so it was, until the dreams. . .

As when I lay in bed aside my wife and amongst the living, the dead infants haunted me. They promised what awaits, what befalls the butchers of bairns, and I believed all.

For the next month, on its first day, Anguselus the knight vanished from his manor. All of court wondered at his disappearance, yet no trace of him could be found. Even Merlin appeared to inquire, though he made public no venture. When his eyes met mine, he looked away.

Ain't Superstitious

The following month, too on its first, another soldier was taken, Gaffere. I'd served with Gaffere at the battle of Bedegraine, and at the rout of Gwynn Collynn, and no fiercer a warrior may be found. Yet by dawn he was gone, as if a flounder snatched suddenly away by an unsparing fisherman's net.

Month by month it was so for Peregryne, and then Ranulf, and thereafter Haweis, each taken by an incremental turn of our Julian calendar. Even Ierimiah was soon lost, he whose pleas that night by the sea for forgiveness surely fell upon ears as unheeding as those who heard the crying babes.

Roisia toiled to ward off this strange bane. She wove spells like golden thread upon a loom of safeguard, and she sought council with the ageless crones underground, chanted songs of babble in the glades, pricked her finger to mine, even while a child of our own coupling took seed in her belly and ripened through the season. And still Roisia wove more, suffering malaise and bemoaning the limitations of her ensorcelled prowess. She was not Merlin, after all, nor Morgana, nor Nimueh, nor even Morgause, the least, but cruelest of them all. But finally, Roisia swore, her magik was enough to shield me, its continuance tolled by the beating of her heart.

And at the next month's start, upon a waning-moon's night, Symounde was vanished. After two fortnights Theoflis followed, and so then Maucolyn. The soldiers were taken, as passed the months, an unremitting progress of time that leads all to its terminus, soon to be gone, gone, gone. . .

After eleven months, eleven men went missing by unknown cause, and by the twelfth, only I and one more remained from that night of horror. I rode to this last soldier, Kenward, and we sought Merlin for help, but he would not hear us. We begged Arthur's audience, but he would not see us. It was as if another spell of secrecy was cast, and we were forgot by those we once served. And as

256

a new month came, I alone stood by Kenward's side for whatever might show. Kenward, who was swarthy and hale, once had hair as raven as my wife's, but of late it turned ashen and listless, much as the man himself.

We waited by torch in his estate, and at the bell's midnight toll they came.

Ne're able to crawl, they showed atop the garden wall like cherub-faced goblins. They appeared when I glanced away, and the sound was of foul mewling: They were the babes we had drowned, surging to us upon an invisible current, their movements in fleeting tumbles, as if tossed to and fro amidst churning waves.

The May Day babes were naked and bloated with brine, skin like blue sponges that hold all they can and ooze excess. Their cries spoke not of vengeance, but still of fright, of pain and despair.

As that tide washed closer and closer, I swung my sword—mercifully—cleaving the first child's head from its wriggling body. But its sobs did not stop, the sound instead turning only hollow, as if blowing through a chafe of wheat, even as the child's head flowed nearer, vanishing, then emerging, dipping and surfacing beneath unseen waves.

Kenward babbled ungodly oaths while cutting through one infant, then another. Suddenly he shrieked at being touched by something most frigid, causing him to abandon wits and flee. At that, the waves broke over him, while skirting me, and the dead children carried Kenward to fathoms from which there is no return.

By morn, I returned home alone, and all distanced from me but my wife, dearest Roisia, whose mother's mother's mother danced by night in the misty bosk of the fae. And days fell away, sloughed-off skin for tomorrows, and I thought less of myself and more of my beloved, preparing to give birth that following month—and a horrible voice filled my head: *Would my fealty have remained so resolute if our own sired were born that day of May?*

And too soon, the thirteenth month commenced. Roisia stayed with me all night, working at her spells. Though I swore to smell a waft of sea salt and cold rot, the dead babes did not come. By my beloved, it worked! Roisia had saved me, and I revered her the more, and we spoke in hope for the constancy of my stayed time.

"It is Arthur and Merlin who are the villains," she told me. As oath required, I only carried out their orders, but they should be held most accountable.

Her sight showed a day not far-distant that Arthur and Merlin will perish, their fall begat by a May Day babe—the cursed son of Arthur himself—who by wonder survived that ocean storm, while the other innocent children perished. Theirs will be tragedies all, in which no peace is ever found.

Some days passed, each a joy in itself, as worries of the drowned babes lessened, while hopes for our own family thrived. And soon that day of celebration arrived, for my wife's belly set to burst, and a midwife called for. 'Tis a most painful labor, I understand, for any woman to give birth, and I did all I could to comfort Roisia whilst in her throes.

My wife's cries were brave at first, but after many hours they turned savage and racking. Her hand gripped mine with the strength of a manticore, and she writhed as her innards clenched and eased and clenched again.

The water broke from between her legs, gushing to the ground, and I unexpectedly thought of stormy ocean waves. Roisia moaned and flailed from her back, and I thought of those babes kicking the air with tiny limbs, squirming so helpless and wretched.

A soft cry rose, a bleating wail from the darkness of her womanhood even 'fore the crest of the infant's head did show. The midwife's face puzzled.

O Shades, My Woe

A second cry joined, frightened mewling from a great distance but drawing near. The midwife's face remade to concern, and by the third crying voice, the fourth, the chorus, she'd taken to frenzy.

I know not why we hadn't considered some wickedness, not braced for an attempt, not thought for this, but that they'd made a way to me.

The first dead babe spewed from Roisia, and she shrieked, for there were more passing through, many more, splitting her womb asunder in terrible rolling waves. Bits of her splattered my tunic, precious lumps colored as wet rust and bitter wine, and incurably ravaged. Roisia's eyes found mine for a trice, then turned up, white, and she convulsed again, splitting at the seams like a burlap sack that bears too many potatoes. The children's number grew. . . Thirty, forty, I dared not count, for all was in crashing fury, lunacy, screams and chaos.

Roisia's magik was enough to shield me, its continuance tolled by the beating of her heart, and at that beating's cessation, the babes were unfettered. My dearest had wove so busily for me, thinking not of herself, thinking not she be menaced, and perhaps 'twas true, but that she'd interfered with reparations of the damned.

Somewhere else the midwife had fallen—Fainted? Taken? I did not know, and I did not probe, for if I looked back further, I would turn unhinged.

I fled outside.

Above stayed a moon so swelled its luster was like filaments snaking down through the sky, and I reached for mercy to take hold and be risen away, but at those hopes its clinquant light thus dimmed. The night turned too dark, and the crashing waves of dead babes surged from behind, and I would flee no more.

Hence here I wait, O shades, knowing my words run low. I resign my fate, for who can escape the ocean that knows no shore?

Ain't Superstitious
And at the last I cry this grief for you, mine sad notes as those whom fall lost, for such is life that we are all babes cast adrift in the great sea of nothingness, wailing for life amongst turbulent waves, until drowning beneath it all.

About the Author

Eric J. Guignard's a writer and editor of dark and speculative fiction, operating from the shadowy outskirts of Los Angeles. He's won the 2013 Bram Stoker Award and was a finalist for the 2014 International Thriller Writers Award. Outside the glamorous and jet-setting world of indie fiction, Eric's a technical writer and college professor, and he stumbles home each day to a wife, children, cats, and a terrarium filled with mischievous beetles. Visit Eric at: www.ericjguignard.com, his blog: ericjguignard.blogspot.com, or Twitter: @ericjguignard

*****~~~~~*****

Credits and Acknowledgments

Illustrations

Cover image and design – Keely Rew

Ebook Only:
Coffee Lake – Coffee bush, commons.wikimedia.org, Coffee bush (Breynia oblongifolia). Paruna Reserve, Como NSW Australia, December 2010, originally posted to Flickr by John Tann
The Necromancer – Still from "King of the Zombies" movie (1940), commons.wikimedia.org, public domain uploaded by User CecilF
What Is Sacred to Dogs – black dog on floor, "jedi puppy kitchen tricks" (commons.wikimedia.org, originally posted to Flickr by user droid)
Upon a Pale Horse – Horses in Battle of Hastings, by Bayeux Tapestry designer and seamstresses [Public domain], via Wikimedia Commons
Gualicho Days – Hands at the *Cuevas de las Manos* upon *Río Pinturas*, near the town of Perito Moreno in Santa Cruz Province, Argentina. Wikimedia Commons, picture taken by Mariano in 2005.
Wind Chimes – Wind chimes, Nagano, Japan. Wikimedia Commons, picture taken by user Fg2
Schrödinger's Schrödinger – (part of Grins section) Schrödinger's Cat, many worlds interpretation, with universe branching. Wikimedia Commons, created by Christian Schirm
A Little Mischief – Illustration by Arthur Rackham of the Cheshire Cat, Drawn for *Alice in Wonderland*, 1907 [Public domain], via Wikimedia Commons

Ain't Superstitious
The Annual Scarecrow Festival – the 2005 Scarecrow Festival, Thornton Hough, Wirral, England. Wikimedia Commons, author: Rept0n1x
Spellcasting – The Love Potion, painting by Evelyn De Morgan, commons.wikimedia.org, public domain. Uploaded by Shuishouyue
Salt and Bone – Keely Rew
Ambrose's Eight-plus-Oneth – Leningrad Symphony conductor Yvgeny Mravinsky, painting by Lev Alexandrovich Russov, Wikimedia Commons, used by permission
The Candlestick – Medusa, by Nikita Veprikov, Wikimedia Commons
Dead Men's Drinks – All Saints Day in Katowice-Dąb Cemetery, Bracka street, Poland, by Ludek, Wikimedia Commons

Readers

Andrew Cairns, Tom Parker, Keely Rew

*****~~~~~*****

Discover other titles by Third Flatiron:

(1) Over the Brink: Tales of Environmental Disaster
(2) A High Shrill Thump: War Stories
(3) Origins: Colliding Causalities
(4) Universe Horribilis
(5) Playing with Fire
(6) Lost Worlds, Retraced
(7) Redshifted: Martian Stories
(8) Astronomical Odds
(9) Master Minds
(10) Abbreviated Epics
(11) The Time It Happened
(12) Only Disconnect

www.thirdflatiron.com

Made in the USA
Middletown, DE
05 March 2016